Fortune Cookie

A novel by 

Carlos Harleaux

My Most Sincere Thanks and Appreciation

First and foremost, I have to thank God for supplying me with the resources, creative thoughts and support to complete my first novel. Without Him, none of this would be possible.

A huge thanks to my parents Debra and Ronnie Swisher and Carl Harleaux for being so loving and supportive of any dream I've had since day one. To my beautiful wife, Alexandria Harleaux, for your endless love, support and understanding throughout this entire process. To all of my family and friends who are too numerous to specifically name here, I love you all and am truly grateful for you.

John Patrick Adams, this whole concept started from a conversation we had about me writing a novel. Thanks for the great support and speaking the vision. Cicely Miller, thank you for this awesome cover and the photography!

Also, as promised, I'd like to give a very special thanks to everyone that pledged towards the Kickstarter that supported this novel, especially John Patrick Adams, Tambria Barnes, Desmond Blair, Michelle Buggs, Danon Carter, Malachi Chimala, Mary Jo Christian, Shana-Lee Dixon, Alexandria Harleaux, Runette Harris, Gabrielle Hawthorne, Tammie Henry, Jai Jackson, Angela Lee, Desire Martin, Cassini Nazir, Shani Harleaux Suber, Debra Swisher and Ronnie Swisher! Thank you all from the bottom of my heart for your willingness to support my writing in an unconventional way!

TABLE OF CONTENTS

One

"Cookie. Cookie. Cookie…baby wake up." Larry shook her so hard that she almost forgot where she was and woke up swinging. "Damn baby. What's wrong? Why are you putting up such a fight with Big Daddy?"

She rolled her eyes and thought to herself that his name should be Little Daddy if the truth were being told. But she played into it because she didn't want to bruise his ego. Men and their egos. "Um, don't you see it's after 3:00 in the morning? You know I have to get up early," Cookie said. He sucked his teeth at her response.

"Yeah, that's what you always say. Come on Cookie, let me just taste you. You don't have to do any work. Just lay there". At that very moment, she wanted to call her line sister Tracy and sarcastically thank her for being the one that started the "Cookie" nick name years ago in college. Born Candice Marie Brighton, few people actually called her by her real name. It has since gotten some interesting (and mostly unwarranted) references when it comes to men and the dating scene.

Finally she gave in. "All right, well since you put it that way….." That was one thing he was good for, if nothing else.

7:05 am and the morning seemed to have come quicker than expected. She reached over to silence the alarm, but had already been awakened minutes before to the sweet smell of pancakes. It had been 3 months but she already decided he had much of nothing to offer. Sure, he was a VP for the fastest growing marketing company in Dallas. He drove a modest, gray Mercedes, which he always kept clean. He was sweet and considerate. But that was just it. He was too nice for her. Cookie knew they were incompatible from the beginning. And she wasn't the kind of woman to stick around just for money. She wanted a man that could hang a suit well (which he did), but also someone that could put her in her place if needed. And Larry was not that guy. She had to find a way to end this….fast.

In walked Larry with just a towel on, carrying a tray of orange juice, water, buttered pancakes with bananas on top (Cookie's favorite kind), a side of large red seedless grapes, and 2 strips of crispy maple smoked bacon. "Hey baby, I made you some breakfast before you get dressed," Larry said.

"Aw, you shouldn't have". Yep, he really shouldn't have. Now this would just make it even harder to break it off with him. Cookie finished the pancakes first, nibbled at the grapes and ate one of the strips of bacon before clearing her throat to make her bold declaration. "Hey Larry…..this isn't….."

"Save it Cookie," Larry said.

"Huh, what are you talking about?" she responded, perplexed.

"Cookie, you've hinted around at this for the past couple weeks now. I know you're not ready for a relationship. So, it may be in your best interest to just get up and leave now," Larry replied.

What the hell? How could he have flipped the script on me like this? I was supposed to be the one dumping him. I'm supposed to be in control. I'm supposed to walk out as he pleads for me to stay! Cookie grabbed her dress that lay next to Larry's bed, her purse and cell phone. She put on her shoes as she said, "Ok, cool. Well, I'll do just that. Thank you for the breakfast". Larry leaned forward to kiss her goodbye on the cheek. She abruptly stopped him. "You know what, it was only a matter of time before I stopped dealing with you anyway. You think you've got a one up on me? Ha, you're funny. Here's a tip for you. Maybe get a few more inches and you might have a chance in satisfying me. But, it's too late for that now. I'm done with your sorry ass." Cookie walked out of Larry's front door before he had a chance to respond. He was disappointed, but not hurt. He knew the kind of woman he was dealing with. He took a quick swig of orange juice and watched ESPN highlights as he got dressed for work.

Cookie briskly walked to her car with purpose, as she always did. But this time her purpose was twofold. Not only was she hurrying to get inside her car and out of the 45 degree weather, but she also didn't want to give Larry the satisfaction of seeing her walk away as the loser. She cranked up her car and immediately turned on Alanis Morisette's "Ironic" with her iPod. It was one of her many morning anthems on her way to work. She loved Alanis and felt her joy, pain and frustration. She was a genius and they were kindred spirits although she had never had the privilege of meeting her.

"Umph.....late again I see Miss Thing." Robert waited until Cookie walked just past his desk to stretch his neck to admire her from behind. He was glad the weekend was over so he could see her again.

"Robert, mind your own business for a change. How about that?" Cookie smirked, but only after she knew she had walked far enough in front him where he couldn't see her face. She was known as Candice at work, but Cookie's presence was still felt.

She switched a little harder as she cleared the double glass doors into her work area. She had just celebrated her two year anniversary at Org Life Essentials, a newly established consulting firm that helped companies resolve internal conflict and grow their businesses. It was right up her alley because she loved nurturing people.....and telling them what to do. She quickly became one of the company's most successful consultants, showing no signs of slowing down. Her psychology background from college her that much more valuable. Plus, it didn't hurt that she was the most desired woman in the office. It was an open secret, but a fact nonetheless. All the men wanted her. Hell, even some of the women did too!

Robert was one of the first people in the office and one of the last to leave. He analyzed consumer data and had a heads up for which clients to recruit. It was the perfect role for him, considering his personality. Robert was that go-to-person that knew everyone's business, but he didn't know, because he pried into their business. Most people just felt comfortable talking to him. And they knew he knew how to keep a secret. But ever since he met Candice, he couldn't stop dreaming about her. He loved everything about her. Her sass and wit. Her trendy auburn bob haircut, with the longest pieces at the sides of her face. Her soft, yet dominant voice. Her almond shaped eyes. And legs to die for. The closest he ever got to any play from her was walking her to her car if she worked late. She seemed out of his league despite the fact that he could break virtually any woman down. Something was different about her. But he couldn't quite put his finger on it.

Candice walked into the up close and personal ambiance at Camden's, an upscale cafe near downtown, for an early business lunch. 11:22 am. She was right on time. She was notoriously late in most instances, but tried her best to be prompt when it came to her clients. Candice, much like Cookie, was cocky and sure of herself and her capabilities. She knew that even if she was late, she was the best person for the job. But, she tried to curtail her pompous air in front of her potential clients.

"Gentlemen, wonderful to see you two," Candice said, extending her hand for a firm handshake. She felt confident and they could sense it. Tim Schleinbergh and Marc Ledeau were co-owners of Wilmington's, a fledging department store that was once the industry standard for all others to follow. Now they were on the brink of filing for bankruptcy and fighting to become the successful company they once were.

"Good afternoon, Candice. Nice to see you too," said Tim. He was the more reserved of the two men. He was also less arrogant. "Yes, we thank you for meeting with us," said Marc. Candice caught him admiring her as they all took their seats. She could see why. She was wearing one of her favorite business suits. A black suit set with a form fitting skirt that flared slightly at the knee and a sleek jacket that showed off her slim waist. Her blouse underneath was burgundy and all of her accessories matched to the T. She felt every bit of the powerful, intelligent, beautiful and independent woman that she was.

"You're quite welcome," Candice said. After a few minutes of small talk and catching up, they began to discuss the current state of Wilmington's. "Well, let's get down to business. How is business at Wilmington's since our last meeting?"

"Things are definitely looking up," Tim said. "We're gaining market share and business isn't exactly booming again yet, but it's growing at a steady rate".

Marc, being the kill joy that he is chimed in with the harsh, bitter reality. "Yes, things have been looking up, but we desperately need a new marketing plan. The bottom line is we have to pull in the numbers," he said.

"Point taken. No business can thrive without successful marketing. But let's not worry about the numbers right now."

Tim and Marc looked at each other with a puzzled look on their faces. "Well, what exactly do you mean, Candice?" Tim asked.

"Let's get down to the core essence of your consumers here. What do they like? Where are they concentrated? What are their habits? What makes them tick? Seduce them. Lure them back by catering to their needs and what drew them to you in the first place," she said, with a glimmer of fire in her eyes.

Tim and Marc both smiled and nodded. Candice could see their gears starting to turn. They brainstormed some possible marketing strategies, finished the remainder of their lunch and exchanged goodbyes. Candice drove back to work in silence to clear her mind. She knew there wasn't much time before her 2:30 meeting and she needed to polish up her presentation a bit beforehand. But before she pulled in to work, she decided to call, Sheila, one of her girlfriends who was always down for happy hour. Plus, she needed to fill her in about how Larry turned the tables on her and dumped her unexpectedly. Sheila eagerly accepted, as Candice assumed she would. 5:00 pm couldn't get here fast enough.

"Cookie! Hey I'm right over here to the left," Sheila screamed. She already texted Cookie to let her know her precise location in the bar. Sheila was fun, loud and a bit out of touch with reality. But she always gave great advice and that's part of why Cookie loved her.

"I heard you the first 10 times....ugghh", Cookie laughed.

"Whatever, get over here and show me some love girl. So what's been going on in your world? And are you still holding on to Larry or have you thrown him to the wolves yet?" Sheila and Cookie had been friends for almost 15 years so they knew each other well. Cookie was always the one dismissing men in relationships, so Sheila just assumed this relationship would follow suit. Cookie felt a wave of embarrassment come over her, but she couldn't lie to Sheila so she just told her the truth.

"Wait a minute? So he told you to leave before you could even get it out?" Sheila asked, with a confused look on her face.

"Yep, I couldn't believe it either but he did. But, oh well, he was sorry in bed anyway. So, on to the next one." Cookie shrugged nonchalantly.

Sheila could tell that Cookie was actually more hurt than she let on to, but she played the game to make her friend feel better. "Bartender! I think we need another round of drinks," Sheila said. The two women laughed in unison.

"But enough about me. What's been going on with you?" Cookie said. Sheila was beautiful in her own right. She had smooth caramel colored skin, short cropped spiked hair, hazel eyes, plentiful breasts and abs that would put women years younger than her to shame.

"Well, I'm still trying to stick it out with Charles". Sheila was the complete opposite of Cookie when it came to relationships. Sheila was the life of the party and appeared flighty on the surface, but she was truly quite a catch. Not only was she beautiful, but she was an excellent cook, loved sports and left no stone unturned in the bedroom. But for some reason, she could never seem to get it right. Sheila, unlike Cookie, loved the idea of being in love, but love never seemed to send her the right man.

"How long has it been now? Three years?" Cookie said, with a frustrated tone in her voice.

"Yeah, but you know….anything worth having is worth fighting for right?" Even Sheila didn't believe the words that were coming out of her own mouth.

"Yeah I guess so….but I would have given up that fight before the first anniversary even hit. You have a good heart. Don't let anybody take advantage of that or make it turn cold," Cookie said.

Although her words stung like alcohol on an open wound, Sheila knew Cookie was right. Charles was a good man, but he came with too much drama. His ex-wife found Sheila at her house when they first started dating. He had only been divorced 8 months at that point, and she just knew there was no way he could have moved on that quickly. Not unless he was seeing Sheila before the divorce. One thing led to another and Sheila found herself in all out shouting match in her own driveway with Charles's ex-wife. Charles tried to put an end to it, but Sheila still catches her driving past her house occasionally. Charles had been faithful to his ex-wife as far as Sheila knew, but she didn't put much past anyone. She knew both sides of the game. She hadn't always been faithful in her past relationships either, but she was faithful to Charles. Financially, he made far less than Sheila and Cookie always told her she thought he was a freeloader.

"I hear you. I promise I do. Enough of this sad talk. Let's make a toast," Sheila said.

"To what?"

"To sisterhood and one day finding true love, with no flaws. Well, maybe just one or two but that's it."

"Ha! Ok I will definitely drink to that," Cookie said.

Cookie and Sheila laughed and talked well after the happy hour window ended. They were just about to call the waiter over for their check when Cookie's phone rang. It was her mother. Cookie answered reluctantly.

"Hello?" Cookie immediately knew something was wrong, as she could hear her mother sobbing uncontrollably on the other end. Sheila could sense something was wrong and waited patiently to make sure everything was ok. "Mom? You there?"

"Yeah Candice. I'm here. I just can't take it."

"What? Can't take what? What's going on mom?"

"It's Chelsea. She's back in the hospital again. They said she may not make it this time."

Two

Chelsea was Cookie's younger sister. They were close in age (Chelsea 31 and Cookie 34), but they were like night and day in more ways than one. Chelsea and Cookie hadn't seen each other in almost 2 years. Cookie already felt bad about not visiting Chicago, her home town, as often as she should have. But, hearing the news of Chelsea being back in the hospital again made her stomach drop to her knees. The last time she saw Chelsea was when she flew her down to Dallas to spend the weekend with her for her birthday. She paid to get her sister's hair done, took her shopping and they stayed up all night laughing, catching up, drinking wine and watching their favorite movies. Cookie also remembered that their fun was short lived. Chelsea fell ill during that time and it wasn't pretty then either.

Cookie caught the first flight out that next morning to get back home to Chicago. Luckily, it was March and right after the major holiday travel rush. She knew it would be an easier commute, without having to fight through so many people. She called her mother once more to let her know she was about to board the flight. But she was still so shook up that her father had to take the phone.

"Candy?"

"Yes, Daddy. Is Mom ok? She sounds pretty broken up."

"She is...she's just tired and wants a better life for your sister. We all do," he said.

Cookie breathed in deeply and exhaled. Almost simultaneously, she let her tears flow that she had been holding back for the latter half of the night and into the morning. "Yeah...me too. But she's strong. I know she's going to bounce back and be ok," Cookie said. Cookie's father was a stern, but compassionate man. He had a calm dominance about him that was very comforting. He was truly the rock of the family but she could tell even his faith was wavering.

"Yes she will. I'm holding on to that. Just get here as soon as you can baby."

"Ok, love you Daddy."

"Love you too, Candy. Be safe."

Cookie boarded the plane and when it was permitted, pulled out her iPod and put it on shuffle. The first song that came on was TLC's "Creep". It brought a smile to her face as she remembered her and Chelsea dancing to it when they were younger and reenacting the music video in their silk pajamas. It seemed so long ago, yet just like yesterday. Cookie continued to let the music play until she fell into a deep sleep on the plane. The plane was only half full, so she had a whole row of seats all to herself. Little did she know how much she would need the rest.

When Cookie arrived at the hospital, she found room 346 and knocked softly on the door. Her dad opened the door and gave her a tight bear hug. Her mother was sitting in a chair, right next to Chelsea's bed, holding her hand and giving a painful smile. She seemed calmer now, but in a dazed state. Cookie bent down to give her mother a hug as she whispered in her ear, "I'm so glad you're here. She has always looked up to you so much." Cookie smiled and then walked over to the side of her sister's bed, rubbed her face gently and kissed her forehead. She was right on time as Dr. Talvin, a tall, slender, and muscular man, arrived to speak to the family before the nurse administered her next round of pain medicine.

"Chelsea's a lucky woman. With the impact that her car hit the esplanade, she could have suffered far more severe injuries. But she'll definitely need some extensive recovery. She has three fractured ribs, a broken arm and her left leg is bruised pretty badly, not to mention her head injuries."

"We understand. Thank you for helping her get back on her feet," Cookie said, as she introduced herself as Chelsea's oldest sister.

"Now....have you and the family considered any type of treatment plans or interventions for Chelsea? She has an alarming amount of cocaine in her system." Dr. Talvin treaded lightly with the family, as he suspected Chelsea was not a first time drug user.

"Yes, we are exploring some different options for treatment plans," said Mr. Brighton. He could see the hurt in his wife and daughter's eyes and wanted to shield them from any further heartache. "Thank you for your help doctor. We truly appreciate it. But the family and I would like to be alone for a moment, if that's ok."

"Sure, I understand. If you need anything, just let me know," Dr. Talvin said. He had become numb over the years with dealing with patients of many different ailments and illnesses, whether self-inflicted or forced upon them. But something about Chelsea really touched his heart.

Chelsea always was rambunctious growing up. As the youngest child, she was able to get away with murder and flash her charming smile to get out of it. But as she got older, she started dabbling into several things that she shouldn't have been involved in. She was able to dodge it all with minimal repercussions....except drugs. She started off occasionally smoking marijuana in college. It was actually one of Cookie's sorority sisters that first introduced her to marijuana at a sorority party that Chelsea's school hosted. Cookie was infuriated when she found out that the woman she was supposed to be bonded to in sisterhood would give something like that to her own blood sister. But everything happens for a reason. That's the motto Cookie lived by. But somehow she always blamed herself for her sister's battle with drugs. There had to have been something she could have done to prevent this.

"Hey baby girl. How did you sleep?" Cookie said. She watched Chelsea as she slept for a few minutes before waking her up. Her parents decided it would be best if she stayed with them for a while until she was able to get back on her feet and be sufficient enough to be at her own home alone.

"Cookie. Before you start going in on me...I know...I know. I'm going to get it together one day. Guess there isn't much I can say to defend myself on this one, huh?" Chelsea said jokingly. It was always like her to try to make light of a serious situation.

"Well you are just blessed that you made it out of there alive. I can't replace my baby sister," Cookie replied, with a serious look on her face.

"I know I'm better than this....I just can't seem to shake it. Everybody has their escape and this just happens to be mine. I'll be alright". Chelsea smiled and turned on her side. Her face was flushed and her bruises were still fresh. Cookie decided to take the rest of the week off from work to help her mom and dad look after Chelsea. They all decided it may be best that she stayed at her parents' house for a few days. Truth be told, everyone was too shook up to leave her unattended again for a while.

"Well this can't be your escape. You've got mom worried half to death. You know daddy is trying to be strong, but he's hurting for you too. I love you Chelsea," Cookie responded.

"I love you too Cookie. You were always the perfect one. But I know your secrets too." The next thing Cookie knew, she was holding Chelsea's hair back from her face as she vomited uncontrollably into the trash can next to the bed. Their parents ran in quickly to help Cookie take care of her sister. "It's going to be ok baby girl. You're going to get through this." Their mother handed Cookie a glass of water to give to Chelsea. "Come on sweetheart. Let's get you cleaned up," their mother said. Their father let Chelsea put all of her weight on him as he helped carry her to the restroom. Chelsea didn't develop her drug addiction overnight and it would definitely take her longer than overnight to break the chains of it.

By Saturday, Chelsea was gaining her color back in her face, getting around the house on her own and even gaining her appetite back. So the family decided to take Chelsea out to The Boiling Pot, her favorite restaurant, to celebrate her recovery. Chelsea was a pretty girl that didn't need much cosmetic enhancement, if any. Like Cookie, she was a natural beauty. But her features were a little less striking. Chelsea used her long auburn hair to her advantage, as she combed it towards her face and masked her eyes with a trendy pair of Michael Kors shades. She wasn't quite able to walk normally yet, but she fixed up well enough not to attract any negative attention to herself as her and the family walked in the restaurant.

The four of them talked, laughed and reminisced about the good ole days. Before they knew it, their food was placed in front of them. "Will you pass me the salt Lisa?" Bill asked.

"Salt!? I will not. Bill, this food is already salty enough. Plus, you know the doctor told you to lay off the salt anyway". It was common for Cookie and Chelsea's parents to go back and forth like this, but the girls never remembered seeing them get into arguments. They were usually able to talk anything out and not let the sun set on their anger. That was perhaps also attributed to their strong Christian background. They raised Cookie and Chelsea to be upstanding Christian women as well. Cookie often wondered what they thought about their children now that they were both grown and out of the nest.

"Chelsea, how about we all go to the movies tonight?" Cookie said. Bill and Lisa's faces gleamed with glee, and so did Chelsea's.

"Sounds like a plan to me. That'll be nice. There are a few movies out I want to see," Chelsea said.

"And maybe if you're feeling up to it, we can go to church tomorrow. How about that?" Cookie must have said something wrong, because her mother's expression quickly saddened and her father's head went down into his plate.

"Church??? You know I'm not going to damn church. You can go sit down with that," Chelsea said.

Cookie couldn't believe her ears and didn't understand why her sister was so bent against going to church. She must have been more out of touch with her family than she realized.

"Cookie, let it go. She doesn't want to go to church. She doesn't like it when we mention church anymore. Ever since she started....," said Lisa.

"Started what? Huh? Go ahead and say it mom. Ever since I got on that shit I haven't been at church, right?" Chelsea screamed.

"Don't you dare talk to your mother like that! You better watch your tone," Bill rarely got excitable, but when he started turning red, things were about to get serious.

"Or what? What are you gonna do? Pray for me? Is that it?" Chelsea was out of control at this point and the other patrons began to notice her emotional outburst. Cookie sat next to her sister in awe and couldn't believe how she was being so hostile with their parents. Especially about going to church.

"You know what? I'm tired of holding this back for all these years. You want to know why I get high? You want to know the real reason? Ooh, look at you. All ears now. You all never paid this much attention to me before. I like this feeling. Oh well, here it is: I was raped right after I turned 18......by Rev. Caldwell".

The room spun around into a deep abyss and Cookie became short of breath. She was rarely speechless and her quick wit was one of her best attributes. But today, she had nothing to say but a deep sigh. Lisa started crying as Bill wrapped his large, muscular arm around her. The waiter reluctantly walked up to the table and asked if everything was ok. "Yes, we're fine thanks. Just bring us the check," Bill said. The waiter quickly brought back the ticket for the meals. Bill put down $140.00 cash on the table as the family walked out of the restaurant to avoid causing a bigger scene.

Outside, Chelsea was furious and didn't care who was around her. "I know...just say it. I'm the daughter you wish you never had! I'm not perfect and prissy like Miss Cookie over here". All of the years of her pent up secret were finally being released. It was therapeutic for her, but her family had no idea how to handle it. Everyone was quiet on the way home. Still in shock, even Chelsea was at a loss for words after her raging rant. The reality of revealing the hurt she kept so closely guarded all these years overwhelmed her.

Bill turned into the driveway abruptly. The Boiling Pot was only 15 minutes away from the Bill and Lisa's home, but every second felt like an eternity. The realization that his youngest daughter had been raped, much less by his close friend enraged him. Lisa was distraught, as she always was when tragedy struck. But this time, she wasn't being overdramatic. She nor Bill knew how to console each other at that very moment, while Cookie kept a protective eye over her sister as the family walked through the front door.

"Alright baby girl, I know this is painful for you. It's a surprise to all of us. I never would have thought Steve would do something like this. He was my friend, my...." Bill said.

"Sometimes you have to watch your friends closer than you would a stranger," Cookie solemnly whispered.

"Baby, please tell us what happened. We need to know and you need to free your soul of this," Lisa pleaded. Cookie sat quietly next to her sister. She was afraid to say anything that would spark her to go left again. She never knew that Chelsea felt like she was the golden child. She thought their childhood and even young adulthood together was like any other sisterly bond. She couldn't believe that Chelsea felt neglected. But at this point, it didn't matter what anyone else thought. Chelsea was entitled to her feelings and that was her reality.

Chelsea leaned back on the couch, took a deep breath and laughed out loud to herself before silent tears began walking down her face. "It was right after my 18th birthday. I went up to the church to grab my jacket that I left there the Sunday before. I remember Rev. Caldwell called me to say they found a jacket there in the lost and found….and he knew it was mine. He always was very attentive. I had just gotten the new Acura you and Daddy bought me for my birthday. I loved that car. I would make up any excuse to get up and go driving around in it. I parked at the front of the church and walked inside. Rev. Caldwell came out of the main office. He must have seen me pull up. That's when he told me to come with him to get my jacket."

"Look at you. Little Chelsea all grown up now. How does it feel to finally be legal?" said Rev. Caldwell.

"It feels great! Have you seen my new car? I love it. I could get used to being 18 every year from here on out if this is what it comes with," Chelsea laughed.

"Ha ha….I see. I would love 18 too if I was the proud owner of a ride as pretty as yours. Why don't you come down to the supply room with me? I just have to get a couple things out for the technician that's coming to do some electrical work here later today. It'll only take a second. Plus, I have a gift for you too."

"Wow, really? You shouldn't have. Ok, sure I'll walk down with you". Rev. Caldwell remained silent and smiled at Chelsea, biting his bottom lip. Once they got to the supply room, he opened the door for her to enter first. She felt a little unconformable once she stepped inside. The room was barely big enough for a few people, but even seemed cramped for two. Plus, it was extremely cold down there. Rev. Caldwell was still behind Chelsea as she walked as far as she could in front of her, looking around the room. Although she had practically grown up in this church for the last 10 years, she had never been in the supply room. She never had a reason to go down there.

"Turn around and come get your present," Rev. Caldwell said. Chelsea turned around quickly, anticipating the gift he had gotten for her. Her demeanor quickly soured and she was horrified at what she saw. Rev. Caldwell stood in a wide legged stance, pants down to his ankles and his hard penis exposed.

Even back then, Chelsea had a potty mouth on her. "What the hell?! Pull your damn pants up! What are you doing?" Rev. Caldwell walked closer to her. He had already locked the door. But if Chelsea was able to move past him, she could break free and get out before anything happened. "Come on baby, you're a full-fledged woman now. I know you've got to be having sex already. But it's time out for playing with the boys....and get yourself a real man. I've been watching you and I feel the sexual tension between us."

"I don't know what you're talking about. I don't like you in that way. You're one of my dad's best friends. Move, or I'll tell him about you". In that instant, Chelsea's life flashed before her eyes. Rev. Caldwell charged at her and pinned her down on the floor with his pants still down. He was 6 foot 5, 235 pounds and just as muscular as he was in his college football days. Chelsea was only 5 foot 3 and 120 pounds soaking wet. Who was she kidding? There was no way she'd be able to get away from Rev. Caldwell in one piece.

"Now you listen here! You say anything to your father about this, and that's the end of you! You understand!?," Rev. Caldwell was breathing heavily on top of her while he pinned her down by forcing all of his body weight on her. He looked her straight in the eye and she didn't recognize the man she thought she knew anymore. His nose flared and his stare was almost demonic. "Now either you're going to give it to me, or I'm going to take it."

The next few minutes felt like forever. A part of Chelsea died that day and never returned. At the most imperfect timing ever, someone knocked loudly on the supply room door. It was Dean, one of the church custodians. Chelsea felt as if God must have been punishing her for something. Why couldn't he have knocked sooner? Or better yet, why couldn't he have already been in the room when she and Rev. Caldwell made their way downstairs? Rev. Caldwell wiped himself off with a paper towel and quickly pulled up his pants. Chelsea thought about leaving her clothes off for Dean to see. But what if he didn't believe her? Plus, Rev. Caldwell already threatened her life if she was to ever tell her father (or anyone for that matter). She pulled up her favorite pair of jeans and put the sweater back on that Cookie had given her for her birthday.

"Coming! Just a second," Rev. Caldwell scanned the room quickly to make sure there was no evidence of his secret dirty deed. "Hey Dean, how are you man? Everything ok?"

"Yes sir, I'm fine. I just couldn't get in the supply room. It was locked from the inside," Dean said. Dean was a very quiet man, but had a warm, contagious spirit. And he was nobody's fool. He couldn't understand exactly why, but he had an eerie feeling when he stepped inside the supply room. Chelsea greeted him with a plastered smile and said hello.

"Chelsea and I were actually just leaving. She thought she left her jacket in here last week and I was just unlocking the door for her," Rev. Caldwell lied. Chelsea was disgustingly impressed at how well (and quickly) he could lie. But Dean seemed to see right through him.

"Ah ok….well, hope you find that jacket pretty lady," Michael smiled at Chelsea nervously.

Chelsea proceeded to walk out of the supply room door when Rev. Caldwell grabbed her arm. "Wait a minute. Don't forget your gift. Happy Birthday. Hope you like it". He pulled out a small orange box, wrapped in a silver ribbon, from his pocket. She wanted to gauge his eyes out with the box and spit on him like the garbage he was. Instead, she just said thank you and walked out of the room. Dean waved goodbye and gave his birthday wishes as well. Chelsea cried all the way home and was relieved her parents were gone when she got there. She immediately jumped in the shower to wash away the scent of Rev. Caldwell. No matter how she scrubbed and washed and cleaned, she still felt dirty inside.

"Oh my God. I'm so sorry Chelsea…." It didn't seem like enough, but it was all Cookie could utter. Lisa ran to Chelsea and held her in her arms while she sobbed uncontrollably. She cried so hard that Chelsea ended up consoling her instead of the other way around. Bill was dangerously quiet. Mute. Almost numb.

"I'm going to go find this bastard. He'll pay for this, baby girl," he said.

Three

Bill went into the bedroom and pulled out one of the many baseball bats he had in his closet. He put his hand on the steel one and walked briskly out of the room. Lisa came running into the bedroom as Cookie sat hugging her sister.

"Bill! Wait! What are you doing?"

"Get back Lisa!! Do you understand what he did to our baby!? Nobody messes with my girls and gets away with it. You stay here. I'll be back."

Lisa, always the optimist, couldn't even find a silver lining in this cloud. As reality sunk in, she felt a disturbing hardening of her heart come over her. "I know. Just please be careful".

Bill was furious, but still methodical. Since it was Saturday night, and basketball season, Rev. Caldwell was likely at home watching the game. He was a devout sports fanatic. His wife detested sports, so she usually went shopping during the game with Rev. Caldwell's sister. Bill and Rev. Caldwell lost touch after the family joined a new church a few years ago. There was previously no bad blood between them. They just lost touch over the years. Bill found his number in his phone and prayed that it was still the same.

"Hello," Rev. Caldwell answered. Sure enough, the basketball game was blaring in the background and from the sound of it, he was at home.

"Caldwell?"

"Is this Bill?! Man, long time no hear brother! Cathy got me this new phone and I lost all my contacts," he chuckled.

"I understand that. These women are trying to get us hooked up to all this new technology just to keep tabs on us. Hey, I was in your area and was wondering if you were watching the game. I wanted to stop by and catch the second half with you, for old time's sake," Bill said.

"Am I watching the game!? Is hell hot!? Sure man, I'll be here. Just knock when you get here. It's just me. You know Cathy went shopping with Marlene like she always does," Rev. Caldwell said.

"Some things never change, right? Ok, I'll be there in a bit," Bill said.

The sun was setting just in time. Bill was about 20 minutes away from the Caldwell residence. He arrived with a purple sky as his canvas outside. Perfect timing. He parked on the street instead of in the driveway, put on his gloves, and grabbed the steel bat from his back seat. He rang the doorbell and then stepped to the side of the house. Rev. Caldwell was slow to answer when basketball (or virtually any sport) was involved, so he'd have plenty of time to hide.

Rev. Caldwell answered the door and said, "Bill! Is that you? He stepped outside; far enough to come completely out of the entry way to his front door. "Ah must be some no good pranksters again. Interrupting my game".

Just as he turned around and headed back towards the front door, Bill called out to him. "Turn around. I want you to see this." Rev. Caldwell recognized Bill's voice, but never heard his tone be so aggressive. He turned around reluctantly as Bill said, "Oh, so you like raping little girls? This is for my baby!" Thwack! The steel bat connected precisely with the side of Rev. Caldwell's head and he instantly fell to the floor. Bill spit on him and kicked him in the chest for good measure. It was the most riveting moment of his life. He felt great power avenging his daughter's pain. He smoothly walked back to his car, threw the bat in the trunk and drove off into the night.

When Bill walked back in the house, everyone was too afraid to question where he had been. He walked over to Lisa, hugged and kissed her. He then leaned down to kiss each of his daughters on the forehead and gently rubbed the top of Chelsea's head. It had been quite an eventful day and when Bill came back home, everyone was ready to get some rest and recharge for the next day.

Cookie fell into a deep sleep after her mind wandered for over an hour about her sister's secret. She didn't know which shocked her most: that her sister was raped or that it was Rev. Caldwell who did it. Soon after she went to sleep, she kept hearing a scratching sound at the window. She decided to sleep in the same room with Chelsea to feel closer to her sister. She thought that maybe she had gotten out of the bed to go the rest room, but Chelsea was still lying right next to her.

The room was dark, but just light enough to see movement clearly. She saw the bedroom door knob turn and her heart started beating fast. She wanted to wake Chelsea up, but didn't want to draw attention to whoever was on the other side of the door. Then slowly, the door creaked open. In walked a man of average height, stocky stature and heavy feet. His footsteps pounded against the floor like bass drums. She knew this was not her dad. He kneeled down on Chelsea's side of the bed and looked intently over her as she slept. He then walked to the other side of the bed where Cookie was. He had a grey hooded sweatshirt on, so she couldn't make out the details of his face. She tried to scream for help as he leaned down with his hands towards her neck. She could see his eyes now, but her vocal chords couldn't make a sound. This is not how she wanted to die….

"Cookie! Cookie! Didn't you say you had to be at the airport by 8:00 this morning? It's already 5:45, you better get moving big sis," Chelsea said. Cookie sat straight up out of the bed and grabbed her sister. "Ouch my arm still hurts. Girl, get off of me," Chelsea laughed at Cookie. Cookie was relieved that her nightmare was not a reality. She called Tina, her supervisor, last night and told her she had to take a later flight and would need to work remotely on Monday. It was a little white lie, but her and Tina had a great working relationship so she didn't mind it.

Lisa cooked a big breakfast of pancakes with bananas (for Cookie), strawberries (for Chelsea), scrambled eggs (over easy for Bill), sausage and freshly squeezed orange juice. She was a very doting mother and wife that loved pleasing her family. Seeing their smiling and satisfied faces brought her all the joy she could ever need or ask for. After the family finished breakfast, they all packed up the car to take Cookie to the airport. Once they arrived, Cookie said her goodbyes to the family and gave Chelsea an extra tight hug before going inside towards the security check in. She promised she would come back soon to visit and maybe stay for a whole week. She made a vow to herself that day to never become distant from her family again, especially from Chelsea.

Cookie was so exhausted from the weekend that she forgot to put on makeup before she left home. She didn't wear much of it anyway, but she felt naked without at least some lipstick and mascara. She was dressed comfortably and more casually than usual. Cookie was a tomboy at heart, but very prissy in her physical appearance. She understood men, because her thought process wasn't too far off base from theirs. Today, her casual clothes matched her demeanor. She wore a black pair of fitted Seven jeans, a pink sweater, calf length grey wool coat, a shimmery black scarf and black knee high boots. Right after she walked through the security gates she noticed a tall, broad shouldered man with hazel eyes and a five o' clock shadow beard. He had a rugged, rough, yet professional look. He had on a pair of tailored jeans, brown boots, a burnt orange sweater and a brown hat and scarf. In other words, he was Cookie's type. He looked like a good guy, but a bad boy too. They exchanged glances as they walked past each other. He quickly looked her up and down without staring too intently.

There were only a few minutes left to board the flight. Cookie logged on to check emails from work. Her follow up with Tim and Marc of Wilmington's was tomorrow. She quickly closed her laptop, put her purse on her shoulder and grabbed her carry-on bag. Her mind was wandering in so many places and she wasn't as aware of her surroundings as she usually was. She needed a mental detox and hoped to get some rest on the flight. Cookie placed her carry-on bag above her head and as she got ready to sit down, she heard a low, strong male voice utter, "Excuse me miss. Is there anyone sitting next to you?"

Cookie was extremely quick on her feet, especially when it came to men. She quickly turned off her surprised expression and said, "Sure. Well, you are now. Go right ahead". It was the same man she exchanged glances with less than 30 minutes earlier. What were the chances of this?

"Good, because it's actually my seat. See," he said as he showed her his boarding pass.

"I believe you. I don't think you're a weirdo. Or at least you don't look like one. But looks can be deceiving," Cookie said jokingly.

"Yes, very true which is why I asked if the seat was already taken. I found it hard to believe that a beautiful woman like you would be sitting on a plane alone."

"Thank you," she smiled quickly and immediately went back to her nonchalant expression. "Just came up to Chicago to visit family for a few days. Nothing major." That was a bold faced lie. There were plenty of major occurrences from her Chicago trip, but she hardly knew this man. She couldn't (and shouldn't) tell all of her business to just anyone.

"So what about you? What brought you to Chicago?" Cookie inquired.

"Well…wait a minute. I don't think I got your name. I'm Ken. And you are?" he asked.

"My close friends and family call me Cookie, but my real name is Candice," Cookie replied. The two shook hands and Cookie was impressed with how strong but soft his hand was.

"Cookie…..cool, I like it. Definitely a pleasure meeting you. I came to Chicago on business. I'm a Regional Innovation Manager for a budding food and beverage company based out of Dallas, called Delicious Delights. We just closed a deal with a very large, but demanding customer. So it's great they've finally jumped on the bandwagon with our product and what we have to offer.

"Sounds very interesting and exciting. A pleasurable trip in some regards I hope." In a round-a-bout way, Cookie was fishing to see if his trip involved seeing any women while he was in town or if he was in a relationship. She didn't see a ring on his finger, so she assumed he wasn't married. But then again, that could be a wrong assumption. She knew plenty of married men who always seemed to conveniently not wear their wedding ring out in public.

"It was nice. I had a great time. But I'm so ready to get back home. The hectic travel schedule can really become tiresome on your body," Ken said. "What do you do professionally?"

"I'm a consultant at Org Life Essentials. We help businesses and individuals brand themselves, and groom their portfolio," Cookie said.

"I know exactly where that's it. Not too far from where I live. That sounds awesome. I can see you knocking that position out of the park. You seem like a natural nurturer and developer."

Cookie loved a man who told the truth. She toned down her urge to give herself kudos and said, "Thanks. It's a challenge but I enjoy it and make it work. So, are you originally from Dallas?" Cookie asked.

"Yes, born and raised. Although I've lived in several different states, I just recently circled back home in the last few months." Ken looked down and noticed a small black spiraled notebook laying at Cookie's feet. The pages were opened and he could faintly read the words:

If you ever get the privilege to
See inside me
You'll find you'll love the woman
Within me
You just have to get to know her
You just have to know how to hold her
Introduce me if you find her
She's afraid and her heart is getting colder

"Um Cookie. I think you may have dropped something there." Ken reached down to pick up her notebook. He couldn't help but inquire about the origin of the writing. "I don't mean to pry, but looks like it may be something important. Don't want you to lose it."

Cookie hardly let anyone see the contents of her notebook. She kept it on her at all times. "Ah, how did this get out? Thank you very much. Yes, just a little bit of writing."

"You wrote that?" Ken asked.

"Yes, it's not finished though, it's…"Cookie said nervously.

Ken cut her off before she could even finish. "Amazing is what it is. I love it. Very mysterious and intriguing."

For the first time in a long time, Cookie felt nervous butterflies at the pit of her stomach. "Oh wow, thank you. I really appreciate that. I'm usually private when it comes to my writing."

Ken and Cookie talked all the way back to Dallas and the nearly two and a half hour flight seemed much shorter. As they were walking out of the terminal, Ken gave Cookie his business card. "Call me. Maybe we can go out for dinner some time," Ken said.

"Yes, I can possibly see that in the future," Cookie smiled. Ken seemed like a decent man. But when it came to love, as good as they were, her perceptions were sometimes way off base. She decided to sleep on it and let her gut instincts guide her on her next move with Ken....if there should even be one.

Four

All things considered, Cookie's day at work on Tuesday went pretty smoothly. Marc and Tim loved her proposals for their new marketing plan. Both of them called in to rant and rave about how personable and professional she was. She went out by herself for lunch at one her favorite Italian bistros. The weather was a perfect 70 degrees, so she decided to eat on the patio. Cookie wasn't afraid to eat (or much of anything for that matter) alone and at times, preferred it. She loved observing people, what they ate, who they were with and even what kind of conversations they were having. After she finished her meal, she called Chelsea on her way back to work to check up on her.

"Hey Miss Lady," Chelsea answered. She sounded surprisingly cheerful and upbeat.

"Hey baby sister. It's so good to hear your voice. How are you?" Cookie asked, with a tone of sincere concern.

"I'll be alright. I always snap back. I'll be back at work tomorrow. Feeling a lot better now." Chelsea was a CPA and owned her own tax business. She was always good with numbers and never was without a job. At least the busy tax season was winding down, so she could get a little bit of a breather.

"You sure you're ready to go back to work right now? Can't Monica cover for you while you're out?" Cookie asked. Monica was the new hire and Chelsea's protégé. She caught on quickly and had a great business sense about her. Chelsea was excited to have her on board.

"Yeah I'll be fine. But I do have something I want to tell you. I'm thinking about going to an anonymous support group and getting some help." Chelsea had tried rehab before, and still relapsed. She was uneasy about even mentioning something similar to her sister.

To Chelsea's surprise, Cookie was extremely happy for her. "I'm so proud of you. You can do it. You can beat this. There's nothing you can't do. I love you".

"Thank you sis. I'll be checking in with you to let you know how it's going. Love you too," Chelsea responded.

Cookie hung up the phone feeling a sense of relief and a burden lifted. She truly believed that Chelsea would be different this time and stick to a treatment plan for her drug addiction. Moments like this made her wish she was still in Chicago, so she could be closer to her sister. But the support group would likely offer Chelsea a level of understanding that Cookie simply couldn't provide.

After spilling the beans to Robert about the real reason she went to Chicago, Cookie decided to call it a day at 5:30pm. It was a good day, but she still felt drained physically and emotionally. She enjoyed cooking every now and then and found it to be relaxing. She spent a quiet evening at home alone and prepared some sautéed shrimp, asparagus, spaghetti squash and a tall glass of red wine. Cookie laid across her bed, turned on Bjork's greatest hits, and pulled out a new romance novel she hadn't started reading yet.

After two hours of relaxation and reading, she decided to take a hot bath and turn in early for the night. She used Ken's business card as her place holder in the novel. She decided was going to call him, but not tonight. Cookie believed that old rules never died and she wanted to build up the anticipation. She turned off her light and cuddled up with her oversized pillow, falling into a deep sleep.

The morning came sooner than Cookie had anticipated, but she felt refreshed nonetheless. She got out of the bed and said her morning prayer and meditation before getting ready for work. The recent happenings with her family brought her closer to God again. She used to always pray in the mornings (and at night), but before last week, she had really been slacking off of it. She reached over to turn her stereo on. She turned up Alicia Keys' "Girl On Fire", smiled at herself in the mirror, and started getting ready for the day. She didn't have much time for breakfast, so she quickly made a mango strawberry protein smoothie with the left over fruit she had in her refrigerator. It was clearly time for her to go get groceries.

Cookie realized she hadn't returned Sheila's call since she got back to Dallas. She decided to dial her on the way in to work. A draining feeling came over her as she waited for Sheila to answer on the other line. Not at the thought of talking to her best friend, reliving everything that happened just a few days ago.

"Hey girl, I was getting worried about you," Sheila answered.

"I know and I apologize. It's just been a long week already with getting back from Chicago and everything. How's your day going?" Although she knew the inevitable would come, Cookie hoped the conversation would take a lighter direction. But that was just wishful thinking. Sheila was too good of a friend not to be concerned about her. Plus, Sheila was well aware of Chelsea's drug problem. But reliving the story of the rape would be hard for her to relay.

"You know me. Just getting these people in line. I swear, some days I question why I even got into this business. But it's my heart." Sheila owned an event planning business. She always had a flare for planning events and creativity. After five years of sporadic clients and some disappointments, her business was finally starting to boom. "But enough about me. Spill it. Tell me what happened. Are you ok?"

"Yeah, I'm fine just mentally exhausted. Chelsea is finally going to try a support group this time. I'm praying for her and I'm so grateful she's trying to shake this. But…" Cookie's voice trailed off.

Sheila could tell there was something more to the story that Cookie wasn't revealing. "But what? What's wrong? That's a great thing that she's making an effort to get help."

"It is…Sheila…Chelsea told us this weekend that she was raped." Cookie said.

"What?! Raped?! Oh my God. Cookie, I'm so sorry. When? Is she ok!?" Sheila shouted.

"Yeah it happened when she was 18. By Rev. Caldwell. You always said something was strange about him," Cookie said.

"We need to book another flight to Chicago to go cut his balls off!! I can't believe that bastard." At this point Sheila was getting so excited that she started to give Cookie a headache.

"Calm down Sheila. Hell, my dad did something to him. But he didn't mention what it was to us. He just went over there. So he might have already taken care of that," Cookie said nervously.

Cookie and Sheila talked all the way until Cookie pulled into the parking garage at work. Although it was painful to rehash all of what happened, she was glad she did it. She felt a cathartic release of weight being lifted off of her shoulders. And she was glad that she had a real friend like Sheila to help her through this difficult time. The day was looking up and she even thought about calling Ken tonight to see what his plans were this Friday. She wouldn't admit it to him, but she wondered if he had been thinking of her as much as she had been thinking of him.

As soon as Cookie walked back into her office, Tina stepped in and closed the door. Oh no…what now??? Maybe Cookie had spoken too soon and this day would take a bad turn after all. But there couldn't be anything wrong. She had just worked another satisfied client this week (Wilmington's) and was in negotiations to meet with two more independent entrepreneurs next week. But she breathed deeply, kept her composure and waited to see what Tina would say.

"Hey Candice. How are you?" Tina asked cheerfully. Cookie could breathe now. Woo. That was definitely a close call. But Tina was a stern business woman and a chameleon, so you never knew what angle she was coming from. They weren't exactly the best of friends, but that was only because of their manager, subordinate relationship. The two had a very high level of respect for each other. The only problem was everyone else in the department picked up on it too.

"I'm doing well, how about you Tina?" Cookie answered.

"Pretty good. Just still trying to shake these migraines I've been having. But I'm pushing through it. Listen, I see your calendar is open Thursday afternoon. Will you have time to meet with me for about an hour?"

"Of course, let me block off some time now. Is 2:00 fine for you?" Cookie said.

"Yes, that will actually be perfect. I just want to meet with you about some possible upcoming opportunities in the department. I know you're open to change, and we may need to make some shifts here soon. Nothing to be alarmed about, just more of a heads up. Let's keep this between us two, if you don't mind," Tina requested.

Cookie left work that day full of anticipation, but for two very different reasons. She had no idea what "shifts" Tina was speaking of at work. But she was also looking forward to speaking to Ken tonight. She had a few errands to run after work but decided to give Ken the privilege of having her full attention. Once she got home a little after 7:00 pm, she decided to dial him up.

"Hello?" Ken answered in his deep, raspy voice.

"Yes, may I speak with Ken please? This is Cookie, from the airport".

"Right, yes I definitely remember you. What gives me the pleasure of receiving this phone call?" Ken was excited to hear from Cookie and he wanted her to know it, while somehow still keeping his cool.

"Hmmm, well I've just been really busy getting caught up at work this week. I apologize. I would have called sooner. I'm not interrupting anything though, am I?" Cookie asked.

"No, not at all. I was actually just getting out of the shower. Your timing is impeccable," Ken replied.

"Just getting out of the shower, huh?" Cookie thought to herself. She'd heard that one before way too many times. It was a way to get her to think about him naked. But with him, it worked. She had secretly been fantasizing about him since their conversation on the plane. And now, she was quite moist. "Oh, I see. Are you free this Friday night after 8:00pm? I was thinking we could pick up our conversation in person."

"Well I think I would love to but I'll actually be busy this Friday evening" Ken said, with disappointment in his voice.

"Oh...ok. Well maybe some other time then. I just know I'll be traveling for work in the next couple of weeks." Cookie couldn't believe he had the nerve to have prior plans. But then again, she did wait a couple of days to call him. He probably had women lining up at his door. No time for sulking though. She had to play it cool and act like she was unbothered.

"Gotcha! Just playing. How about this? I come pick you up at 8:00 and take you to this jazz café downtown? They do spoken word too every Friday at 9:30," Ken said.

"Hmm...yes, you did get me. Ha...ok sounds great. I look forward to it". Cookie and Ken talked for about 30 more minutes before Cookie decided to call it a night. It was getting late and she didn't want to get too flirtatious....at least not yet. She hoped there would be plenty of time for that later.

"Well, have a good night beautiful lady. I'm anticipating our night out on the town on Friday," Ken said.

"You too....just watch out with all that anticipation," Cookie said playfully.

"Something tells me there's some anticipation in that cozy bed of yours over there too." Cookie could hear his smile through the phone. She liked his slight air of cockiness. It was confident and sexy.

"We'll just have to see about that then, won't we?" Cookie said sarcastically.

"Oh yeah, we'll see soon enough. Sleep well." Ken said.

"You too. Good night," Cookie replied.

The rest of Cookie's week was shaping up to be quite nice. Knock on wood, there weren't any stressful issues going on at work and she talked to her sister and parents on Wednesday. Chelsea's first day back at work hadn't been too bad and she was looking forward to attending the support group sessions. Her parents were also doing well and were planning a much needed cruise at the end of the summer. Maybe things were turning around for the best after all.

Now she was just getting back from lunch at her favorite local pizzeria. It was a beautiful Friday eve and she decided to treat herself and deviate from her healthy eating for a change. She arrived back at her office at 1:30 pm, which was perfect timing for her to gather her composure before her 2:00 pm meeting with Tina. She answered an email and returned a couple of phone calls. 1:57 pm. She started making her down the hall for the meeting.

"Hi Candice. Prompt as usual. Thank you again for carving out some time to meet with me." Tina hadn't even turned around in her chair yet. But, she instinctively knew that Cookie had entered her office. She minimized the screen that was pulled up on her computer and swiveled her chair around to face Cookie.

"Hi Tina. How are you? It's been strangely quiet this week. So I took it upon myself to organize some of the files from Q4 of last year," Cookie said.

"Look at you. Always looking for the next challenge. Please, have a seat. I appreciate that and I respect it. You've always hit the ground running since you started here. That's part of what I want to speak with you about today," Tina said.

"Oh, why thank you Tina. This is my passion and I love it here." Cookie could put on a poker face with the best of them. But she genuinely loved consulting. Perhaps that was why she performed head and shoulders above the rest.

"I know you do. Hey…I really don't know any other way to say this. I'm usually pretty direct as you know. But this is a little different. It's a little hard to articulate. Candice, I have a brain tumor. I just found out a couple of weeks ago. They're not sure yet if it's cancer. But, I have to start making preparations now, personally and here as well. Candice, if something happens, I want you to be my successor in this role. You're the only one here that's really got what it takes. So…..there it is," Tina exhaled deeply.

Cookie sat in silence and amazement for a few seconds before responding. She didn't know what to say and was at a complete loss for words. But the uncomfortable silence was becoming more awkward by the second. "I uh….Tina, I am so sorry to hear that. You're going to beat it. I know you will," Cookie assured her.

"No no, don't do that. Please. You're right. I'm strong and I'm going to beat this. A little tumor won't keep me down," Tina smiled weakly at Cookie. Although Tina was a strong woman, the possibility of cancer was a mighty blow that she didn't expect. But then again, who would? Cookie and Tina changed the subject and got caught up on the lighter side of each other's personal lives. Cookie told Tina about her date with Ken tomorrow night.

"He must be special. You've got that glow." Tina raised her eyebrows and smirked. "Oh, he's alright. We'll see after tomorrow how long I actually keep him around." Cookie laughed, while Tina shook her head. "Ugh, men; can't trust 'em. But I hope it works out well for you." Tina was recently divorced and had been hurt by men one too many times. It was a good laugh that Tina desperately needed to take her mind off of her health complications. She was truly happy for Cookie and hoped she would really find true love. She was ready to celebrate love for someone else, since she had no such luck finding it for herself.

Five

Cookie unlocked her door at approximately 5:00 pm. It was just enough time for her to look and feel her best before her big night with Ken. It was the first time in a long time that she was actually excited about a date. She poured herself a glass of cranberry juice and ran a hot bath. She soaked for over half an hour and let the stress of the week wash away. When she got out of the tub rubbed her coconut oil moisturizer all over her naked body. She then slipped on matching black lace boy short cut panties and a bra.

She started looking through her closet for just the right outfit. After several attempts, she finally settled on the perfect one. A black leather skirt, with a form fitting red sweater top that had a plunging neckline. She wore tall black high heeled boots that came up just above the calves. 7:10. She was running ahead of schedule. She teased her short cropped bob in the front and flat ironed the longest pieces at the sides. Cookie wasn't a fan of much makeup, so just used a little eyeliner, eye shadow and burgundy lip stick. 7:45. Cookie sprayed on her favorite perfume, *Gucci Guilty*, and waited to hear a knock at the door soon. She turned on some soft music and anticipated hearing from Ken.

7:55. A knock was heard at the door. Cookie walked slowly towards the door and turned the knob. Ken stood on the other side, smiling with a bouquet of flowers. "Hello. Why, thank you sir for the flowers," Cookie smiled.

"Of course. It's my pleasure," Ken said, admiring Cookie and how stunning she looked. But Cookie was also trying to sneak a glance of looking Ken up and down from head to toe. His large biceps and chest were well defined through his baby blue sweater. She even liked the way his gray wool pants slightly gripped his thighs. But she quickly regained her composure as not to seem thirsty.

Cookie walked with Ken outside towards his black Mercedes. Again, she was impressed but kept her composure. Ken opened the door for Cookie and admired her once again, as she eased down gracefully into the passenger seat. Ken sat down in the driver's seat and put his key in the ignition. Jill Scott's voice began to pour out of the Bose speakers.

"Ah, a Jill Scott fan I see. I love her voice," Cookie said. "Yes, she is nothing short of amazing. What's your favorite album of hers?" Ken said.

"Hmmm....I would have to say *Beautifully Human*, her second album. I can play that one from start to finish," Cookie said, anticipating Ken's response.

"Oh yeah? That is a great one. That's probably my second favorite of hers. Her debut album is actually my most favorite," Ken said.

The two continued to trade favorite musical artists and albums, sports (both were die hard football fans), their tastes in food and aspirations for one day starting a family in the future. Like Cookie, Ken had been married before too and really wasn't into wasting time with someone who didn't seem remotely seem like marriage potential.

After what seemed like only five minutes, Ken pulled up to the valet at exactly 8:30 pm. "Impressions". Cookie remembered seeing this place before, but had never been here. Ken opened the door as the two walked inside and found a quiet table, towards the back of the quaint café.

"You'll love the food here," Ken said.

Cookie smiled and said, "I'm anxious to try it. I can be a little picky when it comes to food. If you hang around long enough, I'll have to cook for you one day," Cookie said.

"Oh, well we can leave right now then," Ken said excitedly as rose from his seat.

"Ha, not so fast mister. Good try though. Have a seat," Cookie replied with a smile.

Cookie and Ken sat in comfortable silence as they both finished their meals. "I must say, that honey-glazed salmon was awesome. How was your steak?" Cookie asked.

"Oh, it was excellent. Seasoned just the way I like it. I'm glad you enjoyed it. There's more to come later...." Ken smirked.

Cookie inhaled deeply and let out a quiet, slow breath. Finally, could this be the relationship she had been waiting on? On the surface, Cookie changed men frequently and the slightest thing about them could her turn her off. But there seemed to be something different about Ken. She told herself to snap out of it for now, and just live in the moment; something she still struggled with doing.

"These open mic sessions are always awesome here," Ken said.

"I love open mics and haven't been to one in forever," Cookie smiled.

"And I'm sure you'll really love this one", Ken gave Cookie a half smirk. She felt a tingling between her legs so strong that she didn't realize her name had just been called.

"Let's get this party started right with a virgin to the open mic stage here tonight. Her name is Cookie because she tastes oh so sweet. But we'll let her tell you all about that. Give it up for Cookie!" As the applause filled the room, Ken gave Cookie a standing ovation. Cookie reluctantly rose from her chair and made her way up to the solitary microphone, illuminated by the spotlight.

"Wow, well I must say this is as much of a shock to me as it is for all of you. I wasn't expecting to be here on this stage tonight. But since I'm here, I'll share one of my recent pieces and hope it will inspire or help someone out there. This piece is called "Teddy Bears".

These teddy bears stare
With their beady black eyes
As the blood stained dresses
Brush against their stubby legs
Her tresses hit the pillow and hold secrets
That she must never tell
If these teddies could, they surely would
Yell so someone would hear them
So someone would pay attention
And believe them
She woke up filled with innocence
And went to sleep full of doubt, anger
And confusion
But she tucked away his mistakes
And stuffed them in bags that
She still carries daily
If these teddies could, they surely would
Have told her that cross

The room filled with a crescendo uproar with finger snaps and cheers. As Cookie walked off the stage, Ken knew he had done the right thing by surprising her. He imagined making love to her as he pulled back her chair for her to sit down again. "Look at you. You killed it! You were completely amazing up there! What a prolific piece. Kinda dark, but I love it." Ken said, with a concerned look on his face. "Ah, thanks. That's nice, but I really think it's time to go," Cookie replied sternly.

"Time to go? I don't understand. The open mic segment is about to kick off. Did you see how hype you made everyone with your poetry?" Ken said, with a perplexed look. "But if that's what you want, fine. I'll ask for the check and I'll take you home."

As Cookie and Ken walked outside, Cookie's could hear her phone ringing inside of her purse. It was Chelsea, but she'd have to call her back. She was too infuriated to speak with her now. "I know you meant well, but I do not like surprises like that. I would have much rather preferred you asked before signing me up for the open mic," Cookie explained.

"I apologize. I just thought it would be something spontaneous to show everyone else how amazing you are. When was the last time you read your poetry in front of a crowd, or even one person for that matter?" Ken said, raising his voice.

"Maybe this whole date just wasn't a good idea. We could be taking this too fast. Please just take me back home," Cookie demanded.

On the way back home, the silence was so thick they could hear each other breathing. Ken, tired of the awkward moments, decided to turn on his radio again. John Mayer's "Your Body is a Wonderland" played from the speakers. That didn't necessarily make things any less awkward. After what seemed like an eternity, Ken finally pulled into the driveway. Although he was upset at Cookie's temper tantrum, he decided to still be a gentleman and open her door for her. He reached for her hand as he opened the passenger door.

"Thank you," Cookie said.

"No problem," Ken responded. Cookie gave Ken a brief, distanced hug and walked briskly towards her front door. Ken sighed and shook his head as he sat in his car, waiting for Cookie to enter inside before backing out of her driveway. Women can be so hard to figure out. "Maybe the relationship thing is just not for me," Ken thought to himself.

Cookie sat her purse down on the couch, poured herself a glass of wine and turned on the TV. The Julia Roberts movie, *Sleeping with the Enemy,* was on. She quickly changed the channel and landed on a re-run episode of *Top Chef*. She sat there and analyzed whether or not she had been too hard on Ken. Their date was perfect up until he surprised her with the open mic reading. A piece of her felt liberated by being on the stage again, doing what she loved. But there was another side of her that trembled with fear. There was fear of memories that she had kept tucked away for quite some time. It's funny how you can live a lie so long that even you start to believe it. Still angry, but ultimately feeling as though she overreacted, she sent Ken a text. "Hope you made it home safely." Ken responded with a curt one word answer: "Thanks".

Cookie leaned her head back on the sofa and closed her eyes for a brief moment. Then she realized she still needed to call Chelsea back. She reached inside her purse to check her phone. There were two voicemails and a text from Chelsea that read, "Call me when you get this sis." It didn't sound too urgent, but Cookie felt an eerie feeling come over her all of a sudden. She checked her voice mails and the first message was from Sheila.

"Um, where have you been?! We are long overdue for catching up. I gotta fill you in on that loser Charles. He's yesterday's news. Love you girl. Call when you can." Cookie shook her head and smiled. Maybe this time Sheila decided to let the dead weight that was Charles go after all. The next message was from Chelsea. "Hey sis, call me back asap. Love you". It had been nearly an hour since Chelsea called, so Cookie immediately dialed her back.

"Cookie?" Chelsea answered quickly.

"Yes, baby sis. Everything ok?" Cookie asked.

"Um, well not quite. Dad just got out of jail," Chelsea said nervously.

"Jail!? Wait a minute. What did he do? What happened? Is he ok?" Cookie had so many questions running through her mind, but she remained silent to let her sister speak.

"Well, the police brought him in to questioning because dad was the last person on Rev. Caldwell's cell phone records. They kept him late last night for questioning. But, they let him go since there was no motive. Dad just told them he just called to check on his old friend since they had been out of contact for a while. Mom and I were on pins and needles. Sis, I'm sorry we didn't call you right away. Everything just started happening so fast. But I had to at least tell you what's been going on".

"I appreciate that. But there's more to this story here. Go ahead….spill it," Cookie said.

"You're right. There is more. We'll have to keep this a closely guarded secret. Dad murdered Rev. Caldwell," Chelsea said coldly.

SIX

Cookie couldn't believe what she just heard. But then again she could. Messing with any man's daughter can cause him to go ballistic, especially in instances like Chelsea's. There was so much running through Cookie's head and Chelsea was able to sense that she needed a moment to take everything in. Her world was turning into a series of colliding dramas. Cookie didn't know how much more she could take.

"Remember when Daddy left the night I told you all about the rape? He called Rev. Caldwell to make sure he was at home. He lied and said he wanted to watch the basketball game with him, like old times. He knew Mrs. Caldwell was probably out with Rev. Caldwell's sister since she detested sports. He had a clear chance at getting back at home. Of course, Rev. Caldwell was receptive to dad coming over. He just told him to ring the doorbell once he got there. Dad was waiting on him on the side of the house….with that heavy steel bat. As soon as Rev. Caldwell opened the door to step outside, dad swung and hit him in the head with the bat. Good thing Rev. Caldwell didn't live to tell it though. Dad made sure he knew it was him before he swung the bat," Chelsea said, slowing down to catch her breath.

Although Chelsea was nervous about her father being found out for Rev. Caldwell's murder, there was a part of her that felt a euphoric release. The man who violated and threatened her had gotten away with it for years. In the end, he had to pay with his own life. It was poetic justice to say the least. Her father's act of vengeance made her feel loved and protected.

"Wow…talk about laying some heavy news. How is dad? How is mom holding up?" Cookie inquired.

"Dad has some nervous energy. You can tell. But he's not sorry at all for killing Rev. Caldwell. At least not today. As forgiving as you know daddy is, I don't think he would have ever gotten over this one. Mom is being mom. She cried when the police took him in. We both thought it was something more serious. She's glad he's been ruled out as a suspect now, but she's still on edge now from knowing what he did. I told them I'd stay with them for a couple of days, more so for mom. Plus, my sessions are over on this side of town anyway."

"How are the meetings going for you?" Cookie inquired.

"They're going well. It's hard. Not every day is easy and these withdrawals are no joke. I'm really going to see it through this time. I'm tired of hurting you and the parents, not to mention myself. Work is going well. Business has really been picking up, so we're going to look at adding some new headcounts."

"Look at you. I'm so proud of you. I love you Chelsea. You know your big sis is here for you right? Let's plan sometime for you to come up and visit me again. It will be like old times. When is good for you?" Cookie said.

"I love you too sis. Yes, I do know you're here for me too. You know I would love that. We haven't done that in forever. How about in May?" Chelsea asked.

"May it is then baby sis. I can't wait. I think we both need this," Cookie smiled.

"Sounds good. I'll keep you posted on anything else I hear. I told dad I was telling you everything, so he already knows. But you can still give him a call if you want," Chelsea advised.

"I will definitely give him a call. I'll wait until tomorrow after some of the smoke clears. I'm sure he may be still a little shook up from the interrogation. I love you Chelsea," Cookie said softly.

"I love you too. Bye Cookie," Chelsea said.

Cookie was tired, but not quite ready to go to sleep yet. She finished watching another *Top Chef* rerun and channel-surfed until she landed on a *Behind the Music* episode with Pink. Cookie decided to text Sheila back while it was fresh on her mind. "Hey girl. Long and crazy night. Got your vm. Wanna meet at the gym tomorrow at 9:00 am? We can get brunch and go shopping after☺". Sheila responded about 30 minutes later with, "Sounds like a plan. See you then girl! Hope everything is ok. Love you."

The morning came quicker than Cookie expected or anticipated. She rolled over at 7:00 am to hit snooze on her cell phone to get a little more sleep. At 7:15 am, she decided to get up and prepare her pre workout fuel snack: a Honeycrisp apple with peanut butter. As she was slicing her apple, she decided to give her dad a call. She knew he would be up because he usually was an early riser.

"Good morning Candice. How are you baby?" Bill answered.

"I'm good. Daddy, are you ok? Chelsea told me what happened," Cookie said.

"Yeah, I figured she probably had reached out to you by now. I'm ok baby. Don't worry about me. He had it coming to him, especially after what he did. I just couldn't let that slide. Was I wrong? Yes. But do I regret it? Hell no," he admitted. Silence filled the air as Cookie really was at a loss for words. She definitely understood the reason behind her father's actions. But never did she think of her dad as a murderer. The reality was that was exactly what he had become.

"I know Daddy. I don't blame you at all for it. Truth be told, he really got what he deserved. I just wanted to check on you to see where your head was at," Cookie said.

"Just trying to keep a low profile and take care of things for your mom around the house. I'm about to go out and grill some chicken for us. You want me to send you a plate baby?" Bill laughed.

"I'll be on the lookout for it. I'll have my fork ready," Cookie smiled.

"Alright, well I love you sweetie. Take care of yourself," Bill said.

"I will. Love you too Daddy. Talk to you later," Cookie said.

Cookie grabbed her keys, gym bag, and iPod and headed to the car. She turned up the radio high, getting pumped for her workout, listening to Justin Timberlake's "Sexy Back". The drive was about 20 minutes from her house, but she felt like she got there in no time at all. Cookie pulled into the gym parking lot and looked for Sheila's car. She saw her walk towards the door, and realized she must have just arrived as well. Cookie caught up with Sheila and the two gave each other a big hug before they walked inside the gym. It had been a while since their last meeting and they had plenty to catch up on. They were the type of friends that never skipped a beat and could always pick up right where they left off in conversation.

"There you go with those pills again. I should slap them right out of your hand," Cookie said, as Sheila took a swig of water to wash down her pill.

"Whatever. This helps me stay slim and trim. Got to keep it tight. We're not getting any younger. I'm sure you'll be asking me for some soon. It's all natural. It won't hurt anything," Sheila said, with a jokingly matter of fact tone. Sheila had been taking some new cardio enhancing workout pills she heard about through some of her clients. Ever since she started taking them, she was hooked on the results.

"You don't even need them though. You were doing fine without all that," Cookie said.

"Maybe you're right. I'll stop taking them tomorrow," Sheila said sarcastically. The two laughed as they put their bags inside of the gym lockers. Both of them were physically fit and usually worked out for over an hour straight. After closing their workout with a two mile run on the treadmill Sheila asked, "Ok, so where are we going to eat? You know I'm always hungry. I have some juicy news to fill you in on anyway. And I still have to hear more about how your trip went," Sheila said.

"Girl, that's your problem now. If you gave up all that eating then you wouldn't have to kill yourself in the gym. Let's go to Great Thai. We haven't been there in a while," Cookie said.

"Oh no. Don't look now, but there's Desire over there lifting weights," Desire Martin was Sheila's ex-boyfriend that she hadn't seen in probably four years. Truth be told, he was the one that got away. They remained cordial and texted each other on birthdays, but nothing more than that. She wondered if he ever moved on. The very next moment, a woman came up behind him and wrapped her arms around his midsection.

"Sheila? Cookie? Wow, this is quite a surprise. Good seeing you both. It's been a long time Sheila. Oh hey baby, this are some old friends of mine. Sheila, Cookie, this is my fiancé Rita." Desire said.

"Well, congratulations are definitely in order," Sheila said, keeping her composure. Her and Cookie complimented Rita on her ring and said their goodbyes to Desire and his fiancé. Judging from their conversation, Desire may not have told Rita that Sheila was his ex.

"Now I bet the adrenaline from seeing him will work better than those fat burners. Don't you think?" Cookie joked, trying to lighten up the mood.

"Whatever, he knows what he's missing," Sheila laughed. "But he deserves to be happy though. Good for him." Sheila and Cookie worked out for about an hour, showered and then headed over to Great Thai, one of their favorite restaurants. They loved the ambiance there, not to mention the great food. The ladies could barely get their food on the table before diving into conversation and filling each other in on the latest happenings. "So, how is Chelsea doing? Is she better now?" Sheila asked.

"She is. She's trying to take it day by day. She's been going to these narcotics anonymous meetings. They seem to be helping and I think that sense of community there will do her some good. As bad as I hated to hear it, I'm really glad she got everything out in the open about her rape. I think facing it will help her heal. What's going on with you though and what happened with Charles?" Cookie asked.

"Ugh...Charles. Let me tell you about that no good dirty dog. You know how I was telling you about his ex-wife showing up at my house and acting crazy? Well, he got tired of me nagging him and he decided to run back to her. But get this. They get back together and in less than two weeks, she dumps him! I thought that was too funny. And to top it all off, now the woman is trying to be friends with me," Sheila explained, talking a mile a minute.

"Wait, you're going to make me choke on this food. I can't believe it," Cookie laughed.

"Yeah, they're both crazy. She finds my number, I'm guessing from his phone, texts me and says, "Girl, I don't know what I ever saw in Charles. This is Melissa. You can have him. I can't believe I made a fool of myself over this bastard," Sheila said.

"Wow, they are crazy. How juvenile is that? Why would she even text you? She's doing way too much," Cookie said.

"Yep, same thing I said. But I'm happy. And I owe a lot of it to you. You told me to leave his ass a long time ago. I knew you were right, I just thought things would work out for the best. But oh well, single and ready to mingle again now," Sheila said, tilting her head to the side with a seductive smirk.

"Oh, I see. Is that the reason why your girls are playing peek-a-boo with the waiter?" Cookie laughed.

"Hey, a girl's gotta do what a girl's gotta do, right?" Sheila joked, shimmying her shoulders back and forth to further accentuate her provocatively low cut blouse.

Cookie shimmied back and laughed at her friend's antics. "I met a guy on my way back from Chicago. He seemed really nice but I think he may have already blown it with me."

"Do tell. How does he look? And what happened? You know you're known to kick em to the curb prematurely. Or better yet, was he the premature one?" Sheila laughed.

"Well I don't know if he's a preemie or not. That was Chris. Don't remind me about him," Cookie said, rolling her eyes. "But this guy was nice. Easy on the eyes too. He's tall, broad shouldered, beautiful teeth, big arms, and his chest is woo....something amazing. I didn't even feel that weird when he found my journal and read one of my unfinished poems. It was like we kinda had this connection, you know? We went on our first date last night and it turned out to be a disaster."

"The only disaster I hear so far is that you were stupid enough to let him go. We're not 25 anymore. I'm not saying lower your standards but...," Sheila explained.

"I know. I know. I gotcha," Cookie interjected. "But ok, this is the deal. He signed me up for an open mic last night without telling me. It was a total surprise. I was so embarrassed. Granted, I've been saying forever that I want to get back into performing my poetry, but not like that. I have to ease my way back in. You know, get my feet wet first. I told him to just take me back home."

"Cookie, if you weren't my sister I would slap the hell out of you right now. Get your feet wet? Sounds like you missed out on getting some other things wet too. You can't keep doing this. Maybe it was wrong, and I would probably be upset too if that happened to me. But every man is not Steve, Trent or even Brandon, for that matter. I hate to say it like that, but you have to let him go. Letting him go means giving someone else a chance. You can't compare everyone to him."

Cookie stared blankly at Sheila for a few seconds before responding. Their brutal honesty to each other was one of the strengths of their friendship, but Sheila's words cut Cookie deeply to the core this time. "I know, and I'm not comparing him to anyone else. I just.....it's just hard starting over, that's all. My trust has been broken and sometimes I don't know how to get it back".

"Believe me, I understand that. But you definitely won't get it back by shutting out every good man that comes your way. Nobody's perfect Cookie. We know that. He didn't call you out of your name. He didn't use his friend's car to pick you up for the date. He didn't try to get you in the bed the first night. Come on, give the man some credit. I don't think you should give up on him so easily," Sheila said, in a matter of fact tone.

"Alright, alright. Enough with the soap box. I get it. I'll reach out to him again this week," Cookie said reluctantly. The two ladies paid for their food and proceeded to go to the Galleria mall for a little retail therapy; a woman's favorite pastime. They shopped for about two hours and decided to make it an entire girl's day out of it by checking in at a local spa. It was the release and relaxation they both needed. They decided to go see the new movie The Rock. They both preferred action movies over the typical chick flicks women were usually interested in. But this was a part of their appeal. They were prissy tomboys in many respects, which made them irresistible to many of the men they came in contact with. They also knew how to be sexy as well.

After the movie, both ladies headed down the street to the spa. They lay across the warm massage tables, dressed in only towels with a clay mask with cucumbers over their eyes. "Girl, this will work wonders for the sagging skin under your eyes," Sheila said.

"Sagging skin?! Who are you talking to? My skin is not sagging. I'm 34 and still look good," Cookie exclaimed.

Sheila snickered to herself before responding. "I just like getting you fired up. It works every time. Ugh...Miss Sensitive. But for real, we do look good, don't we?"

The two women laughed and reminisced about their college days. They made fun of themselves for the crazy fashions they wore and the silly men they dated. Two ladies soon entered the room and asked if they were comfortable and ready for their massages. Sheila and Cookie responded with a calm, yet resounding, "Yes".

Cookie didn't realize how all of the stress with her sister's drug episode, finding out about her getting raped, her disastrous date, and ill boss was taking a toll on her. She could feel the knots being loosened from her shoulders. The pleasurable pain made her exhale deeply. Suddenly, the masseuse's hands seemed stronger than normal. Now, she began to feel only pain. The stature of the masseuse even felt different standing over her. She was still face down on the massage table and could only see the baggy pants of what looked like the same sized woman standing over her. But then again, it was hard to tell because her presence seemed so much larger over her now.

The room was awkwardly silent; so much so that Cookie couldn't even hear Sheila or the other masseuse in the room. "Sheila?" Cookie tried saying her friend's name, but her voice was only audible enough for a whisper. She could barely hear herself breathe. The hands were digging deeper and deeper into her shoulders. Now they were squeezing her neck. Whoever this person was had her pinned down so hard that she couldn't even move to try to fight back. Finally, Cookie was able to use her legs to swing off the table and attempt to make an escape. But that moment was short lived, as the person who stood over her suffocated her face with their hand. It had to be a man. There was no way an average woman was this strong.

"Cookie! Cookie!" Sheila shook Cookie hard, as the masseuse working on her friend stepped back. "Are you still having those bad dreams?" she asked.

"Oh no...I am so embarrassed. I guess I must have dosed off for a bit. I just felt so relaxed until.....it just felt so real. I'm so sorry" Cookie apologized to Sheila and her masseuse.

"It's quite alright, she tends to have that effect on people," the masseuse that worked on Sheila said. The women all laughed together and made light of the whole ordeal. Sheila and Cookie got dressed, paid for the spa visit and tipped the masseuses graciously on their way out.

"Cookie, I gotta tell you something. You're scaring me girl. You think that maybe you might need to talk to someone about those dreams you've been having? Seems like they're more frequent now," Sheila said, in a concerned tone.

"What do you mean see someone?" Cookie asked, although she was well aware of what Sheila meant.

"I mean like a counselor or something. Someone professional. Someone who can maybe really help you get to the bottom of all of this and maybe that will stop the dreams. It's worth a try. I'll even go with you if you want," Sheila offered.

"Hmmm...maybe so. Ok, I'll at least think about it," Cookie said.

Seven

Mario stood at the opening of her bedroom door, with just his boxers on. His hands were above his head, grasping the frame of the bedroom door. He leaned forward and gave her a look like he was going to eat her alive. His eyes were seductive and said, "Come and get it" without him ever saying a word. He was cocky, but his confidence was sexy and turned her on even more than his looks. Although at 6 foot 3, with full, soft lips, a chiseled eight pack and legs to die for, he definitely was an amazing looking man.

"It's been a while. Why did you make me wait so long, baby?" Mario said.

"I know....I've been such a bad girl. What are you going to do to punish me Daddy?" Cookie uttered softly. She lay across her bed with a royal blue lace bra and boy short panties to match. She felt and looked desirable and she needed this release. Mario was one of her on and off again flings that she always knew she could call for some mind blowing sex, with no strings attached. A woman should always keep at least one an in between man on hand – the guy you call in between relationships when you need your back blown out. For some, he's also the one they still sleep with while they're in a relationship. But Cookie wasn't that kind of girl. Deep down, she knew Sheila was right about Ken. She planned on calling him later this week to even see if he was still interested in her – and apologize. But for now, she had a one track mind on having fun.

Mario walked towards her slowly and intently, with a bow-legged swagger. His oiled physique glistened under the dim lighting in her bedroom. Cookie laid there waiting for him to get closer to her. He climbed on the bed, leaned forward and proceeded to take his boxers off. "Oh, who gave you permission to do that?" Cookie said. "Pull those back up."

"Yes, mam. Is there anything else I can do to please you?" Cookie just stared in his eyes silently. She liked pretending to be dominant. Although she did have an aggressive personality, she was no match for Mario. He knew how to take control at just the perfect times. Since he was so good in bed, she always let him have his way. "Playtime is over. Come here". In one fell swoop of his massive right arm, Mario pulled in Cookie close underneath him. He climbed on top of her and whispered, "Slippery slope, huh? Mmmm…"

Mario got caught up in the heat of the moment and proceeded to insert himself inside of Cookie. Slowly….deeply. She knew it was wrong, but she enjoyed the feeling too much to stop now. Wait. She had to regain her composure. "Hold on, where's your condom?" Cookie said, in a forced tone of concern. "I have it….just wanted to feel you first. Skin to skin," Mario said. Neither one of them wanted kids right now, so Mario reached for his protection before continuing with Cookie. Before she knew it, her legs wrapped were tightly around his back and her arms around his shoulders. Mario's hands rested firmly on her ample behind. The two moved together like waves of the sea – much like making love and less like casual sex.

Then all of a sudden, he pushed her forcefully on her back and began kissing her roughly. It was almost as if he sensed the unusually romantic vibe and wanted to change their focus back to sex, with no strings attached. But this was different. He then placed one of his strong hands around her neck as he began to move faster and harder while hovering over her. Cookie felt herself gasping for air. She immediately started having flash backs. "Bitch, you think you can leave me?" "Nobody wants your tired ass." Normally, she would try to block out these thoughts. But tonight she embraced them. In a sadistic sort of way, they even turned her on.

"Yes, choke me Papi!" Cookie screamed. Mario, caught off guard by Cookie's request, did just as she asked. He kept one hand on her neck as he squeezed tighter, while the other hand aggressively massaged her right breast. Cookie's legs began to quiver uncontrollably. Mario knew she was reaching her climax. "Yes! Yes! I'm...." Cookie could barely speak and felt as though she was about to lose consciousness. "Ah.....oohh. Damn!" Cookie lay lifelessly on the bed as Mario collapsed on top of her. Her reaction turned him on more and they both climaxed simultaneously. Only at that moment did he loosen his grip on her neck. Cookie loved it.

After what seemed like endless hours of stress relieving, sheet biting, breathtaking, pillow grabbing, amazingly fulfilling bliss, the two lovers lay sprawled across the bed holding each other as they fell into a deep sleep. Cookie wasn't one for overnight guests, but Mario deserved to spend the night after his performance tonight. He was one of the very select few that ever spent the night at her house. Usually, those who were lucky enough to get in her bed also left the same night.

Cookie awoke to the sunlight peering through her window, and Mario getting up from the bed naked, walking to find his jeans in the living room. "Call me baby....don't make it so long the next time. You know I'm like a fiend when it comes to you. I can't wait too long for my fix," Mario said, with a half crooked smile. "But I know you won't. I won't let you. I'll just show up to your house in a trench coat and naked underneath," Mario danced as if he was giving her a strip tease. "Go on boy," Cookie laughed and said, "but seriously, I'll give you a call".

As she locked the door behind Mario, she went to her phone to check her messages. She didn't want any interruptions last night, so she put her phone on silent. The first text she saw on the screen was from Ken. "Hey...I'd like to make it up to you. No surprises this time. What do you say?" the text read. Cookie felt really dirty now. But the feeling was well worth it. Now she definitely felt obligated to give Ken a call. Her next message was from Tina. She was surprised since Tina rarely texted her on the weekends, unless there was a big company event going on....or a hot issue to resolve.

"Hello Candice. Please contact me at your earliest convenience. I have some urgent matters to discuss with you." Cookie immediately called Tina to see what her message was all about. It was just after 9:00 am, but she was sure Tina was up since she was an early riser. She waited anxiously as the phone rang and eventually went to voicemail. "Tina, this is Candice. I got your text and was just giving you a call. Feel free to give me a call whenever you can". As soon as Candice was about to hang up, she heard her phone beeping and saw that it was Tina calling her right back.

"Tina?" Cookie answered abruptly. "I was just leaving you a voicemail".

"Yes. Hello Candice. How are you? I was just tending to my garden outside and couldn't make it to the phone in time. These weeds are a mess," Tina said.

"It's ok. I figured you were probably up and about. What do you want to speak with me about?" Cookie said.

"Well, remember that conversation we were having a few days ago? It's time….I'd like to meet with you, if you have some time today. I think it will be easier than trying to discuss everything in the office. But if you're busy, I understand. I can just tell you everything over the phone."

"No, I'm not busy at all. Where would you like to meet?" Cookie inquired.

"How about that new sandwich shop that's a few blocks up from work, at 1:00pm? The one you and Robert went to a couple weeks ago. My treat," Tina said.

"That sounds great. I'll see you then," Cookie said. As she hung up the phone, she sighed deeply. She sensed that Tina's health must be getting worse. But she didn't want to speculate too much before their meeting. She decided to get a quick run in before getting her day started and meeting with Tina. She pushed through her soreness from last night's rendezvous with Mario. It was an understatement to say that he had really worked her over. Cookie laughed to herself and took in the outside elements as she started on her run. There was a trail just five minutes up the road from her house that frequently got a lot of traffic. The trail had beautiful landscaping and people were always running on it.

Cookie inhaled the outside elements and tasted the cool, crisp wind on her lips. The weather was breezy, with just the right amount of sunshine. The day couldn't have been more breathtaking. She closed her eyes for a brief moment, taking it all in. When she opened her eyes, she realized she almost ran into a man jogging the opposite direction from her. "Sorry....I guess I'm enjoying this weather a bit too much," she said.

The man, who was quite handsome with a stocky, muscular build, said, "It's quite alright Miss Lady. Enjoy it while you can," he smirked. That was the extent of their interaction as each of them continued in their prospective directions. She looked back just as she passed him and turned forward quickly in case he decided to turn around too. There was something eerie about his response that rubbed her the wrong way. What did he mean by, "Enjoy it while you can"? There was something dark about his presence that seemed to have latched on to her and she couldn't shake it. But, she couldn't focus on that. She had three more laps to complete before returning home to get ready to meet Tina.

The sound of Lorde's "Royals" poured form the speakers, as Cookie drove to meet her boss. She arrived at the restaurant a few minutes early and decided to grab a seat inside, next to the entrance. Tina walked in a couple minutes later, dressed in jeans, a form fitting purple blouse and purple high heeled boots to match. Purple was Tina's favorite color and it looked good on her. The ladies traded compliments on each other's outfits (Cookie wore jeans as well with pink heels, a turquoise blouse and pink feathered earrings) and shared some memorable moments from work over the years.

"Cookie, it's such a beautiful day outside. Why don't we go sit on the patio?" Tina pleaded.

"Sure, that's a great idea. I went running this morning after we talked and I just love this weather. If only Texas could be this nice every day, right?" Cookie laughed.

"Yes! So very true. But there's beauty in the abrupt changes of life, don't you think?" Tina smiled, with a glossed over look in her eyes. "Well, let's get right to it shall we? The transition is going to have to start being put into action now. My cancer hasn't spread, so I'm counting my lucky stars for that. But I am going to need surgery to have this tumor removed. What a price to pay for getting rid of those migraines, huh?" Tina laughed to try to lighten the mood.

"Of course, Tina. Whatever you need, I'm here. I'll fill in wherever I'm needed", Cookie said. As driven as she was, Cookie wasn't actually a corporate minded woman. She did it because she had to and just happened to excel in it. However, this was a first. She had never received a promotion because of someone else handing over the position to her.

"That's great. I'm so glad. I wouldn't trust anyone else with handling our business besides you. This surgery is pretty risky and it could take a few months for me to recover. It may take a year or more to gain all of my functions back, provided everything goes as planned with. But, there's something else I want to tell you….Cookie, nobody's perfect in this world. But you really have an aura, a glow about you. I've seen it since the first day you walked through those doors. Don't let anyone steal that from you. Watching you and living with this tumor has brought me closer to God. Your energy is evident without you preaching to everyone. I respect that about you. Maybe I was supposed to go through all of this to acknowledge Him. That I don't know. But I think I've finally learned what faith really means," Tina said.

"Wow, thank you so much Tina. God loves you. I've been praying for you," Cookie said. As a flashback of being pleasurably choked by Mario last night flashed across her mind, she felt somewhat like a hypocrite. How could she be a Christian example for Tina? If only she knew her dark secrets, would Tina still respect and admire her faith as much as she did?

"I'm learning that, slowly but surely," Tina said. "Let's continue to keep this between us for now. I'll announce my resignation on Friday. I know you'll be great and continue to push the envelope for success like you always have." Cookie was well aware that even with such an expensive and risky surgery, Tina would be set financially. Not only was her salary from Org Life Essentials pretty substantial, but she was also very wise with investments. It was no secret that Tina openly discussed and encouraged the importance of investing, whether inside or outside of the company, to all of her employees. Cookie could only assume that Tina must have cashed in on a couple of them, which further supported her decision to resign from the company. "In the meantime, I'll be funneling information to and through you until my official leave. But, you won't need much of my coaching anyway."

"I'm truly honored. Thanks again for even entrusting me with the department," Cookie said, with a heartfelt tone. The two ordered a Turtle flavored cheesecake for dessert, which they shared, and talked for a little while longer before saying their goodbyes and parting ways. Cookie was reflective of her and Tina's lunch meeting in her car and decided to stop by Barnes and Nobles before returning home. She called Ken on her way there. The phone rang a few times as Cookie was preparing to leave a voice mail. Finally, Ken answered.

"Hello," Ken answered, slightly out of breath.

"Hey Ken, this is Cookie. Catch you at a bad time?" Cookie asked.

"Not at all. Your timing is actually perfect. I was just wrapping up my workout. And how are you pretty lady?" Ken inquired. He was still a little upset at Cookie for the way she reacted on their date, but he was so infatuated with her, that he didn't want to miss an opportunity to talk to her. He wasn't expecting this after his phone calls and texts went unanswered. Usually, his temperament would not have allowed him to even keep trying to pursue a woman like Cookie. But there was something different about her that made him feel she was worth every bit of the chase.

"Pretty lady?" Cookie thought to herself. This man must have a lot of patience, after the way she acted. "Thank you.....I just wanted to give you a call to apologize to you. You didn't deserve the way I treated you on our date. That was uncalled for and in your defense, you didn't know the reason why that was so impactful to me," Cookie said.

"Apology accepted", Ken said. "But I do have to ask, what was the big deal about the open mic? I will say though, I'll definitely steer clear of that one if I do get the chance to take you out again."

"I know......it may seem strange. I'm sure I'll be able to tell you one day, but it's just so much to get into. I know it wasn't right though and I'm sorry. I know it's a little late notice for tonight, but I was wondering if you have a free night any time this week coming up. I'll take you out this time," Cookie stated.

"Hmmm...oh really? Taking me out, huh? What if I told you my schedule is wide open tonight?" Ken said.

"Great. How does 8:30 sound? I'd like to take you to a new seafood spot I heard about. Everyone says they have the best salmon in town." Cookie said.

"I love it. Sounds like a plan then. I'll be ready at 8:30. I'll text you my address too so you'll know how to get here. I'm not far from you," Ken said.

"Ok, I look forward to seeing you soon then," Cookie smiled.

"I look forward to seeing you as well. Take care." Ken said.

EIGHT

Cookie felt like she really needed to make it up to Ken for how she acted on their last date. Sure, she was sexy the last time they went out, but she wanted to look extra special as part of her apology to him for being so curt. She decided to go to her favorite specialty boutique to find just the right outfit. Cookie never needed much of an excuse to shop, but she did have good reason this time. She had an affinity for designer clothes, but rarely shopped at malls. There was no sense in paying full price if she didn't have to. Plus, she loved fashionable clothes that she would likely not see another woman wearing.

Cookie finally settled on a black sheathe dress, with a row of small diamond holes across the midriff. She picked up a few gold accessories too and she knew just the right shoes to match. They were a pair of black Christian Loubitin pumps with spikes right above the heels. She had only worn them twice and kept them tucked away at the back of her closet. When she got home, she trimmed the ends of her hair to give her bob a fresh look.

Then she climbed into a hot bath filled with almond and shea butter oils and soaked for about an hour. She felt especially sexy and pulled out the black and gold Gucci Guilty perfume bottle from the front of her cabinet. She always felt delicious and irresistible whenever she wore it. She liberally applied lotion to her naked body and slipped on her pink lace boy short panties and matching bra. At 8:05 pm, she was fully dressed and practically ready to leave. She sprayed a couple more mists of perfume, one on her chest and one between her thighs, before she turned off all the lights and walked out of her front door.

Cookie started her car, plugged in her iPod, and pulled up Ken's address in her phone. She was only 15 minutes away. She decided to call and give him a heads up that she was in route.

"There she is. Hello Beautiful," Ken answered in a smooth, unhurried tone.

Cookie blushed and was speechless for a moment, before she quickly regained her composure to respond. She was fascinated at how many times he was able to catch her off guard in such a short time of knowing her. It was a euphoric, refreshing feeling. "Why thank you. Especially coming from such a handsome man as yourself. I'm in route to you and should be there in about 15 minutes," she said.

"Alright. I'll be waiting. See you soon," Ken responded.

At 8:28pm, Cookie pulled into Ken's driveway and was immediately impressed. Although it was dark outside, she could tell the landscaping of his yard was immaculate. Not to mention the house was all brick and sat on a substantially sized lot. But Cookie was still full of pride and couldn't let on to any signs of vulnerability.

Cookie dialed Ken's number once more to tell him she was outside. As he stepped through the front door and towards her car, she noticed they were dressed alike. He wore a thin black sweater that showed off his chiseled chest and arms, dark gray wool slacks and what appeared to be black Cole Haan boots. Damn. Once again, she had to remember to keep her composure.

In actuality both Cookie and Ken were nervous about how the night would go. When Ken sat down in her car she jokingly asked, "Oh, do I need to get out and open the door for you? Where are my manners?"

"No mam, not at all. But I will make sure you won't have to open a single door for the rest of the night. How about that?" Ken rebutted. Cookie was attracted to his quick wit and confidence, something that many men boasted on the surface but actually lacked when the rubber met the road, let alone the bedroom.

The two drove in a comfortable silence for a couple minutes before conversing again. "Should I prepare myself to be kidnapped?" Ken asked. He was a little apprehensive and liked to be in control at all times. But the vulnerability of not knowing was about to happen next felt spontaneous and exciting. It made him want her that much more.

"Who knows, I might tie you up against your will," Cookie teased. "Mmmm….I might have to play hard to get then," Ken slyly answered. "Oh, putting up a fight. I think I like it," she laughed. "I've heard this restaurant is phenomenal and they have a live band that plays on the weekends. I thought we both could try something new to redeem myself from the last time. I hope you enjoy it, "Cookie said.

"No sweat, I'm just happy to be spending some time with you now. Sounds great, and even better since I'll be there with you," Ken stated.

Cookie pulled up to the valet at the Ocean Crest parking lot, as her and Ken stepped out of her Lexus SUV. They were greeted with a warm greeting and an opened door that led to the buildings main entrance. Ken let Cookie walk in first, not only because he was a gentleman but also to admire her physique from behind. She looked amazing and he felt proud to have her by his side tonight, even if nothing more serious transpired between them. Well, truth be told, Ken was going to make it a point to take things further with Cookie. She was too phenomenal of a woman for him to let go of.

"So tell me a little more about yourself. I know you're into poetry obviously, but what else are you into? What makes Cookie click?" Ken asked.

"Well, yes that's right I do love poetry," Cookie laughed. "Other than that, I absolutely love to travel. I haven't had the chance to do it as much lately. Oh yeah, and I love music too…..action movies, sports, cooking. Sometimes I think I was a man in another life. I love fashion and dressing up, but I'm not a girly girl all the time. I can get rough with the guys too. What about you?"

"Interesting. Well I'm glad we crossed paths in this life then," Ken laughed. "I actually love traveling too. I have to travel a lot for my job, so I get to have a little fun here and there, but not as much as I'd like to for leisure. I love golf, and I like doing a little construction work too every now and then. Also a music lover, as I'm sure you've picked up on," Ken said.

Cookie and Ken thoroughly enjoyed each other's conversation and their delicious meals. Cookie ordered seared shrimp and scallops with sautéed asparagus spears and garlic whipped mashed potatoes. Ken had a lobster tail, with a crab bisque soup and a side Caesar salad. When the check came, Ken took the bill and paid for the both of them. Although Cookie offered, he insisted otherwise. They stayed for another hour and danced while the live band played a mix of current popular songs, jazz and blues.

"This place really has an amazing ambience. We'll have to come here again. I hope I'm not being too forward," Ken said.

"I'm pretty sure we can arrange that. It's not too forward," Cookie smiled.
Cookie and Ken left the restaurant right before 11:30 pm. It was slightly later than Cookie planned on being out, but she didn't regret the time spent with Ken. They talked all the way back to

Ken's house and Cookie pulled into his driveway just before midnight.

"I had a really good time tonight. You're more than welcome to come inside. I know it's late, but I just want to extend the invitation," Ken said.

"Well, if you're inviting me, I can come in for a little while," Cookie said. As they walked inside, Cookie was immediately impressed with how clean and well decorated Ken's home was. Plus, it was very spacious. "Would you like a glass of Chardonnay?" Ken asked.

"Sure, I'll take one," Cookie replied. Ken handed Cookie the glass of wine, sat next to her on the couch and turned on his stereo. The Isley Brothers' "For The Love Of You" oozed out of his Bose speakers.

"Great taste. I absolutely love this song. Mmm….this one takes me back," Cookie said, gently swaying her head to the music from side to side.

"Thank you. I know a little bit when it comes to music. I have a very eclectic and wide range of tastes though," Ken said.

"Well looks like we definitely have something in common then," Cookie smiled, as she could feel the temperature rising inside of her.

The sexual tension between Cookie and Ken was getting stronger. Ken moved in closer to Cookie and put his arm around her. He leaned in and kissed her slowly as they both tasted the wine on each other's lips. He sucked on her bottom lip softly and caressed her neck. Cookie felt he had more than earned his right to kiss her and she was not going to stop him from going any further.

Ken wrapped her inside of his other arm, pulling her against his chest. Cookie raised her leg up over Ken's knee as she continued kissing him, rubbing her fingers through his closely cropped hair cut. "Wait….um," Cookie breathed deeply.

"Do you want me to stop?" Ken asked, panting and pleading for Cookie to not deny him of indulging in her body with his eyes. Truth be told, Cookie wasn't one of those women that necessarily made a man wait for a certain amount of time (two weeks, three months, etc) before having sex. She tried to at least not have sex on the first date, but they had already surpassed that point and she was too hot herself to turn back now.

Cookie straddled Ken and pulled him close to her as she began kissing him again, firmly yet slowly. "Could you take this as a no?" Cookie asked.

"Umph…sounds good to me cause I can't stop myself," Ken said. He slid his hands up across the back of her knees and then up to the fullness of her back side. He groped her with both hands and kissed the top of her breasts. It turned Cookie on as he removed her dress and continued caressing her. Cookie then removed Ken's sweater and was turned on by his full, defined chest and washboard abs. Ken unhooked Cookie's bra with one hand as he squeezed the back of her neck. Her bare breasts touched his chest before he grabbed them with both hands and sucked them.

Ken unbuckled his belt and Cookie finished taking off his pants. He stood up and removed the rest of his clothes, which pleasantly surprised Cookie. She began to slip off her boots when he told her, "No, keep those on". Ken was obviously kinkier than she imagined, but she liked it. He picked her up, sat down on the couch and placed her directly on top of him, wrapping her legs around his back. The sharp heels of her boots digging in his back turned him on more as he began to thrust back and forth inside her.

"Do you have any....?" Cookie could barely talk. "Yeah....I do," Ken gasped back. He then stood up while still inside of Cookie and walked them into his bed room. He laid her down gently across his bed, and reached inside the night stand drawer to get a condom. He climbed on top of the bed, and pulled her by her hips. Her legs were now resting on his shoulders as he made love to her. Cookie was not used to this. Something was different. Ken was very dominant in bed, but he had a certain sense of gentleness that made her feel alive and cautious at the same time. They continued exploring each other's bodies and pleasing each other for the next couple of hours before climaxing and ultimately falling asleep.

Cookie woke up just as the sun was peering through Ken's bedroom window. She felt so relaxed and comfortable lying on his chest, but didn't want to make her heart at home with him just yet. Everything was too soon and she had made the same mistake in the past. She got out of the bed quickly and walked to the front room to gather her clothes. Ken awakened just as she was about to walk out of his bedroom door and said, "Alright now, you ready to start a round 2? Looking at you walk like that is getting me excited all over again."

"Well not so fast Mr. As tempting as that sounds, I probably should go. I have a really busy day ahead and have to work for a couple of hours too. I'll give you a call later?" Cookie asked.

"Sure, I'd love that," Ken said, with a plastered smile, attempting to hide his disappointment. He opened the front door and walked Cookie out to her SUV. "You know Cookie, you can't run forever. I don't know what he did. But he's sure making it hard for me. But that's ok; you're worth the fight."

"Who said I was running?" Cookie said, with a half smirk.

"Mmm....touche. Well, I'll just be looking forward to that call later then pretty lady," Ken said.

"Will do," Cookie said, kissing Ken on the cheek before she got inside her car.

Cookie was still in awe at the phenomenal night she had with Ken. He effortlessly checked off everything on her list, but she didn't know how to handle it. On top of all that, the sex was delectable, incredible and unforgettable. She shivered just thinking about it. But she had no time to time allow herself to get engulfed by her emotions. At least that's what she had to keep telling herself.

NINE

Cookie turned the key to her front door and sighed deeply as she walked in. It was only Sunday morning and it had already been one hell of a weekend – in more ways than one. Chelsea was on Cookie's mind for the last few days, so she decided to give her a call to see how she was doing. Cookie dialed her number, but only got her voice mail. She texted her sister (since she rarely checked voicemails) and said, "Your big sis is just checking on you. Call me back when you can. Love you". Cookie poured a tall glass of orange juice and sat on her couch as she turned on the TV.

As she hung up the phone, Cookie remembered how Chelsea used to always follow her around and admire her when they were younger. Although Chelsea never said it, Cookie felt like life (and her own doing) separated Chelsea from this feeling and may have even contributed to her drug usage. She felt partially responsible for it. She would give anything back to have those precious moments when life was easy and all she had to worry about was making sure her sister could look up at her and flash her beautiful approving smile. She had a flash back of that day at the restaurant when Cookie asked Chelsea about going to church and how enraged she became. It all made sense now, but it was still disturbing to see her sister so angry. It was a side of her that she never wanted to see again.

Just as Cookie was about to put her cell phone back in her purse, it rang. She looked at the screen and it was her dad calling. "Daddy?" she answered. Her heart skipped a beat as she felt a wave of uneasiness come over her. "Hey sweetie, have you heard from your sister? Your mom is worried sick and I'm starting to get concerned too. We haven't heard from her in the last few days. She would have called or at least sent a text by now. But we've heard nothing. She's not returning our calls either," her dad said.

"That's really strange. No I haven't heard from her Daddy. I literally just called and left her a message though because she was on my mind. You know how that girl is. Probably running around town and so excited she's back on her feet and feeling herself again. I'm sure she'll call us back soon."

Cookie's dad laughed. "You know, you do have a good point. You're right. She'll turn up here soon. In the meantime, please let us know if you hear from her baby. We love our girls and we're always concerned about you both."

"I know Daddy. I love you and I'll definitely let you know if I hear from her. I'll try calling her back in a little while too if she doesn't call me first," Cookie said. "Ok, that sounds like a plan then. Well, your mom just walked back in the room. I don't want to get her stirred up again. I'll talk to you later baby," he said.

Cookie smiled and told her dad that she loved him as she hung up the phone. Although she did believe Chelsea would call back soon, she had to admit she wasn't so secure in that. Something felt eerily strange this time. Something was different. She immediately prayed for her sister and asked God for her protection wherever she was and whatever she was doing.

Almost immediately after she finished her prayer, her phone rang. She was half expecting it to be Sheila. They hadn't really talked since her embarrassing outburst at the massage parlor and she did promise her that she would call to let her know how the meeting with Tina went. But, to her surprise, it was Chelsea. Excited to see her sister calling, she almost dropped her phone trying to answer it.

"Hello!? Chelsea? I was getting worried about you. You ok?" Cookie spoke excitedly.

There was dead silence for what seemed like an eternity.

"Chelsea? Chelsea? Are you there?" Cookie thought that maybe there was a problem with the phone connection and she was about to hang up and call her sister back. But she could distinctly hear a soft echo of whimpering in the background. Nervous and not knowing what to expect, her intuition led her to stay on the line.

"Chelsea?" A dark and distorted voice finally answered on the other line, with a sinister laugh. "This ain't Chelsea bitch".

Cookie's heart sank to the very pit of her stomach. She was speechless and couldn't catch her breath as she felt her chest tighten with a vice grip of fear. "What?! Who is this? Put my sister on the phone right now! Who the hell are you!?" Cookie screamed.

Silence again.

"You're bold. You always were. I like that about you. But if you keep it up, you just might be wishing you had shut your pretty little mouth." Cookie then became quiet as a mouse and could hear her own heart beat pounding through her chest. The man's voice sounded somewhat familiar, but the distortion filter he was using made it impossible for her to decipher exactly who he was.

"I'm sorry...I'm just scared...pl..please put my sister on the phone. What have you done to her? Where is she?" Cookie was totally out of control, a feeling she rarely experienced. At this moment, she was totally helpless and at the mercy of the crazed man on the other end of the phone.

"I will not. She can't come to the phone right now. But she knows I'm talking to you. She's so precious.....Hmmmmm. I'm going to have some fun with her. She's got that feisty spirit like you. But your courage was learned. We all know that, don't we?"

What was he getting at? Cookie thought that this man must have been someone close to her. What in the hell did he mean by saying her courage was learned? How dare him. But she quickly changed gears to focus back on her sister. She had to find a way to free her from this lunatic.

"Just tell me what I need to do to get Chelsea back," Cookie cried.

"Well for starters, don't think about calling the police. They won't be able to get to me. I've made sure of that. But I've got eyes on you. I'm always watching. Remember that. So don't think about doing anything stupid or something you'll live to regret later. We're going to make this fun. Let's play a little game."

"A game? What? Ok, I'll do whatever you say," Cookie said reluctantly.

"Ooh what a conundrum you're in sweetheart. Play the tough girl role or follow the rules? Decisions, decisions," the man toyed with her. "The first task will be simple enough. Do yourself a favor and try to get some good rest tonight. You'll need it." The mysterious man that was holding her sister hostage abruptly hung up the phone.

Cookie dialed Chelsea back as the man quickly answered. "Hello, my darling. That was a really short nap. Goodbye for now. Sweet dreams." The call ended again as Cookie stared in disbelief at the phone. She was truly entangled in a moment of utter shock, confusion, anger and fear all at once. What would she tell her parents? How would she even break the news to them? She was scared to make any moves and felt as though she was being watched at every angle.

She got up from the couch and filled her glass with mostly vodka this time and a few ounces of orange juice. As she tossed her head back on the couch, her phone rang again. She looked down and saw that it was her mother calling. It was hard enough talking to her dad about Chelsea. She really couldn't deal with her mother's dramatics right now. Cookie was trying to be strong, but the thought of hearing her mother break down would likely push her emotions over the edge.

"Hey Mom. How are you?" Her greeting was fake and she was almost certain her mom would be able to pick up on it.

"Candice....baby, why didn't you say anything!!? Your sister is gone. She's gone..." her mother sobbed.

"Mom...wha-what do you mean gone?" Cookie stuttered.

"Some man just called here from Chelsea's phone. He has her with him and said he just talked to you. He hung up on me after I told him to put Chelsea on the phone. Did he really talk to you?" Cookie's mother asked, confused.

"Mom, I was so scared to say anything. Everything literally just happened a couple minutes ago. I called Chelsea earlier. She was on my mind. I thought it was her calling back.....but, it wasn't. This guy knows us whoever he is. I can just tell by the way he talks," Cookie said.

"Well I don't care about that. What are we going to do? We have to call the police. They'll find her. They'll find my baby," Cookie's mother cried hysterically.

"Wait. Mom, no we can't call the police. He's watching us. I'm telling you. We have to be really careful with this," Cookie said. "This is bullshit! We have to get her back! I can't....I just can't.....no. She was just getting her life back on track. She's not going out like this," Cookie's mother screamed. Lisa was not one to use profanity often, but when she did it usually was for good reason.

Chelsea laid motionless inside the dark room as water from the ceiling dripped steadily across her forehead. The room was damp, cold and hollow. He stood above her, pleased at his work and it turned him on to know that she was completely helpless. Finally, he had complete control and he reveled in it. His black steel toe boots made a resounding thud each time he took a step, pacing around her makeshift bed.

Suddenly, Chelsea moved her right arm and rubbed it across her head. She could tell that she wasn't in a regular house and was starting to feel a slight twinge of her energy coming back. She barely had enough strength to utter the words, "Where am I?" Her voice bounced off the walls in a jarred pattern of echoes, as she realized she was in the room alone now. She licked her lips as she tasted what seemed to be blood. At the same moment, she realized that her upper lip was bruised and swollen. She felt a cool breeze come across her abdomen. Chelsea's clothes were off and she was laying there in just her bra and panties.

Chelsea attempted to seize the moment of potential freedom by easing herself out of the bed, but was stopped dead in her tracks. There were two ropes tied in double knots at her ankles. She didn't know how in the world she would get out of this one. She looked around quickly in the dimly lit, cave-like room she was hidden away in for anything that could help free her from bondage. The only thing she found was a stray piece of long metal. Maybe that could be her golden ticket to freedom. There was just one problem. The metal was too far for her to reach. She stretched as hard as she could, without trying to make too much noise. She had to think fast and right now her need to escape overshadowed her fear of being caught by whoever was holding her hostage.

In a last ditch effort of desperation, Chelsea unhooked her bra and stretched again, this time, using her bra to extend her reach further to grasp the metal rod. There was hope still yet. She finally was able to bring the metal close enough to her reach, as she picked it up off the floor and quickly tried to put on her bra again before wiggling herself free. But maybe that wasn't her fate, because she started to hear heavy footsteps inch closer towards her vicinity.

"Think fast. Think fast. Shit! God help me please," Chelsea silently panicked. There's no way she would have enough time to break free from the shackles of rope at her ankles without causing a ruckus. For the time being, she decided to lay back down and tuck the metal rod underneath her makeshift pillow. The very next moment, the door to the room swung open so swiftly that it banged against the wall. She pretended to be still sleep, dead, unconscious or whatever would keep her alive at the moment. The man who was just standing over her a few minutes ago, began to whistle as he took off his jacket and removed his shirt, exposing a dingy wife beater. Although she still pretended to be still and motionless, Chelsea's eyes were opened just enough to see what was going on.

"Mmmm...wake up, you sexy bitch," the man whispered in Chelsea's ear. She cringed at the thought of humoring this nasty scumbag that she didn't even know. His breath reeked of alcohol – some kind of brown liquor, Jack Daniels or Crown Royal perhaps. She thought it wouldn't be wise to start moving so quickly. He may suspect she had been up moving around while he was gone. So she lied motionless for a couple more minutes – that is until he reached back and poured a huge cup of ice water over her face. She couldn't keep her composure and before she knew it she sat straight up and screamed. She panted heavily, trying to catch her breath; still in shock from being doused with the ice cold water.

"Ah, that's it....," the man said as he took off his shirt and hovered over Chelsea's scantily clad body. "I've been waiting for you my dear. So sweet and so beautiful. I'm going to make you crawl and beg for your life tonight though. You're gonna love it. You'll see."

"What do you want from me?" Chelsea asked, with her signature attitudinal tone. Although both sisters were feisty, Chelsea had a little less couth than her older sibling. But even she had sense enough to know that right now wasn't the best time to test her luck with the maniac standing over her. As he leaned closer over her, he kissed her on her neck. She was trying to make out his face, but the knitted skull cap he had on made it difficult to see his features. Even in the shadows, he somehow looked eerily familiar.

"Let's not play the game baby. You and I both know what I want now, don't we?" the unidentified man said as he firmly cupped her breasts through her bra. He then tore it off her and at the same instant, Chelsea felt his very erect penis rub against her through his jeans.

"No, please! I can't....I'll do anything. Just please don't do this to me please. I can go get some money for you if that's what you want," Chelsea pleaded. The 18 year old girl that was raped by Rev. Caldwell immediately flashed before her eyes. She was still scarred from that and couldn't imagine having to now heal again from another man who violated her more than a decade later.

"Shut up! If your memory serves you right, you would know that I don't need your damn money. I can buy you," he said.

Chelsea fought back a smart rebuttal, but couldn't hide the perplexed look on her face. Now was the time to pull out that metal rod from behind her pillow. But maybe she should wait. He had a rather stocky build. She was in a vulnerable position and could only think of one way to really break free. She would have to play along with his games for a while – even if that meant letting him have sex with her.

"Now spread those legs for daddy. I've been waiting a long time for this," he said. He proceeded to unfasten his jeans and pull down the zipper. He then started to pull Chelsea's panties to the side and thrust his penis into her. As the tears began to run to her ears, Chelsea held on tightly for just the right moment. "I knew you would feel good. Damn, it's so tight."

The forceful act went on for the next few minutes and then finally there was a light at the end of the tunnel. He began to pump harder and faster, so Chelsea knew he was about to reach his climax. She stretched her right hand behind her and hid it under the pillow until she was certain he was about to come. She stared him directly in his eyes and made him believe for a second that she was actually enjoying it. "Aaagghh, yesssssss!!!" he exclaimed.

Chelsea immediately flung the metal rod from underneath her pillow and stabbed him in the neck with it. It all happened so quickly and he was too weak from climaxing to even react. His eyes widened with surprise and terror as blood spurted out of his neck, onto Chelsea's face and breasts. She felt a cool warming sensation of revenge that was smooth and sweet like honey. She laughed out loud, although she was still afraid. He jerked a few times before collapsing on her chest. "Get off of me you bastard," Chelsea grunted as she pushed him to the ground, next to the bed. She then proceeded to use the metal rod to free herself of the rope tied to her ankles.

Freedom. Her left foot was now free. She had more of a struggle releasing her right foot though. The knot was tied much tighter on that side. She kept trying to wriggle herself out of the knot, but nothing seemed to work. After several minutes of failed attempts, the knot finally loosened. Chelsea felt like a weight of two tons had been lifted from her shoulder. She survived, yet again.

She got out of the bed and took a brief, but thorough look around the room. She touched the walls and realized they weren't sheetrock, but stone. The room was shaped similar to an igloo and she still couldn't figure out where the running water sound was coming from. She had to find her way out of this tortuous dungeon. But first, the curiosity burned inside of her to really see who her assailant was. She remembered him making subtle references about the past and always wanting her, so it must have been someone she knew.

She kneeled down beside the bed and removed the skull cap. He actually did look familiar, but she couldn't make out the full features of his face since the room was still dimly lit. She searched along the walls for a light switch and then felt a single string tickle her shoulder as she moved closer towards the bed again. She looked up, pulled it and the room lit it up so brightly that she had to squint her eyes to adjust to the sharp contrast to the dark lighting she had been subjected to for the last few hours.

Chelsea looked down on the floor, where the man was lying on his back, eyes wide open and burning a hole through the ceiling above him. He was still bleeding profusely and a small pool of blood was now starting form on the floor. She couldn't believe her eyes as she realized who she had just killed. Brian.

TEN

Brian and Brandon were the "it" guys in college. Everything got its jump start there and it's where everything took a turn in Cookie, Chelsea and Sheila's lives. Although Chelsea was a couple years behind them, she was still very popular and fit in easily with the older crowd. The sorority that Cookie and Sheila were a part of even tried to recruit Chelsea, but she declined. She loved Cookie dearly, but usually ran in the opposite direction of anything that seemed remotely close to being in her sister's shadow.

Brian and Brandon were identical twins (Brandon was the oldest by seven minutes), and very easy on the eyes. They looked so much alike that the only way to really tell them apart was that Brian had an eagle tattoo on his left shoulder and light freckles just above his cheek bones. They were both around the same height – 6'2, with broad shoulders, chiseled abs, and a stocky, muscular physique. Every girl wanted to be with them. They were corporate bad boys – street smart, but extremely intelligent. It was no wonder Cookie was the envy of the whole female population on campus when she started dating Brandon.

Cookie was always a hard catch though. Brandon loved the thrill of the chase and in some ways she humbled him. She was very attracted to him, but didn't let on exactly how much she liked him. She saved that until after she fell hard and deeply in love with him. Brandon and Brian quickly gained a reputation on campus as being heartbreakers. Although both of them were smooth, Brian was a little rougher around the edges and more quirky than his brother. Brandon's smooth persona was exactly what he needed to win Cookie over.

After three years of dating, Cookie and Brandon got married. Her parents reluctantly approved. They had a hunch that something wasn't quite right with Brandon. They heard of his reputation as a bad boy and weren't quite convinced that he was the best pairing for their lovely daughter to marry. But unlike Brian, Brandon was a smooth talker and able to sell himself like none other. Brandon really seemed like a changed man and convinced a very skeptical Cookie that he was ready to settle down and be a one-woman man.

Specifically during their first year of marriage, Cookie always had an itching intuition that Brandon may have been slipping back into his old womanizing ways. He never cheated on her that she knew of, but she was well aware of how much of a ladies man he was when they first started dating. But she was proud that she could keep his attention for three years. Plus, Cookie had the envy of what every woman secretly wants – to change a man (or at least be perceived as the catalyst that changed him).

Brandon always had a bit of a temper, but Cookie had no idea exactly how deep his angry roots were. The twins really turned out well considering their background. Their mother was an alcoholic that left them when they were just two years old. Their father did his best to raise them as a single parent. He loved those boys to the moon and back. But possibly the stress of his wife leaving him and raising two rambunctious boys really caught up with him. During their junior year of college, he passed away. Brian and Brandon were distraught by it. To make matters worse, their mother actually showed up at the funeral. It was their first time seeing her in more than 20 years. From that point on, she tried to be more involved in their lives, but both brothers had become numb to her absence. They tried for a brief period to forgive her for walking away from them years ago, but just couldn't move past their hurt to sustain a healthy relationship.

One evening Cookie came home later than Brandon expected from a girls' night out with her friends, including Sheila. It was barely midnight when Cookie called Brandon to let him know that her evening out on the town was coming to an end.

"Hey babe, I'm on my way home now. Just dropping off Sheila. What are you up to?" Cookie asked.

"What the hell you mean what am I up to? Just get home soon," Brandon said abruptly and hung up the phone.

Cookie gasped and stared at the phone in disbelief. Sheila could immediately sense something was wrong and asked why her friend's face looked so disturbed. "Everything alright girl?" Sheila asked.

"Oh yeah, it's all good girl. You know how these men are. So possessive. He's ready for his wife to get home. Guess I can't blame him for that," Cookie laughed it off.

Sheila could smell the bullshit in the air, but she played along with the game anyway. It was one of the great aspects of their friendship. They were both able to read between the lines of what the other one was saying. "Yeah, I hear you girl. Tell him to stop sweating you! You were out with your girls. Isn't it time for the playoffs anyway? Tell him to pay attention to the game and don't worry about you. You're out with your girls," Sheila laughed.

Cookie appreciated the lighthearted joke her friend was trying to make and replied, "I know, right! Get off my back". The two ladies laughed and recounted some highlights of the night until Cookie pulled into Sheila's driveway.

"Alright sweetie, well I know the hubby awaits, so I won't keep you any longer," Sheila snickered.

Cookie rolled her eyes as she said, "He is not the boss of me. He can wait. Alright, girl. Had a good time tonight. Take care."
Truth be told, Cookie was a little nervous on her drive home. Although she knew Brandon was short fused, she never quite

heard him talk to her like that before. But, she psyched herself out and chalked it up to maybe he just had a bad day at work. He worked as a marketing analyst and it was near quarter close.

She pulled into the driveway and sat in the car for a couple minutes to get her thoughts together before walking into the house. Cookie was dressed to kill (as she usually was) with a short cropped auburn, spiked haircut, minimal makeup, large silver leaf earrings, an off the shoulder purple form fitting dress and bright blue heels, with straps that wrapped around her calves. She turned the key and slowly walked through the door. "Babe, I'm home. You in here?"

Cookie didn't hear Brandon respond, but she could hear the TV playing ESPN highlights in the living room. As she walked closer to the side of the couch, she could tell that he was sitting there without his shirt on. As she continued to walk towards him, he said, "Hey. Wait, don't come any closer. Take your clothes off now. Leave the shoes on."

Turned on and perplexed at the same time, she did as she was instructed and then walked closer towards the couch to greet her husband. He stood up and she realized he was sitting on the couch butt naked. "Come sit over here on daddy's lap. He grabbed her by her wrist and led her to the couch as he turned off the TV." He then picked her up, as she wrapped her legs tightly around his back. He sat down on the couch gently and began to insert himself inside her slippery love land. Cookie moved like a steady wave on top of Brandon, slowly at first and then more passionately (following Brandon's forceful, steady thrusts).

He stood up, slowing pulling himself out of her and led her to the bedroom. Before climbing on top of her in a missionary position, he squatted down with her bottom half hanging off the edge of the bed as they both began a constant push and pull with each other in rhythmic motion.

Brandon then proceeded to climb on top of Cookie and kiss her passionately on her neck. This felt different and much more aggressive than any other time they had made love. But for now, she wasn't going to question it. It felt much better to just lay back and enjoy the ride. He then took his right hand and squeezed her neck, gently at first. As he got closer to climaxing he squeezed harder, and now with both hands. "Ah so you wanna come home late, huh? Keep me waiting, huh? What's next, you just gonna walk out on me too!?" Brandon yelled. "Ohhh….baby. Yes! Right there. Don't move. Don't move."

Cookie was caught in a perplexed moment of pleasure and confusion. She didn't struggle to free herself from Brandon's grasp, although his statement really made her concerned. He began to violently thrust his hips as she felt him release inside of her. The motion triggered her to orgasm as well as she began to feel herself slip out of consciousness.

"Here baby, I brought you some juice," Brandon said. Cookie had been lying there motionless for a while, but he didn't seem too concerned. He did bring her some grape juice though. That was her favorite after sex. She never understood why, but she had a strong desire for it afterwards. She finally came to when she felt his hand on her arm. She sat up slowly and said, "Aw, thanks babe. Um, how long have I been sleeping?" Cookie asked. "You've been knocked out for a little while babe…maybe 45 minutes or so," he confirmed.

"Hmmm…that was different. Amazing, but different. Feels like I blacked out. I don't remember anything after…well, you know," she smiled nervously. "What was that all about?" She was scared to ask the question, although they both knew that the latter portion of their sexual episode was out of the norm and borderline abusive.
"What do you mean?" Brandon asked, with a genuinely dumbfounded look on his face. "I just aim to please baby. I

missed you, that's all". Cookie smiled and said, "Well that, you definitely did sir." They didn't continue the conversation anymore from there, but deep down Cookie felt that something wasn't quite right. It was her most sexually pleasing encounter ever, but also the most disturbing. She figured she wouldn't complain, since it was so good, but she still left it as an open thought in the back of her mind.

Brandon continued to show his aggressive side throughout the course of him and Cookie's marriage. Things escalated quickly, so much so that Cookie often felt like Brandon had split personalities. She conditioned herself to the new normal of their rough style of sex (and truth be told, she loved every minute of it). But she never felt totally safe and secure with him. The kind of feeling that a wife should always have with her husband.

The first time that Brandon put his hands on her, Cookie vowed she would never let it happen again. But as many women often do, she stayed. It all started when one of her college friends, Michael, whom she hadn't seen in a while was in town for the weekend. He was her closest guy friend since high school and they remained friends through college and even after they graduated. Their communication was less frequent after Cookie got married though. Brandon knew of him as well and even hung out with him a couple times. He had a clear understanding that they were just friends, but things somehow took a turn for the worst.

Michael called Cookie on a Friday afternoon and let her know that he would be in town for a couple weeks. He respected her marriage, although there was an unspoken sexual chemistry between the two of them that they kept well hidden and under control. He never voiced it, but deep down, Brandon knew there was a spark there between the two of them. If there was anyone that he felt she would have cheated on him with, it would have been Michael. But he always kept his composure when it came to him, which went against his possessive nature.

"Um, yes may I speak to Miss, oh I mean Mrs. Cookie? I forgot, she's an 'ole married lady now," Michael said in a joking tone as Cookie answered the phone. She was pleasantly surprised to hear from him, seeing as how they hadn't spoken in great detail much since the wedding. He was always a jokester and had a witty sense of humor. Plus, he was easy on the eyes too. He stood about 6'3, 200 lbs, with broad shoulders and a very pronounced chest. He was lean, muscular and always wore clothes that complimented his physique.

"Still crazy I see," Cookie laughed and smiled from ear to ear. She was feeling down the last several days for no apparent reason. Hearing Michael's voice was the refreshing commercial break she needed from the cloudiness going on in her mind. "Mike! Now, to what do I owe the pleasure of this phone call sir? You just forgot about me, huh? You know married women do still have friends and a life," Cookie said.

"Oh yeah, they have a life. To split half the bills and give up the goods on the regular. Like it or not. Well for your sake I hope you like it...that's your life in a nutshell, Sweet Cakes. Plus, we all know how that husband of yours has a bit of a jealous streak. I don't want to have to give my regards to the undertaker after fighting him off," Michael said.

"Whatever. He is not that bad," Cookie laughed.

"Oh ok, I'll take your word for it. So how is married life treating you?" Michael asked, with a tinge of genuine concern in his voice.

"It's great. You know, just living, loving my husband and enjoying life. But enough about me, tell me about you. What's new in your world, Mr. Mike?" Cookie responded.

"Ah ok, well hey it sounds like it doesn't get much better than that then. I'm happy for you. As for me, I'm about half way through this MBA program. I should have done the fast track like you did. So, between that, work and random dating here and there, I don't have much time for an active social life. But that's part of the reason I was calling. I'll be in town for a couple weeks, leading up to Thanksgiving. I don't know what your plans are, but maybe you, Brandon and I can all go out to dinner one while I'm there," Michael said.

"That would be great! Yes, let's do it," Cookie exclaimed. She was so excited about the prospect of seeing Michael, but quickly had to reel herself in. "That sounds like a plan then. I'll talk to Brandon about it tonight. I'm sure he'd love to catch up with you too".

"Cool beans then Mrs. Cookie. Just keep me posted. I'll be just catching up with family and a few other people here, so I'm wide open for the most part," Michael said.

"Ok cool, sounds good. I'm thinking Monday might be best, but I'll still let you know either way." Cookie said, her voice smiling through the phone. Although she didn't admit it to Michael, they both knew it would be a little awkward if Brandon really did decide to tag along. Nonetheless, Cookie was going to respect her husband by asking. Hopefully they could all go together and just have a great time enjoying each other's company. She thought about how she would frame up her proposal to Brandon on her way home from work. It was a little after 5:00pm, which would put her at home around 5:20. Her timing was perfect for her to get home, change clothes and cook dinner to have it ready around 7:00 pm.

As Cookie walked through the door, she didn't hear Brandon in the house and there was a quiet stillness that made her feel like she was inside alone. She was actually grateful for it. It gave her a little more time to decide how she was going to frame up the dinner request with Michael. Just moments later, Brandon walked through the door with his duffel bag in his hand, smelling like a fresh bar of soap and Bleu Chanel cologne.

He kissed her on the cheek and said, "Ooh is this fine lady all mine? I think I'll keep her".

"Oh, little 'ole me? Thanks babe….mmm, I think this sexy man is a keeper. You just coming from the gym?" Cookie said.

"Yeah me and some of the guys finished up a bit early from work and played some basketball and got a little weight-lifting in. You know I have to stay fine for my baby. How was your day, babe?" Brandon asked. Cookie saw this as her segue way into talking about the potential dinner with them and Michael. She was apprehensive about bringing it up, but decided to just go for it and get it over worth.

"Really good. We closed the deal on that big account we've been trying to secure. So that was good news. Oh and I talked to Mike today. He called this afternoon and said he'll be in town for a couple weeks, around Thanksgiving. He wants to have dinner with us one night while he's here. What do you think?" Cookie said.

"Both of us? Oh, ok that sounds cool. But baby, you should go. He's more of your friend and I know you haven't gotten a chance to catch up with him in a while. You should go and enjoy yourself," Brandon replied, approvingly.

"Are you sure though? I know you used to hang out with him too sometimes. You don't think it would be cool for all three of us to hang out?" Cookie asked cautiously.
"Oh yeah, I'm sure, babe. What's that you're cooking up over here?" Brandon asked, looking over her shoulder to see what she was dicing up on the cutting board.

"Some tilapia, shrimp skewers, green beans and new potatoes. It should be ready in about an hour. Hope you have an appetite," Cookie smiled.

"Most definitely. I'm starving. Can't wait for it," Brandon said.

Cookie and Brandon ate their meal primarily in silence, besides a little small talk. "The food is amazing babe, you put just the right amount of seasoning on it. Now I know why I married you," Brandon smiled.

"Oh really? Is that all you married me for?" Cookie chuckled. "I'm glad to know I can keep you satisfied." As the two finished their meal, Cookie cleared the plates from the table and excused herself from the kitchen. "I'll be back in just a second. You need anything else?"

"I'm great, just maybe a cold beer from the refrigerator," Brandon replied.

"Sure, baby. Here you go," Cookie sat the beer on the table in front of Brandon, kissed him and then went into the bedroom. She took just a few minutes, but it was perfect timing as she heard Brandon walking down the hallway towards their bedroom. She stood right outside of their bedroom door and stretched her arms across the hallway. "Where do you think you're going Mr.?" She asked with a coy tone.

Cookie had changed clothes quickly into a form fitting turquoise teddy, which pushed her already perky breasts up to kiss the sky. The back of the teddy was made into a thong style with a gold bow right above her full, round ass. She topped off the look with six inch silver pumps. Brandon noticed she was also holding a black leather whip in her hand.

"Ooh damn, baby. Look at you, turning the tables on me. You ready for daddy to give it to you right?" Brandon asked, lifting his shirt and leaning in to kiss Cookie on her neck.

"Unh uh. Wait. Not so fast. In there. Come on. Let's go. On the bed. Butt naked. Let's get to it. Time's ticking sir." Cookie was nobody's prude, and considered herself to be very well experienced in the bedroom, but even she surprised herself at how aggressive she was being. She proceeded to walk into the bedroom slowly and cracked the whip against Brandon's wash board abs as he laid there, standing at attention.

Brandon, being the usual aggressor, was out of his element being so submissive. Cookie would let him have his way with her soon, but not now. She climbed on top of him and started kissing on his chest, biting his nipples, clasping his hands and stretching them high above his head. She could feel him pulsate involuntarily as she sat on his lap, rocking slowly back and forth.

"Enough of the role playing baby. It's time for me to take what's mine," Brandon grunted. He rolled Cookie over until she was flat on her back, pulling one leg up above his shoulder. He began kissing her calf as she swiveled her foot right next to his ear, admiring her stunning shoes. He slipped the crotch of her teddy to the side, gripped her breasts firmly and inserted himself slowly inside her. Now, both legs were on his shoulders as he thrust his pelvis slowly at first in long, slow strokes. Then he began to really build a rhythm, moving faster and harder inside of her.

Cookie breathed in deeply and squeezed her hands on top of his as he continued to grope her breasts and hard nipples. They were in sync with each movement, which made it hard for either of them to even think about switching positions at the moment. Brandon could feel her insides becoming more slippery and he knew she was close to climaxing. He thrust deeper and slower as Cookie's legs began to shake. "Yes daddy! It's yours! I'm coming for you!!" Brandon held out just long enough for Cookie to climax, before erupting waterfalls inside of her.

"How's that for dessert?" Cookie murmured jokingly in a raspy tone.

"Pretty delicious if I do say so myself. Didn't even need a plate to put it on," Brandon rebutted, collapsing on top of her and kissing her softly. Neither one of them remembered falling asleep. But Cookie felt this was just what Brandon needed to help take some of the edge off her dinner with Mike. She decided she would call him tomorrow to confirm for Monday night. It was the last thing she remembered before closing her eyes.

Eleven

The sunlight danced on Cookie's eyelids until she awakened, with a smile on her face. "Mmm.... Somebody's happy this morning. Did you sleep well, babe?" Brandon asked, kneeling down to give her a kiss on the cheek. He had just gotten out the shower and was getting ready for work.

"Oh yeah, like a baby. Look at you. That new workout plan has really got you ripped up. My husband is so hot," Cookie smiled like a shy schoolgirl.

"Well my favorite routine was the one from last night. I can't wait for another one of those," he smiled.

"Who are you telling? Ah, guess I should be getting up too, huh?" Cookie stretched and swiveled her feet to the edge of the bed, sitting there for a few moments and then getting up to brush her teeth.

"I'm out baby. Gotta get on the road. I'll see you tonight sweet thing. Love you," Brandon hugged her and kissed her on the forehead.

"Love you too babe," Cookie answered.

She was in an exceptionally good mood and decided to put on one of some music while she got ready for work. She let the hot water run down her back and enjoyed its steady streams for longer than she even realized.

She stepped out of the shower, grabbed her robe, and opened her closet to find something to wear for work. She decided on a hunter green sweater dress and knee high black boots with silver accessories. Truth be told, she was getting tired of working at the start up accounting firm she had been at for the past two years. But today, she wasn't going to let anything get her down – not even her job. The day ended up passing more swiftly than she imagined and she decided to give Mike a call to confirm what day would work best for their dinner. He wasn't available so she left him a voicemail. "Hey Mike, this is Cookie. How about Monday night for the dinner? Let me know if that works for you. Oh and it'll just be us two – no Brandon this time. Talk to you later. Call me back. Bye".

Cookie went on with her day and wouldn't admit to anyone else that she kept checking her phone to see if Mike had called her back yet. As fate would have it, he did call her back while she was in a meeting around 3:00 pm. She called back right after the meeting ended. "Hey Mike, it's me. You get my message?" Cookie eagerly asked.

"Yes, I sure did get it. I hate Brandon can't make it too, but we'll have a great time catching up. How's your day treating you so far?" Mike asked.

His attentiveness was always refreshing and after such a long gap in communication, it still was. It made her feel wanted and appreciated – something she honestly never had with Brandon. "You know what? I just got out of the most boring finance meeting ever, but it's a great day. I'm not letting anything get me down," Cookie laughed. "How about you?"

"That's awesome. I love it. Nothing wrong with a positive attitude. I might need to bottle some of that up from you. My day's been well all in all. No major complaints. You know how family is. I've only been here a few days, but I'm already ready to get back," he laughed. "But there's a light at the end of the tunnel. And Monday night sounds perfect by the way."

Cookie could hardly wait to have dinner with her long lost friend. But, she hid her anticipation well as she told Brandon about her and Mike's dinner plans that following evening. He still seemed pretty calm about it – almost too clam. Deep down, a woman loves a jealous man. She felt a tad bit deflated that Brandon didn't seem concerned about her going out to dinner with Mike without him.

When Monday finally came, Brandon had to work late. Cookie was actually glad about it so that she wouldn't have to face her husband right before she left for the dinner. The time was about 6:30pm and Cookie called Brandon before she left home. "Hey baby, I'm about to leave here in a few minutes. How's your day going? Sorry you have to work late today."

"It's ok baby, I'm just glad the day is finally winding down. I should be out of here in about an hour or so. Where did you and Mike decide to eat at?" Brandon asked calmly, again without a hint of jealousy in his voice.

"Ah, I'm sorry baby I should have told you that already. We actually didn't decide it until today. But we'll be at Sliders – the one right next to the movie theater you took me to a couple weeks ago," Cookie responded.

"Cool, well sounds good babe. Have a good time and tell Mike I said hello," Brandon said.

"I will. I love you," Cookie told Brandon.

"Love you too," Brandon replied.

Back at home, Cookie sprayed just a couple of mists of perfume, as she didn't want to seem like she was going on a date. She kept on what she wore to work that day, a sexy outfit but not over the top. She wore a mustard colored dress, with modest gold jewelry, including one of her favorite pairs of hoop earrings, brown leather boots and a brown pea coat.

She pulled into the Slider's parking lot right at 7:00 and to her surprise, she saw Mike already sitting down at a booth as she walked in. He usually was not very prompt, but it made her feel good to see him sitting there waiting for her.

"Hey you! Look who finally learned how to be on time?" Cookie laughed.

"Ah, you've got jokes I see. Well, I figured since you've done me the honor of fitting me in your busy schedule, I'd at least make it on time," Mike smiled.

Cookie and Mike laughed and exchanged gazes before Cookie noticed a black Range Rover. Her nervousness must have been written all over her face, as Mike quickly caught it. "What's wrong? You look like you've just seen a ghost," Mike questioned.

"I uh...I'm...I'm good. I'm good. What were you saying? I'm sorry I just saw an SUV that looks just like Brandon's. Just caught me a little off guard that's all," Cookie responded nervously.

"Well, that's great. You think maybe he changed his mind and decided to come?" Mike asked

"I don't think so. He was adamant about it being just you and I hanging out. Plus he had to work late. It would be a shocker to me if he did decide to come. I don't think that's him though". But Cookie's intuition didn't match the conviction of her words. She caught a quick glimpse at the license plate and it even looked very close to Brandon's. Maybe her mind was just playing tricks on her. She decided to let it go and just enjoy her time with Mike. Besides, the Range Rover did just pass by and they never parked – so it couldn't have been Brandon.

Mike and Cookie laughed, talked and reminisced about the old times as they rolled from one conversation to the next. After chips and salsa, a full meal and a cocktail for each them, they decided to share a skillet chocolate chip cookie. Cookie looked down at her watch and noticed it was almost 9:00 pm. "Well, good sir, I guess I better get going. We will have definitely have to do this again soon. I almost forgot how hilarious you are. Between the food and all the laughs, my body's going to pay for this in the morning." Cookie laughed.

"It was totally my pleasure. This is definitely one of the highlights of my trip, hanging out with my girl Cookie. We can't let it be this long before we see each other again. I've missed you. And tell Brandon to bring his ass out of the house next time." When the waitress came back to the table, Mike asked for the check and confirmed that it would be on one tab.

"Mike, thanks, you didn't have to do that," Cookie said

"Yes, I did. I invited you out, so I'm footing the bill. Don't worry, I'll let you get me next time," he laughed.

As the two exited the restaurant, Mike offered to walk Cookie to her car. "Well, I know it's cold out here and it's getting to be late hours for married folk, so I'll let you get to it," he joked.

"Whatever man," Cookie smirked and playfully punched him on the shoulder. "Gimme a hug boy." Mike held on to Cookie about two seconds past appropriate but she didn't push him away. He caught himself and stepped back, with his hands still slightly gripping her arms.

"Alright, well it was good seeing you as always. Be careful," Mike said.

"I will, you too," Cookie said, lowering herself into the front seat. Just as she was about to close the door, Mike called out to her.

"Hey. Uh, let me know when you make it home, ok?" Mike said.

"Sure thing, long as you promise to do the same," Cookie smiled and closed her door as she watched Mike get inside of his truck. He waited until she exited out of the parking lot safely before pulling off. Cookie wasn't one to cheat. Sure, she had done it a couple of times as an unmarried woman with other guys she dated. But something about Mike felt so familiar and safe. Truth be told, had he tried to kiss her, she probably would have let him.

Cookie texted Brandon to let him know he she was on her way home and then turned on the radio. Maxwell's "Pretty Wings" poured out of the speakers. She basked in the moment of euphoria from a great dinner with Mike. Just then her phone rang. She placed her Bluetooth on her ear and looked down at the screen. It was Mike.

"Hello?" Cookie said.

"I'm just checking on you. I know you used to be a light weight with your liquor, so I'm making sure you're staying in your lanes over there," Mike laughed.

"Oh, whatever! I saw you stumbling out your seat when you stood up. Looks like somebody else may be a light weight too," Cookie chuckled.

Cookie and Mike both played it off as if he was just calling to check on her. But they knew that they didn't want to leave dinner and thoroughly enjoyed each other. Before she knew it, Cookie had pulled into the garage at home. She said goodbye to Mike and took a deep breath in the still silence. She grabbed her purse and coat from the front seat of the car and turned the door knob to walk into the house. To her surprise, the door was locked. She turned on the light so that she could see better to unlock it. She noticed there were three empty Heineken bottles on top of the mini fridge. Brandon must have had a few beers earlier. She shook her head and prayed silently. He was a bit much to handle when he had been drinking.

"Babe? I'm home...you still up baby?" Cookie asked cheerfully. Brandon was usually a night owl, but she wouldn't be surprised to find him already asleep since he had such a long day. Then again, he never slept too hard if she was not in the house. She turned the corner, down the hallway and into the bedroom. Brandon was sitting across the bed, watching TV, with some sweatpants on, barely tied at the waist, and his shirt off. He was wrapping up a phone conversation as she walked in. There was a half-gallon of Rocky Road ice cream sitting in his lap, with a spoon in it. She hated when he ate ice cream straight out of the container, but nothing in life is perfect. She still loved him nonetheless. Although she did feel some kind of spark while she was out with Mike, she was truly elated to see her husband.

"Hey babe, how was your dinner?" Brandon asked, without looking directly at her.

"It was nice. We had a good time catching up. Mike said he's dragging you out of the house next time though. I told him I tried hard to get you to join us," Cookie smiled.

"Oh next time, huh? You two already set another date?" Brandon questioned.

"No. He's only in town for a few days remember? Who knows when he'll be back again? He is thinking about moving back to Chicago though after school. But enough about me. How was your day? I didn't mean to cut your conversation short earlier. You could have kept talking," Cookie said.

"That was just Tim. If you want to know who I'm talking to, just ask," Brandon responded defensively.

Tim my ass. Cookie caught a glimpse of Brandon's cell phone as he laid his phone on the bed. The face on the screen appeared to be a woman with long, curly hair instead of one of his guy friends.

She often questioned his faithfulness, but never actually catch him in the act. After so long, she realized she would rather not know if he was cheating.

"Well, no need to get offensive. I was just saying," Cookie rebutted nonchalantly, trying to keep the peace.

Brandon knew deep down that Cookie had just busted him in a lie. He decided the best way to take the attention off of himself would be to direct the discussion back at her. He noticed her Bluetooth clipped onto her ear, as she ran her fingers through her hair in frustration. She texted him to say that she was on her way home, while he was on the line with another woman. Seeing the Bluetooth on her ear just confirmed his suspicions about her and Mike. Driving past Slider's and seeing them interact so lovingly and now the Bluetooth on her ear, he was convinced he had the proof he needed to accuse her of cheating.

"I got it. The dinner must have been so good, you couldn't tear yourselves away from each other, huh?" Brandon asked with a stoic expression.

"Brandon, what the hell are you talking about?" Cookie responded, now raising her voice. Clearly it couldn't have been that obvious that she was attracted to Mike.

"Oh what am I talking about? I think we both know what I'm talking about. Don't play dumb with me," Brandon inquired in a very low, controlled tone.

"You're crazy. Let's face it. You got busted talking to that whore and now you're trying to turn the tables on me. This is unbelievable." Cookie was a no nonsense type of woman, but as soon as those words escaped her lips, she was well aware of the sting and repercussions they would have with Brandon.

His jaws tightened as he stood up from the bed, with the half-eaten container of ice cream in his hand. He scooped out a big chunk of ice cream with the spoon and devoured it. Cookie stood her ground as he walked slowly towards her, stopping within arm's reach in front of her. "Don't you ever call me crazy again. You got that?"

Cookie stared him down with a look of disgust and didn't utter a word. Just as she turned around to walk away, he grabbed her arm and turned her back towards him. He brought his other hand up and smashed the container of ice cream in her face.
"Don't you walk away from me!" he screamed.

She jumped and yelled, "You crazy bastard! What's your damn problem?! Cookie immediately grabbed the iron sitting on the dresser in a furious rage and hurled it directly at Brandon's head. She barely missed and he felt the quick wind of the iron whiz past his earlobe. Her force was so strong that it broke the bedroom window.

Brandon was taken by surprise, although he expected a quick reaction from Cookie. He watched in a frozen state as she immediately began to throw clothes, toiletries, her laptop and her phone charger in large duffel bag. She grabbed her keys and coat from the bed and stormed out of the room towards the front door. Brandon began to chase after her and she turned to him and said, "This shit is over," throwing her wedding ring at his chest.

"You damn right it's over bitch!" Brandon replied as she stormed out of the door.

TWELVE

Brandon walked into the garage after Cookie left and grabbed two more beers from the mini fridge. He downed the first one in less than three minutes. As he popped the top of the bottle off of the second one, he heard a loud knock at the front door. He didn't think it was Cookie, because the knock sounded too forceful to come from her or any woman. But then again, she did single handedly break their bedroom window with the iron, so he wasn't sure. Either way, he was ready for her if she was coming back to start a fight with him.

He looked through the peephole and to his surprise, two police officers were standing on the front porch. He grabbed a T-shirt from the drier and threw it on before he answered the door. "Good evening. How may I help you, officers?" He asked. Brandon was not one to crack under pressure and his demeanor came off as slightly arrogant as if to say, "Why the hell are you at my doorstep?" The officers looked at each other quickly before one of them answered. "Officers Mitchell and Frankston here. We received a noise complaint for disturbance. Is your wife home?"

Brandon quickly glanced down at his hand. Obviously, his wedding band clued them in that he was married. "No, she's actually not in right now, but what can I help you with?"

"The complaint filed stated that there was some violent activity being heard. It didn't exactly sound like you were just having a normal conversation. We're watching you. Don't try anything slick," Officer Mitchell said, running his hand across his gun. "Good night, sir. Keep the noise down".

"Will do. Sorry for the disturbance gentlemen. It won't happen again. Good night," Brandon responded calmly.

"Oh wait. Sir?" Office Frankston said.

"Yes?" Brandon replied, clearly showing his irritation by now.

"Where exactly did you say your wife was?"

"She went to the store. She should back soon. You guys have a good night now," he responded, closing the door before finishing his sentence.

Meanwhile Cookie was furious and driving in no particular direction. She felt the stickiness of the ice cream stuck to her hair and face. She reached in her glove compartment for some napkins to wipe the residue of it off. There was no way in a million years she would have expected Brandon to act like this. Sure, she knew he was jealous. But this was totally uncalled for. She didn't know what to do or who to call, but she knew she wasn't going back home to sleep with one eye open. There was one person she knew she could call that would keep the situation between the two of them – Chelsea. The flipside was that Chelsea's temper was even shorter than Cookie's. She was a rebel in more ways than one.

Cookie reluctantly dialed Chelsea's number, not knowing what to really expect. Unlike Cookie, Chelsea was usually up late. So Cookie didn't expect Chelsea to be sleep, even at 11:30 at night. But to her surprise, when Chelsea answered the phone, she sounded very out of it – almost inebriated.

"Uh...hey...hello? Cookie? What's a married woman like yourself calling here so late for? I know Brandon didn't let you stay in the streets this late," she said.

"Funny you mention his ass. Girl, you won't believe what that fool did. Long story short, we got into a big argument and he smashed a container of ice cream in my face. I'm so pissed at that bastard. I mean, I know that..." Cookie was clearly on a rampage and her feelings started boiling over again as she recounted the story to her sister. But before she could finish her sentence, Chelsea quickly cut her off.

"Come again? He did what!? Threw ice cream in your face?! Who the hell does that shit? I knew he was crazy, but this has reached a new low. Where are you now? What you need to do is let me take you to the shooting range. I'm telling you. My gun is in the closet, we can take care of this right now," Chelsea exclaimed.

"Whoa, whoa! Chelsea….slow down. We are not about to go kill anybody. That would be crazy. Come on now, we can't do that. But I am leaving him though. I can't live like this," Cookie said softly.

"Crazy huh? No what's crazy is him throwing some damn ice cream in your face. How did all of this….? Nevermind. We'll talk it out. You on your way here?" Chelsea asked.

Yeah I'm on my way. I'm almost there. About 10 more minutes." Cookie confirmed.

"Ok, well in that case, just give me a ring when you get here. I can't believe this shit. Call me. Love you sis," Chelsea said abruptly, hanging up the phone.

Cookie looked down at the phone in slight surprise that Chelsea just ended their conversation so curtly. But she didn't have the mental capacity to really dive deep into that. She started to turn on the radio, but decided against it. She opted for the painful silence instead. As she pulled into Chelsea's driveway, she unhooked her Bluetooth from her ear, and grabbed her duffel bag from the front seat. The Bluetooth. That's why Brandon was so upset at her. She could have kicked herself for being so careless. The fact that the Bluetooth was still on her ear indicated that she was previously talking on the phone to someone else – and not to him. It surely did nothing but heighten his already insecure suspicions.

She still could not believe what he had done to her. Sure, he had a temper and they had gotten into verbal altercations before— maybe even a little pushing and shoving. But she had never seen him in such a rage like he was tonight. He was a completely different person. She toyed back and forth with the idea of really leaving him for good. After all, she really wasn't happy anyway and Brandon was probably someone she never should have married in the first place. She can just hear her father's voice in her head now. "Something about this guy is bad news. I just can't put my finger on it." Maybe she should have listened.

Cookie snapped out of her daze, got out of her car, walked towards Chelsea's front door and rang the doorbell.

"Girl, get in here!" Chelsea said, giving her sister an extremely tight hug. "I love you. I can't believe this shit. Oh my God, look at your hair. Just say the word and we'll have this fool erased. You know I'll do it. You want me to fix you a drink?"

"Ooh yes, you know I love your Amaretto Sour. You have anything to make one of those? It can be a strong one too. I'm sorry to barge in on you like this. I know it's a weeknight.

"Hush! Be glad you have someone to tell all of this to and that you got away safely from that fool. That's what family is for, right? One Amaretto Sour for my big sis coming right up. Now spill the beans....I'm all ears."

"Well, do you remember Mike from college?" Cookie asked.

"Do I remember Mike?! Of course, how could I forget him? You and he were thick as thieves in college. Woo...just the thought of that man still gives me chills. I bet he's still fine too. You know I always told you that he was sweet on you," Chelsea was going a mile a minute, but paused to process her next thought before vocalizing it. "Cookie……you didn't….did you?"

"No! Come on now. I wouldn't do anything like that to Brandon." Cookie's voice trailed off and her eyes shifted quickly to the left.

"But you thought about it, didn't you? No judgment here. Hey, a thought isn't cheating, so I say think away," Chelsea said.

"Focus baby girl," Cookie cut her off. "He did call me this week though, out of the blue. It was such a pleasant surprise. He wanted to meet up with Brandon and me for dinner."

"So what's the problem then? I'm sure Brandon tagged along didn't he? If he has half a bit of sense, I'm sure he did," Chelsea responded.

"No….he didn't. I was really shocked by that too. He just told me to go on without him and have a great time. He even said it would probably be good for us to have that time alone to catch up. You know, now that everything has gone down, I think he was following me too," Chelsea said.

"Wait a minute. That asshole followed you and Mike to dinner? Did you catch him there?" Chelsea inquired.

"Well, not exactly. But when we were at dinner, I swear I saw his SUV pass by the window. I even caught a glimpse of the license plate number and it looked like his. I don't know. I just know I gotta get away from him," Cookie sighed deeply.

Just then, Cookie's cell phone rang. She made sure her Bluetooth was off, so she didn't accidentally answer the call. It was Brandon. "Speak of the devil, this is him calling me now. Probably trying to figure out where I'm at," she said.

"Gimme that," Chelsea reached towards Cookie's phone to push the ignore button. "Now, that takes care of that. Getting back to this story. So let me guess. You came home and he got jealous and tried to fight you?"

"Well not exactly. He was on the phone when I walked in. He lied and said it was his friend Tim, but when he hung up, I saw some chick on the screen when he laid the phone down. I didn't say anything at first, but he just started drilling me about the dinner with Mike. I mean question after question, until finally I let him know that I knew he was talking to that bitch. I told him he was crazy too. That's when he snapped," Cookie sighed as she concluded her recount of the night's events.

Chelsea handed her sister the amaretto sour and said, "Well, you know my door is always open. Stay here as long as you like".

"Thank you. I love you girl. Damn, this drink is so good. I needed this. Wooo...." Cookie exhaled deeply. The two sisters talked for a little while longer before getting ready to turn in for the night. Cookie took a nice long shower to not only cleanse her body and wash the sticky traces of ice cream off of her, but to renew her mind as well. She couldn't quite put her finger on it, but something was different about her sister. Maybe it was just the stress of the night, but she had a good hunch that her intuition was on point. Whatever the case, she truly didn't have the energy to exert on it, but she did keep the thought at the back of her mind.

Cookie looked at herself long and hard in the mirror after stepping out of the shower, as the minute droplets of water that she missed from drying off slid down her body like warm molasses. Many men looked at her as desirable, but tonight she felt like the ugliest woman in the world. The man who she loved and dedicated her life to had disrespected her in a way that she thought was impossible for him to do. But the reality was that he did. And the reality was that she couldn't go back.

THIRTEEN

"Baby, I didn't sleep good at all last night without you here. I'm so sorry. Please forgive me. I'll do anything – anything to get you back. I love you….I'm sorry." It was the 12th text message (not to mention four missed calls) from Brandon. This was the most recent one Cookie saw when she naturally awakened a little after 8:00 am. Although her body woke up on its own, she slept hard and needed the rest. Brandon's incessant communication was flattering, although highly annoying. At least he did seem remorseful for his actions. After all, he didn't hit her, but he was way out of line and Chelsea still insisted that she leave him and never look back.

When Cookie woke up, she realized she was home alone. There was a faint, fresh smell of Yves Saint Laurent perfume in the air. Chelsea must have not been gone too long. Cookie got out of bed, rinsed off her face and brushed her teeth before walking to the living room. She found a note on the kitchen counter that read, "Love you sis and didn't want to wake you. Make yourself at home. There's food in the refrigerator, in case you get hungry. How about a girl's happy hour tonight after work?" Cookie smiled as she placed the note back down on the counter.

She then checked her voice mails as she poured herself a glass of cranberry juice. Right before the back to back voicemails that Brandon left last night and into the early morning, Cookie realized her mother had called and left a message as well. "Hey baby, this is your mother. You know, the lady you haven't talked to in about a week now? Just checking in on you baby. I miss you and I love you. Call me when you can."

She opened her laptop and sent a quick email to her supervisor to say that she would be working from home today. Work had been a little hectic this week, but she needed the mental break.

Cookie then decided to give her mother a call back. Her mother answered the phone, sounding surprised and elated. "Hello. Aye my baby. I wasn't expecting to hear back from you so soon. It's so good to hear your voice. Wait, isn't a successful business woman like yourself supposed to be at work right now?" Lisa asked. Cookie was always amazed at her mother's quiet keenness. She noticed everything and she may not have known all of the details, but just like her dad, she could always tell when something was wrong with one of her daughters.

"Hey Mom. It's so good to hear from you. I'm doing ok, how about you? Yeah I decided to work from home today. Woke up this morning with a terrible migraine. But I'll be ok. I think the extra rest will do me some good."

"Oh no, do you need me to come over and bring you some soup? It's that time of year. Did you get your flu shot yet?" Lisa asked, concerned about her daughter.

"Yes, I sure did mom. You're right; the flu season is definitely upon us, isn't it? I don't think it's anything major though. We should have lunch soon and do a little shopping. Maybe some time in the next couple of weeks? How's Daddy?" Cookie asked, trying her best to deter her mother from coming over to visit.

"You must have read my mind. I was just telling your father how much I've missed our Sunday dinners. You know, we'll be leaving for our cruise tomorrow with the Swishers, so you and your sister will be on your own for Thanksgiving this year." Ronnie and Debra Swisher were a fun-loving couple that were similar, but just opposite enough of Bill and Lisa to make a great trip. Ronnie and Bill were both excellent cooks, but Ronnie was a little more reserved, yet just as perceptive as Bill. Debra was much less emotional than Lisa, but more spontaneous and fun. Both couples were adventurous, which would make the trip that much more memorable and enjoyable.

"What are you and Brandon up to next Sunday? What do you say we celebrate Thanksgiving together then? I'll make one of your favorites – my homemade lasagna and a pecan pie, plus all the food your dad usually makes. What do you say?" Lisa asked with glee.

Her mother sounded so cheerful and Cookie didn't want to burst her bubble. She honestly had forgotten about her parents' cruise, let alone the fact that Thanksgiving was next week. She went ahead and told her yes against her better judgment. This meant she would have to make up (or at least fake it) with Brandon before then. If she changed her mind, she would just have to think of another lie early Sunday morning, before her mother started cooking. "That would be so wonderful mom," Cookie smiled. "Just like old times. I can't wait for it. I'll be sure to let Brandon know."

"Excellent. Your daddy tries to act all big and macho, but he's really been missing his girls. I'm going to call Chelsea and let her know too, but if you talk to her first, you can pass the message on. Hope you feel better baby. Let me know if you need anything at all. I mean anything. Ok?" Lisa asked.

Again, Cookie felt as if her mother could read right through the tone of her voice and could really tell what was going on. Her last statement chilled to the bone and Cookie fought the urge to spill out everything that happened between her and Brandon last night. "I sure will mom. I love you so much. Kiss Daddy for me. Talk to you later," Cookie responded.

"Ok, love you too baby. Bye," Lisa replied before she hung up the phone.

To be absent from the office, Cookie got quite a bit of work done while she was at Chelsea's house. Before she knew it, 4:00 pm had come and Chelsea was walking through the door. "Hey sis!

How's my big sister doing in here? That bastard call you again today? I know he was just blowing up your phone."

"Whew. Not already. You haven't even put your bags down yet girl," Cookie laughed. "Yeah he has been calling though, but I haven't answered," her voice trailed with a bit of uneasiness at the end of her statement.

"Hmmm...you sound sad. Please don't tell me you're thinking of going back to that loser," Chelsea said.

"Well Chelsea, he is my husband. This kind of things has never happened before. I'm going to try to stick in there as best I can. Within reason of course. He can never do anything like this to me again. But anyway, how was your day? I'm sure mom has already called you by now about next Sunday."

"She did," Chelsea responded. "And she said that you and Brandon would be there. Just don't sit his ass next to me. I just might stab him. You can put up with this bullshit if you want to, but I'm not having it. Let me change clothes, because you're not going anywhere tonight. I have the perfect movie for us. I figured we'd have a better time staying in rather than going out. We can drink Amaretto sours and get tipsy and dance to some music. What do you say to that?" Chelsea asked.

"Sounds good to me. I think we could both use some sisterly bonding time. Thanks again for letting me stay here girl," Cookie smiled.

Two hours later, Chelsea and Cookie were on their second Amaretto sour and in the middle of watching *What's Love Got To Do With It?* After they finished watching a couple more movies, they put on some music and danced around the house like they didn't have a care in the world. Cookie felt liberated and at that moment she was happier than she had been in a long time. Just then, her phone rang. It was Brandon. She reached over to silence it, but accidentally answered.

"Um...hello," Cookie answered nervously and out of breath, as she motioned for Chelsea to turn down the radio. Chelsea turned down the music, but not before she shot the middle finger up in the air, directing her frustrations to Brandon.

"Thank goodness you're ok baby. I've been calling you. Where are you? Was that music in the background?" Brandon asked.

"You know, right now, I think interrogating me is the last thing you need to be doing right now," Cookie defensively answered.

"I know baby, I'm sorry. I've been calling and texting you. Where are you? I'm so sorry. I was wrong and way out of line. Please come back home," Brandon pleaded.

"Well that's not an option right now. Brandon, things can't just go your way this time and go back to normal. This is pretty major what you did this time. Look, I gotta go," Cookie responded curtly.

"Gotta go? Ok, just make sure you bring your ass back home soon," Brandon answered.

"I knew it. Same shit, different day. You're not sorry," Cookie hung up the phone abruptly.

"Ugh....what a damn buzzkill. Here's another drink. Oh let me guess what he said. "Baby please come back home. This bed is so cold. I can't live without you baby." Oh go chew bricks why don't you? Geeshhh, he's begging harder than Keith Sweat. I say let him beg some more if you really do go back. He hasn't suffered long enough yet. Make his ass pay," Chelsea ranted.

"You are hilarious. You know he probably knows I'm here. I don't want to put you in any kind of compromising position in case he comes looking for me," Cookie said.

"Oh trust me, he'll be the only one in a compromising position if he shows up at my door step. And you know he knows Daddy is crazy, so I doubt he'll show up at their house either," Chelsea assured her sister. "Like I said, my house is your house. You stay here as long as you want or need to."

"I know…..and I appreciate it. I do," Cookie slurred.

"Girl, you are either really tipsy or really tired. This is too funny. Wow, it is after 2:00 am though. Guess we can't hang like we used to. If I feel like this now, I'm scared to see 30 come. I'm starting to get sleepy myself. We can go ahead and shut it down for the night," Chelsea said.

Cookie fell into a deep sleep, before she heard the bedroom door creak open. She looked over in the bed and her sister was still there. She didn't know where the noise was coming from, but considering her conversation with Brandon earlier, it definitely made her nervous. Would he really be that bold to come and look for her at Chelsea's house? It didn't reassure her feeling of safety once she reminded herself that most men would, which means Brandon definitely would. The next thing she knew, she heard very heavy footsteps right outside the bedroom door. She was tempted to get up and look, but didn't want to endanger her life or her sister's. She laid there still, anticipating to see if the noise would stop. She was probably overreacting. Yes, that had to be it.

Just when she started to let her guard down, a tall figure with broad shoulders walked into the room. She could barely make the person out from the moonlight, but their silhouette was definitely one of a man. He was wearing dark sweat pants and a matching hooded sweatshirt. Chelsea turned over in the bed and coughed. It startled Cookie, but she stayed still and quiet as a mouse. She could practically hear her heart pounding through her chest, as the man walked closer towards her side of the bed – making very slow, heavy steps.

Cookie prayed silently as the man hovered over her body. He then reached his hands down towards her throat. She had to do something – and quickly. She grabbed the porcelain statue Chelsea had on her nightstand and slammed it against the man's head. But it did nothing, as he shook off the broken pieces and charged at Cookie. She screamed as he began choking her.

"Bon appetite. Morning sunshine," Chelsea said. "Breakfast is ready, so you might want to get up soon. I made buttermilk maple pecan pancakes, eggs, grits and turkey sausage."

"That sounds so good. Ok, let me get up now. Did you hear anything last night when we were sleep? Any noises? I had the craziest dream. It felt so real, but thank God it wasn't. I probably was just really tired," Cookie concluded.

"Hmmm, that's weird. No I was knocked out. I didn't hear a thing. I made those drinks stronger than I usually do, so I could have slept through an earthquake," Chelsea laughed.

"I understand. I slept pretty hard too. I guess my mind was just wandering. Chelsea, what's that under your nose?" Cookie asked.

"What do you mean? Ugh don't tell me something is hanging out of my nose," Chelsea responded, as she snorted, thinking that would help.

"Kinda looks like powder or something," Cookie said.

"Oh girl, that's baby powder. I put some on after I got out the shower this morning and I must not have wiped my hands off good. Thanks for looking out. Don't want to walk around looking like a druggie," she laughed.

"No I wasn't saying that. Just looked a little strange," Cookie laughed.
The two sisters ate their breakfast and continued to talk, trading laughs about last night. "So what you gonna do?" Chelsea asked abruptly during their conversation.

"Ugh, can't we just talk about this wonderful breakfast my sister made for me? These pancakes are out of this world. You always could cook better than me," Cookie responded.

"Thanks, but let's stay on topic. I have to keep you on your toes. Seriously, what are you going to do?" Chelsea asked, with a stern look of concern written across her face.

"Who's the big sister now? You're right. I know I have to do something. I'm going to go back today just to get some more clothes. He should be gone by the time I get there. He's always at the gym around 11:00 am on Saturdays. It's like clockwork. I just need a little bit of time to get in and out of there. After that, I guess just take it day by day. I don't really want to see him right now though. Just too much drama to deal with," Cookie responded.

"I'm not trying to pressure you. Just asking because I love you. And I'm going with you to your house. I can follow behind you. That way we'll catch his ass off guard in case he tries something," Chelsea said.

"Ok, I'll start getting ready now and maybe we can leave in about 30 minutes?" Cookie said.

"Sounds good to me. I'm ready to go, you just say when," Chelsea responded.

As Cookie drove to her house, with her sister trailing behind her, all of Thursday night's events began replaying in her mind. She got a text message and checked it while she was at the red light.

It was Mike. He said, "Just checking on you. Hope your weekend is going well. Had a great time Thursday. You ok?" Cookie smiled, but was a little puzzled at why Mike asked her if she was ok. Did he sense something was wrong with her? She surely hoped not. Perhaps she was just being sensitive and overly paranoid right now. She placed her phone back in the passenger seat, as the traffic light turned green. She finally pulled into the drive way and didn't see Brandon's car in the garage. She saw Chelsea rolling to a slow stop on the street, a couple of houses down from hers. Cookie let up the garage and didn't see Brandon's car – great. He was holding true to his normal routine, something Cookie sometimes complained about. But now couldn't have been a better time for him to be gone.

Cookie motioned to her sister that everything was ok, before walking into the house from the garage. She walked to the bedroom quickly and grabbed a few pairs of panties and bras, before going inside the closet to get a couple of outfits. She saw her wedding ring sitting on top of the pillow in the bed. The sight of her ring punched her in the chest and she stopped to look at it for a moment. She quickly snapped out of it and continued throwing clothes in her bag. She grabbed a couple of pairs of shoes and then walked out back into the garage. She let the door up, pulled out and waived to Chelsea in the mirror that everything was ok.

Just as she turned the corner, she thought she saw Brandon's SUV turn onto their street. Her phone rang and it was Chelsea calling her to confirm what she saw. "Did you see that? That was him coming in behind us. You made it out of there just in time. He wouldn't expect to see my car, so good thing you were driving in front of me. How do you feel?" Chelsea asked, this time with no sarcasm and genuine concern.

"I don't really know. I walked in and saw my wedding ring on the pillow. I can't lie, that kinda shook me for a minute. But I'll be ok," Cookie responded.

"Yeah. I know you probably felt some kind of way after being in the house again since everything went down. Well, I'll let you clear your head. I can let you go if you want, and see you back at the house," Chelsea said.

"Ok, sis. See you there. Love you," Cookie said. She waited until the next traffic light and texted Mike back. "Yes, we will definitely have to do it again. You know, same ole thing here. Just running errands and whatnot. How about you?" She purposely dodged his question of asking if she was ok.

Mike immediately texted her back and said, "Nice, sounds good. Well you take care of yourself. I'm heading back right after Thanksgiving. I'll be sure to keep in touch. Make sure you do the same."

"Of course, will do. Be safe! Let me know when you make it back," Cookie replied. Even after all of his crazy antics, Cookie was still loyal to Brandon. She felt guilty because of her feelings for Mike. Brandon could sniff it out no matter how hard she tried to fight it. But it was a good thing Mike didn't live in town anymore. After Thursday night's fiasco, she wondered if she just should have followed her desires and cheated anyway.

Fourteen

Cookie stayed with Chelsea for the next few days and her mind constantly wandered between whether or not she should stay or leave Brandon. She weighed out her pros and cons and found that ultimately, she still loved him. She packed her bags and walked out into the living room, knowing Chelsea would have something to say about it.

"Um, and where are you going with those?" she asked. "Please tell me you are not about to go back to that sorry ass husband of yours."

"Yeah, I am. I'm going to give it another try. I love you. I know you're only looking out for me," Cookie said.

"Anytime. That's what sisters do. Love you too sweetie. Call me if you need backup," she laughed. Chelsea despised her sister's decision, but as much as she disagreed with it she understood why Cookie was going back. After all, she had made a vow to love him for better or for worse, even if their relationship had momentarily turned for the worst that ever was. She just hoped things wouldn't escalate more than they already had.

Friday afternoon was going smoothly at work for Cookie. She was knocking off things on her check list and pleased with the tasks she had completed. Shortly after lunch, she received a call from Brandon. She had still been ignoring his calls. But today, she decided to answer. "Hello?" she picked up, with a friendly, but curt demeanor.

"Candice, I really miss you. I've been hurting….hurting so badly, without you here. I know that doesn't matter compared to how I've hurt you. But I need you in my life and I'm willing to do anything to get you back."

Cookie was silent for a long time and gathered her thoughts before responding. "Brandon, I love you. I really do. And I'm committed to you and only you. I'm willing to stay and work through this, but there have to be some visible changes. What happened this week can never happen again."

"You have my word, never again. I promise," Brandon apologetically replied. "Will you come back home, please?"

"I'll see you tonight after work. I should be out of here around 6:00," Cookie responded.

"Ok, I'm really looking forward to it. You won't regret giving me another chance. I'm going to make sure of it." Brandon reinforced his apology to Cookie.

"It's going to take some time to build back my trust in you again. But I'm willing to make it work. See you tonight," Cookie said.

"Ok, see you then. I love you," Brandon responded.

"I...I love you too Brandon," Cookie said. She kept the whole ordeal with Brandon a secret from everyone. Not even Sheila, whom she told everything, knew exactly what was going on. Cookie did mention that her and Brandon got into an argument, but failed to mention how heated it became. She felt ashamed and was glad that Chelsea was the only person who knew the whole truth. Although she was even uncomfortable disclosing the information with her sister, she knew that she had to tell someone to get away that night. Chelsea was the safest bet and would keep the information to herself.

At 5:45 pm, Cookie started packing up her things and preparing to leave the building. She was feeling particularly apprehensive about seeing Brandon, but she vowed to just go with the flow and calm her nerves. As she walked closer to her car in the parking garage, she saw a gold box with a crimson bow wrapped around it sitting on the roof. Underneath the bow was a plain white card, with an embossed framing around it.

"Baby, I know I haven't been the best husband I should be towards you. In fact, I have been pretty selfish, insecure and inconsiderate. I beg that you please forgive me and allow me another chance to treat you how you should be treated – like the queen that you are. There's a surprise in the box...." Cookie began to feel the butterflies fluttering at the pit of her stomach. It was the kind of feeling she remembered having for Brandon once upon a time. She inhaled deeply and took in its familiar fragrance.

"What are you still doing in this parking lot? It's Friday. You should be spinning your wheels out of this place," said Malachi. Malachi Chimala was one of the new managers who recently transferred from New Jersey. She had a keen business sense and spunky attitude, which quickly made her well liked within the company. "I don't know about you, but it's been a long week."

"Oh, hey Malachi. I'm sorry. I'm sure I looked quite silly standing here with my eyes clothes. My husband surprised me with a gift. I'm headed to meet for him dinner tonight," Cookie smiled, still feeling excited, yet slightly embarrassed.

"Well let me not interrupt you! Sounds like someone has an exciting weekend planned. Have a good one. I'll see you on Wednesday. I'll be traveling on Monday," Malachi responded.

"Ok, have a safe trip and a great weekend," Cookie said. She couldn't wait to finally open the box to see what was in it. Inside, she found a pair of brown leather boots with gold diagonal zippers. There was a note attached at the sole of the left shoe that read, "Just because you deserve it." A few weeks ago, Cookie pointed out these exact boots to Brandon in the mall and told him how much she liked them. She decided against purchasing them and opted to wait until they were on sale. It was honestly not a ploy to get him to buy them for her, but she was truly shocked that he even remembered their conversation enough to pick them up.

She smiled, opened her car door and gently placed her things, along with Brandon's gift, in the front seat. That's when she noticed another note on her windshield. She grinned from ear to ear, and reached to pick up the note on the front of the car. It said, "Meet me at Mi Amor". Mi Amor was a quaint coffee and tea café where Cookie and Brandon had their first date. On Friday's they had a small jazz ensemble that performed from 7:00 to 10:00 pm. When Cookie entered the café, Brandon stood up and greeted her with a bouquet of pink roses.

"Hello beautiful. These are for you. Thank you for meeting me here," Brandon said, handing her a Spiced Chai Tea Latte, her favorite kind of tea. She thanked him as he kissed her softly on the forehead. The two talked and shared a few laughs, although their conversation started off somewhat bland and forced. By the end of the night, Cookie started to loosen up to Brandon again and believed she made the right decision to take him back.

As they arrived home shortly after 9:00 pm, Brandon took Cookie by the hand and led her into their home. As soon as they got inside, he turned and kissed her tenderly on the lips while he massaged the back of her neck with his hand. Cookie groped his chest and caressed his back with her free hand. Brandon started licking and sucking right underneath her jaw bone. He then knelt down and lifted up her dress, breathing feverishly between her legs before tasting her and taking her juices into his mouth. Cookie never felt such passion and desire for Brandon. She returned the favor and she could tell she was driving him wild. She was so attracted to him at that very moment, she felt like she was about to explode. They were too heated to move to the bedroom. Brandon laid her across the kitchen table, with her legs up over his shoulders. Unlike recently, before the climactic buildup last week, he was taking his time and thoroughly enjoying every piece of her. It was a foreign feeling, but Cookie had no complaints. She enjoyed every second of it.

Brandon rubbed his fingers through Cookie's hair with both hands as he moved slowly, but forcefully inside her. Cookie could tell he was about to climax and pushed herself away so they could switch positions. She raised up, clutching his chest and sat him down on one of the kitchen chairs. She then mounted herself on top of him and moved her hips back and forth in circular motions.

Pretty soon, neither one of them could hold out. So they both gave in and climaxed at almost the exact same time. Cookie, still on top of Brandon, wrapped her arms around his neck, laid her head on his chest and whispered, "I missed you," in his ear. He responded and said, "I missed you more. This house was cold here without you. I'll make sure you never have to leave again. I promise, you're going to see a change in me."

Fifteen

Cookie enjoyed a fabulous weekend making up with Brandon. He was such a gentleman and it felt like in the very beginning when they first started dating. However, as Sunday evening drew nearer, she was quite apprehensive about visiting her parents for dinner. She could manage playing the game well enough in front of them, but not Chelsea. She knew everything and wasn't supportive of Cookie's decision to take Brandon back. But she promised she would be on her best behavior to keep the peace for her sister's sake.

At 5:30 pm, the time had finally come for her and Brandon to leave home to arrive at Cookie's parents' house by 6:00 pm. "Are you sure they don't need us to bring anything babe?" Brandon asked. "Oh yeah, we're fine. I asked her the same thing too, but she said her and dad will have everything there. From all the food they're cooking, we may need a designated driver to get back home," Cookie laughed.

"Well as long as your mother is still making her pecan pie and I can get some of your father's ribs, I'm set. That's well worth us being rolled out of there," Brandon responded, rubbing his chiseled stomach. "Everything ok babe? You look a little flushed all of a sudden. Anything on your mind?"

"Oh no, I'm fine. Just remembered something I forgot to wrap up at work on Friday, but it will be fine. I'll just get in to work a little early tomorrow. For now, I'm just enjoying the moment and enjoying you. How about that?" Cookie said.

"I love it. And I love you," Brandon smiled.

When Cookie and Brandon pulled into the driveway, Chelsea's car was already parked there. They both got out of the car and rang the doorbell. Cookie heard Chelsea shout, "I'll get it!" Cookie didn't know what to expect from Chelsea when she opened the door. But to her surprise, Chelsea acted very calm about the situation. Almost too calm. "Hey Cookie! Come on in here and give me a hug, girl. Hey my favorite brother-in-law! How are you? Good to see you." While she was hugging Brandon, she rolled her eyes and made a gag face where only Cookie could see. Cookie smiled and tried to contain her laughter.

"Is that my oldest girl I hear in there!?" Bill said. He came out of the kitchen, with his apron still on and walked quickly to give Cookie a tight squeeze. "Ah, and how's my main man Brandon? How about those Bears? Did you see the game last week?" Bill asked, giving Brandon a hand shake and a pat on the shoulder.

"I did! It was a great one, wasn't it? It was a close one. They almost let that one get away from them," Brandon replied. Him and Bill never had the best relationship, although Bill eventually gave Cookie his blessing (if you can call it that) to marry him. But sports was their common thread that allowed them to have some form of conversation, without things being so awkward.

"Aww, look at my oldest girl and my son! Come give your mom some love," Lisa said, coming out of the bedroom. She was so elated to have both of her daughters home at one time and it was written all over her face.

"Hey mom! Look at you with that post vacation glow," Cookie smiled and hugged her mother tightly. She exhaled deeply and her mother could tell there was something different about the way her daughter embraced her. She gave her a quick glance as if to say, "We'll talk about this later." She then looked over at Brandon and stretched her arms out wide, as he walked briskly towards her. "Now there's my handsome son. Don't tell me you have even more muscles since the last time I saw you," she said, squeezing his arms.

"Well I had to burn off some calories to make room for this delicious meal you and Mr. Brighton have prepared," Brandon laughed.

"Aw, aren't you quite the charmer?" Lisa smiled. Bill let out a barely audible grunt as he finished setting the table. "Well kids, let's eat!" Mr. Brighton said.

Everyone ate relatively quietly. There was still a bit of tension in the air and Cookie's parents were trying to subtly sift it out. But the food was so delicious that there didn't seem to be much time for conversation. After dessert was served, they all sat around, watched TV and talked for a couple of hours or so. Cookie soon gave the cue that she and Brandon were heading out. They said their goodbyes and Chelsea stayed behind a little longer before she left as well. As Cookie walked back to Brandon's SUV, she whispered in her head, "Crisis averted. Thank God".

When Brandon and Cookie finally arrived home, they were both still full from the meal and recounted how great the food was. Cookie hopped in the shower, while Brandon watched ESPN highlights. A couple of minutes later, he pulled back the shower curtain half way, standing there completely naked with a glass of wine in his hand. "Would you like a taste?" He asked charismatically. "Well that depends mister. Which taste are you talking about? A taste of you or the wine?" Cookie answered, glancing down between his legs. "Hmmm….how about I see to it you have some of both?" Brandon asked. "Well come on in," Cookie answered.

Brandon tilted her head back and poured some of the wine in Cookie's mouth. He also took a sip before pouring the rest of it at the top of her breasts and chasing it down with his tongue before it rolled off her wet body. They made love, less urgently than Friday night, but still passionately. Cookie felt sexy. She felt powerful. She felt grown and in control. And most of all, she felt loved by Brandon in a way she never experienced before. She welcomed the feeling in and all it had to offer. Things were definitely looking up for their marriage. She was convinced she had made the right decision, reminding herself all couples experience some bumps in the road to paradise.

Cookie slept incredibly well that night, in Brandon's arms. She even woke up on her own, right before her alarm was set to go off. Brandon had already left for work. He left an oatmeal cream pie on the nightstand with a note that read, "Remember these babe?" In college, Cookie used to eat oatmeal cream pies all the time and Brandon made fun of her for it. It was one of their inside jokes.

There's always a wakeup call that snaps us back into reality when we've traveled a little too far into fantasy land. For Cookie, that call came around 10:30 am that morning. It was Mike. Cookie stepped away from her desk to answer her phone. She was excited to see him calling, but also nervous. "Hey, Mike how are you?" Cookie answered, with a forced gleeful tone. "I'm doing well, just running some errands on my last day of vacation before heading back in to work tomorrow. Just checking in on you to see how you're doing," he answered.

"I'm so sorry," Cookie exclaimed. "I totally meant to call you yesterday to make sure you made it back into town safely. I was over at my mom's and I..."

"No, no. It's ok, really it is. I promise I didn't think anything of it. I do have a question for you though, if you don't mind me asking," Mike replied.

Oh no, this has got to be something bad, Cookie thought. She tried to play it off with a nonchalant answer. "Sure, you know neither one of us are good at biting our tongues. Fire away, sharp shooter." Deep down, Cookie had a hunch that Mike's question had something to do with Brandon.
"Are you really, truly happy?" He asked curtly.

"Excuse me. What do you mean? Mike, yes I'm very happy. What brought this on?" Cookie asked, genuinely puzzled.

"Just making sure. You're one of my best friends and just want to make sure that you're ok. You know I can tell when you're lying though, right?" Mike answered calmly.

"Whatever Mike," Cookie laughed. "Did you add a shot of whiskey to your coffee this morning? You're on quite a roll."

"I'm perfectly fine. Cookie, I heard what happened Thursday night after we had dinner," Mike said.

There was a still, thick silence that spliced itself right between Cookies thoughts and the words she so desperately tried to formulate to say. What exactly had Mike heard? And perhaps more importantly, how much of it had he heard? "Mike, exactly what are you saying that you heard on Thursday?" Cookie asked. She thought it would be better to try to pull information out of him, rather than volunteer details herself. Details that she really didn't want to relive again, if she could keep from it.

"I only heard a piece of it, but I could tell you and Brandon were in a heated argument. I heard you say, "This shit is over" and then I heard him say, "Damn right, it's over bitch". I started to call the police, but only didn't when I heard you leave in your car. Cookie, were you and Brandon arguing about me? I promise I'm not trying to cause any problems for you at home. That just really burned me up to hear him talk to you like that. No matter what you were arguing about, that's unacceptable," Mike said.

"No, no. Of course not. It didn't have anything to do with you. You know how relationships are. Sometimes the other person just pisses you off to no end. We had a pretty harsh exchange of words, but it's just the way we are sometimes. We've been arguing off and on lately....and over the smallest things. Funny thing is I don't even remember what that argument was about Thursday," Cookie replied.

"Ok well I understand. Just want you to be ok, that's all. I'm going to try and come back again for Christmas. Maybe Brandon can join us this time and we can all go out for drinks?" Mike asked.

"That sounds great. I don't see what could stop us. Just let me know when," Cookie said

"Awesome. I'll hold you to that. I'll probably be there a few days before Christmas, maybe the beginning of that week. But I'll let you know either way," Mike responded. "I'll let you get back to it then. Talk to you later, Candy."

Cookie knew that Mike was really concerned about her. Considering how much he could have actually heard, it was easy for her to see why. The tipping point was when he called her "Candy". He usually called her Cookie, like most people, but would often refer to her as Candy if he was upset with her.

"Ok, well it's always good talking to you Mike. I'm glad we've reconnected again. Oh, and thank you. Thanks for looking out for me. I know you've got my back and that's priceless to me. It really means a lot," Cookie replied.

Cookie and Mike exchanged their final goodbyes and went back to their respective tasks for the day. However, their conversation stayed on Cookie's mind well into the afternoon and even when she was leaving work that evening. She decided to just brush it off and follow her instinct, that she was a loving and devoted wife for working it out with Brandon. She picked up her phone to call him as she was walking out of the door, but he called her before she could even dial him. "Well, hello there handsome. Believe it or not, I was just about to call you," Cookie answered cheerfully.

"Is that right? Well I sure am glad to hear your voice pretty lady. What do you say we go to the movies tonight? We haven't been in a little while. I know there's a lot out that we want to see. We can grab dinner first and then see which one is playing. Would you like that?" Brandon asked.

"Sure, that sounds so good. I'm on my way home now. Just need to freshen up a bit. Meet you there?" Cookie said, unable to hide her excitement. Brandon was much more romantic lately, even with small dates like tonight that he was planning all on his own. Their relationship had seemed to shed the worst of times and was now flourishing in the joy of an easy going love.

Their revitalized honeymoon period lasted for about a couple of weeks. Things began to get comfortable between the two of them again. Those comfortable feelings caused both of them to let down their guard. It was a week before Christmas when their relationship started to experience some turbulence again. Cookie had already been home from work for a couple of hours and Brandon hadn't made it home yet. She tried calling, but wasn't able to reach him.

She made a large pot of spaghetti, one of his favorites, while she was waiting for him to come home. Right as she was draining the noodles, she heard the garage door open. It was perfect timing as her sauce had stewed to delicious perfection. She was a great cook, much like both of her parents. Cookie grabbed her favorite wooden serving spoon from the kitchen drawer and scooped up some of her meat sauce for Brandon to taste.

"Hey, my sexy hard-working man," Cookie said, smiling from ear to ear as she kissed Brandon. "Come here. Taste this. I made you some spaghetti. I think I may have added a tad bit too much cayenne pepper. What you think?" Cookie asked, standing on her tip toes and lifting the spoon towards Brandon's mouth. She could tell he was in a sour mood, but hoped it was just something minor. Instead of tasting the spaghetti sauce, he just waved her hand away and put his bag down on the dining room table. "I'm good babe. Can't eat right now," he replied.

A wave of disappointment blanketed Cookie's spirit, but she smiled and tried to hide it. She could now see something was seriously wrong with Brandon. "Here babe, let me help you with your coat. We'll eat later. Talk to me. Everything ok?" Cookie asked, rubbing Brandon's back.

"I got laid off today, babe. Those bastards said they're downsizing and decreasing our pay by 16%. Said either take it or leave it. So, I stood up to em, you know. I couldn't believe the bullshit they were trying to feed us. I told them I wasn't standing for it. They said, "You have two options – keep your job with the pay cut or we're going to have to let you go."

"Oh no, baby I'm so sorry," Cookie rubbed his head, while she sat down in his lap. "Well, what did you tell them?"

"What you mean 'what did I tell them'? The same thing anybody with good sense would have: I told them how big of a mistake they were making and I was walking. I quit!" Brandon said, with wrinkled eyebrows. Just talking about it was getting him revved up all over again.

"So you quit and you didn't really get laid off?" Cookie asked, trying to erase the puzzled look she knew was forming on her face.

"Hell yeah. I mean, what was I supposed to do? They backed me into a corner. I did what I had to. I couldn't let them give me that kind of ultimatum and stay there. That would have been crazy," Brandon responded, with an angry look on his face.

"Yeah baby, I totally get that. Of course. I really do. Just maybe next time something like that happens, can we just talk about it first?" Cookie asked.

"Talk? You women love talking, don't you? Yeah, I'll see what I can do. Sometimes you can't talk about it. You just gotta do it and worry about the rest later," Brandon said.

"Cool, well no more talking from me about it. Us women like me made sure you had some hot food on the table waiting for you when you got home. I hope that's still worth something," Cookie rebutted dryly.

"Cookie....I'm really not up for no shit right now," Brandon said.

"Neither am I, so fix your own damn food. I'll be in the bedroom reading. Or maybe I'll fold the clothes in the drier. Does that count as a womanly duty?" Cookie said.

"Wait, I didn't mean it like that. It's just....you know how stressful that job was. All of the profits I earned for them. Gave them my best and this is how they repay me. I just can't stand for that. I'm not that kind of man. If it's the money you're worried about, I'll find another job in the next couple of weeks. We shouldn't even feel a hit from it," he assured her.

In her mind, Cookie knew that wasn't exactly true. Or at least it was highly unlikely. Not many companies are looking to hire new employees at the end of the year and especially right before Christmas. Brandon worked for an online marketing firm that helped grow traffic for small to medium sized businesses. He was one of the best on the team, but when downsizing creeps up, hardly anyone is really secure.

"Well I can reach out to some contacts and make some calls for you. I'm here, whatever you need," Cookie said lovingly. "I know you've had a long day. Why don't you get more comfortable and I'll set the table for us?"

"Ok, thank you baby," Brandon said, as he walked over to Cookie and kissed her softly on the lips. "I'm sorry. Wow, you know I love your spaghetti. It smells amazing. I'll get changed up and be back in a couple minutes."

"Sounds good, I just might have a surprise up my sleeve for you too," Cookie smiled. As she was setting the table, she thought she heard Brandon's voice in the other room. At first, she thought he was talking to her, but then she realized he must have been talking on the phone to someone. She really thought nothing of it until she heard him say, "Love you too. Gotta go. I'll talk to you later." Her heart skipped a beat and she quickly reassured herself that she didn't know who he was talking to or hear the conversation. Her snap judgment was based on a fraction of what she heard.

Brandon walked back into the kitchen right as Cookie had just finished setting the table. The night's meal included Cookie's famous spaghetti (literally everyone that ate it loved it), a fresh spinach salad tossed with strawberries, candied pecans and feta cheese crumbles, garlic bread, an Italian Chianti red wine and homemade Oreo cheesecake. Brandon was crazy about cheesecake, especially Cookie's.

"Damn. I knew I married you for a reason. This looks so great baby. And cheesecake too?!" Brandon uttered in excitement.

"Sit down silly. Now the truth comes out. You married me for my cooking huh?" Cookie asked playfully.

"Well, that's not the only reason. There are definitely a couple of others too," he said, leaning sideways to look at her behind as she sat down to join him for dinner. Cookie rolled her eyes and laughed.

Cookie made sure to keep the conversation light during dinner, as not to further upset Brandon. She was honestly pissed that he didn't consult her before quitting his job, although she did understand the reason why he did it. Maybe this was a blessing in disguise. The stress of his job trickled into their marriage other times before. She silently prayed that he find something more fulfilling and stress free....quickly.

The next few days weren't as unnerving as she expected. Brandon kept the house immaculately clean since he had more time during the day. It was something they both hadn't really had the time to tackle with their busy schedules. He applied to several jobs in the area, but of course most of them were on a hiring freeze until January.

Brandon still seemed very optimistic about finding a job. Cookie tried to be as supportive as she could and share his enthusiasm for being able to find a new place of employment. In the meantime, she felt like she was walking on egg shells to keep peace in their home. She already prepped her parents and Chelsea that they she would come over to visit them and drop off some small gifts, but things would be tight since Brandon had just lost his job. She made them promise that they would keep the news a secret among themselves.

When Cookie woke up on the morning of Christmas Eve, she wondered why she hadn't heard from Mike yet. In a sense, she was relieved. If he had really come in town, it would have been even more awkward dealing with him now. Just then the text message alert on her cell phone went off. She was home alone for the time being, as Brandon left to go for a run. As Cookie picked up her phone, she had a hunch that the message was from Mike. She was right.
"Hey Cookie. Came down with the flu. Wasn't able to make it back this time. My parents came up here instead. Love u and Merry Christmas! I'll be checking in on you tomorrow," he said. He was always very in tune with what was going on with those he loved, even if he wasn't feeling his best. It was one of his best traits and it made Cookie love and appreciate him even more as a friend.

"Oh no! I hate to hear that. I understand. Make sure you rest and get better! Lots of fluids ☺. Love you too and tell your parents I said hello. Merry Christmas!" Cookie responded. She put her phone back down on the night stand next to the bed. She then picked it back up and decided to delete the text messages. There was no need for additional drama in her life right now.

When Brandon arrived back at home, they went out for brunch at one of their favorite local restaurants. Being out of the house and alone together did them both some good. They both thoroughly enjoyed their food and the complimentary mimosas. "Hey, what do you think about us going to the spa today? I think we both could really use it. I still have a couple free passes. They're open until 5:00. I know how much you loved that massage last time."

"That actually sounds really great. I say let's go for it. You'll be relaxed just right for me to give you a rub down under the mistletoe later," he smiled.

"Well, bring on the mistletoe. Mrs. Claus will be ready to have all of these goodies unwrapped," Cookie responded seductively.

After spending majority of the day out, the two returned home. Cookie made some hot chocolate and homemade s'mores, while Brandon lit the fire place. Thankfully they had already put up the Christmas tree and lights last week, right before Brandon quit his job.
They enjoyed each other's company for the rest of the evening and watched some of their favorite holiday movies. Tired from the events of the day, they both fell into a deep sleep on the couch. The morning sun of the dawn creeping in didn't initially awake Cookie. But she felt something moving tickling her chest. It felt hard and metallic, but she wasn't sure what it was. She jumped out of her sleep and saw Brandon walking towards her with a glass of ice cold milk and freshly baked cinnamon rolls. "Good morning beautiful. Merry Christmas", Brandon said.

"Hey, good morning babe. Aw, thank you sweetie. Merry Christmas," Cookie said. She looked down at her chest and saw a diamond heart shaped pendant hanging on her neck from a silver chain. She gasped, gripped the pendant and looked at Brandon with the warmest smile ever. "Oh my goodness. You remembered. I love it!" Cookie jumped up from the couch and wrapped her arms tightly around Brandon's neck.

"That's the smile I love to see. Your eyes lit up when we first saw it together, so I had to make sure it was yours," he said.

"It's simply beautiful. I'll always cherish it. Oh and you just might have a surprise too. Make sure you look through your bag well the next time you go to the gym," Cookie replied.

"Hmmmm....ok let me go grab my bag now then." When it came to gifts, Brandon was like a little boy in a sense. It was one of the traits Cookie really loved about him. He walked into the laundry room to get his gym back out of there. He looked through it and pulled out some black and yellow Nike's with some work out pants and a shirt to match. "What?! Ah, babe you didn't have to do this."

"Well going by your philosophy, I actually did. I wasn't the only one with a twinkle in their eye. I guess great minds think alike. Funny that we saw these things the same day and ended up getting them for each other. I guess it's a meant-to-be thing," she smiled. After exchanging gifts, Cookie and Brandon stopped by to make their family rounds, first at Cookie's parents' house, where Chelsea was as well, and then to Brian's house. When they were on their way home from Brian's house, there was one comment he made in particular that really disturbed her. He always made inappropriate statements, so that part was nothing new. But this time, he had gone further than Cookie ever recalled.

Cookie and Brandon were preparing to say their goodbyes to Brian. They even shared a meal with him that he had prepared. The food was actually very tasty (baked Cornish hens, dressing, macaroni and cheese and green beans), but Cookie was reluctant to eat it. Out of respect for her husband, she ate it any way.

"Well, brother we're about to head out. Love you man," Brandon said as him and his brother exchanged hugs. It was always surreal for Cookie to see them interact. They weren't as close since their father passed. Although she wanted their relationship to have more frequent interaction again, something about Brian made her fearful.

"Hey, Cookie," Brain said as he hugged her goodbye. "Why don't you tell that baby sister of yours to stop fighting the feeling and go ahead and give in? I've been watching her for a while now." Brandon gave a nervous laugh, as he could tell Cookie despised that comment.

"Um, excuse me?" Cookie replied. "Give it up Brian. That's not happening with her."

"In due time.....you have a good night now. Merry Christmas!" Brian responded as he closed the front door behind them.

Despite a few road bumps, the holidays were mostly pleasant for the newly rekindled couple. There were still moments though when Cookie felt as if she was the only one she was trying to convince that her and Brandon's marriage would truly last for eternity.

But things took an ugly turn on New Year's Eve. Cookie suggested that they celebrate by going to Blu Fox, the new night club that opened up downtown. It had only been open about a month, but she heard from several people that it was the place to be on a Saturday night. Her and Brandon were both far removed from their college partying days, but Cookie was excited to get out and try something different. The two really hadn't been out to a club since they had gotten married.

She could hear Sheila's voice in her head now telling her, "You never ever take your man to the club with you. It just never ends well." She laughed to herself and decided to go against her friend's warning, especially since Brandon seemed cooperative about going. They shared a champagne toast before leaving home around 9:00 pm. Cookie and Brandon were both very attractive in their own right, but as a couple they looked like a pair that just stepped out of a magazine.

The weather that night was chilly, but not with the usual Chicago winds one had grown to expect around this time of year. Cookie wore a shimmering silver dress that was off the shoulder on the left and had a long sleeve on the right. It stopped just above her knee, but her ample behind pushed it up a bit in the back. She wore red and silver stilettos with red accessorized jewelry to match. She was quite stunning to say the least. Brandon was dressed in fitting charcoal grey slacks with exaggerated pockets, a gray, purple and white buttoned-down shirt, and black leather boots. It wasn't so much his clothes that made him attractive to Cookie (and most other women), but the way he wore them. He could wear almost anything and still turn heads because of his physique and swagger.

Cooke and Brandon hadn't been inside the club 15 minutes when an obviously drunk woman came staggering towards them. She stretched out her hands to greet Brandon, totally ignoring Cookie. "Heeyyyyyyy!!! I didn't expect to see yooouuu here tonight. I thought you had some family stuff to go do. This place is jumping, isn't it?" Brandon had a bewildered look on his face, as he knew he had some deep explaining to do. He tried to brush the woman off, but could tell that Cookie was able to read between the lines of what was going on.

"Whoa...you're drunk. Back up Donna. Are you here alone?" Brandon asked.

"Hi. I'm Candice. Brandon's wife. And....who are you?" Cookie interjected.

"Babe, this is my former coworker Donna. She's a hoot...as you can see," Brandon responded, with a nervous smile.

"Brandon, come on. Let's dance! Yeah!! New year, new beginnings! Hmm...that's if wifey doesn't mind. Excuse me, I'm so rude. Would you like to dance with us?" Donna said, barely able to hold herself up.

"Are you going to handle this tramp, Brandon? Because I will if you don't," Cookie said, clearly infuriated with Brandon at this point. Just then, everything flashed back in front of her eyes from the night that she and Brandon got into their big argument. When he put his phone down, the woman on the screen looked similar to the woman standing before them now. Of course he said it was his friend Tim, so she never knew her name. After seeing her now in person, she was certain she saw the right person on Brandon's phone that night.

Cookie didn't even wait for Brandon to walk away from Donna. She walked swiftly towards the bar to order a drink. She needed something strong, so she asked for a Patron and Sprite, with a double shot. Just as she was about to walk away, a man tapped her on her shoulder and asked if he could buy her next drink. He looked to be a little older than her, but very debonair. He didn't look like the type of guy that would frequent night clubs and seemed a bit out of place. Cookie found him very attractive, but of course turned down his offer. "Thank you. I appreciate the offer, but I'm here with my husband," Cookie smiled politely.

"Husband? He must not be too wise to let a stunning beauty like you get out of his eye sight. He's an extremely lucky man. I hope he knows that," he said as he looked her up and down in admiration.

"Well, as much as I am totally flattered, I've really got to get going. He's waiting on me," Cookie said. Just as she turned around, Brandon walked up to her. Although he said Donna was just a drunk coworker, deep down, she knew he was lying. At that moment, she didn't even want to look at him.

"Who the hell was that? And why did you walk away from me?" Brandon asked Cookie in a frustrated tone.

"Look, you can try this shit on somebody else you can play for a fool. I was just at the bar getting a drink until you figured out what you were going to do with your side hoe over there. Don't try to flip this around on me," Cookie said, as they walked out of the club.

"I would tell you about her if you'd just let me explain. But I can't reason with you. I can't ever get a word in when you get these crazy ideas in your head," Brandon responded.

"Well let me shut up then. Go ahead, I'm being quiet now. I'm all ears," Cookie said, with an attitude. She knew that whatever he came up with, it would be a lie.

"She was a new hire at the job a few months ago. I had a feeling she was crushing on me, so I kept my distance from her. Just didn't expect to see her here tonight," Brandon continued to tell his side of the story on their way home. Cookie listened intently, without saying a word. After fully listening to what he had to say, she decided it was the right time to interject, just as they were pulling in to the garage.

"You know what Brandon? Maybe it was a mistake for me coming back," Cookie said.

"What?! You're talking crazy now. What do you mean?" Brandon asked.

"I really want to believe you. I do. But I just can't. The night that we were arguing, I saw the screen of your phone when you laid it on the bed. If that was Tim that you were talking to that night, he sure looked a lot like Donna. I'm not a fool Brandon and I'm not about to be played for one either."

At this point Cookie was tired of acting like she was ok with Brandon and everything was completely back to normal. Their normal was never all it should have been anyway. She felt it was way past high time she let him know it.

Sixteen

"What did you say?" Brandon asked, while he and Cookie were still in the car. Cookie didn't show it, but she was now starting to be fearful of him. She really didn't know how her words would impact him, but she did know she had to get her feelings off her chest. And it felt mighty damn good too.

"I don't know Brandon. I really don't know. Tonight is making me second guess whether or not we've made a mistake reconciling".

"Let's go in the house so we can really talk about this," Brandon said. As the two walked in, he placed the keys on the kitchen table and stood there with his hand on his forehead as he exhaled deeply. "Cookie, I need you. If I've never told you, I need you now more than ever. I know the stress of me not working is a big part of this. I know it is. I promise you, I'll be working again in the next couple of weeks. Just believe in me baby, please," he said.

Brandon seemed genuinely crushed at the thought of Cookie leaving. Maybe she should have shut her mouth after all. But then again she knew what she saw and she couldn't let that go unaddressed. "Brandon, I'm not saying I'm going anywhere. And for the record, this isn't about your job. That place was causing you so much stress it's a good thing you quit. They were making you a ticking time bomb. But that woman tonight, she was so disrespectful. If nothing is really going on, it just seems like you would have stood up for me more. You wouldn't have let her carry on like that in front of me," Cookie explained.

"Baby, I'm sorry," Brandon said, coming towards Cookie to embrace her. She reluctantly let herself fall into his arms. "You know what? I won't ever talk to her again. How about that? I don't ever want to do anything to hurt you. We can work it out.

I'll be better. But you just can't leave me. I can't allow that to happen," Brandon said in a calm, still voice.

"I love you Brandon. I'm here to stay. I made a vow for us to be together forever. Nothing will take us apart. We're just in a rough patch, that's all. We'll look back on this one day and laugh. I know it," Cookie smiled. She felt a little uneasy all of a sudden and said whatever she thought Brandon wanted to hear. That was even if she didn't fully believe the words coming out of her own mouth.

"Good," Brandon kissed her hard on the lips and grabbed the back of her neck. "You relax babe. I'm going to run you a hot bath. You look a little flushed."

"Oh....thank you. Ok, I just have a surprise for you after that too. Don't tell my husband though. He'll get a little jealous if he finds out what I'm going to do to you," Cookie smiled. She began undressing to her panties and bra and looked at the clock above the TV in the bedroom. "It's almost that time, 11:45. I'll go pour us a glass of wine so we can toast in the New Year together."

"Ok, that sounds good baby. I'll be waiting for you," Brandon turned around and responded.

As Cookie walked to the kitchen to pour two glasses of wine, she thought about the old saying of however you end the current year was how you were going to spend the whole next year. She quickly brushed the thought out of her head, as she walked back into the bedroom with two room temperature glasses of wine in her hands. Brandon had turned the lights out in the bedroom and there was only the dim light of a few candles coming from the bathroom.

"Babe? You in there? Are you hiding from me?" Cookie smiled and walked into the bedroom slowly and seductively.
"Nah, I'm not hiding. I'm right here!" Brandon charged for Cookie from the bathroom and startled her so much that both glasses of

wine fell to the floor. He grabbed her inside of one of his arms and covered her mouth with the crevice of his arm. At first she thought this was a sick joke, but she quickly realized he was serious. He had a major advantage by catching her so off guard. She stepped on his feet and tried to scream, but it was useless.

Cookie bit the inside of his arm and jerked him off of her just long enough to catch her breath. He quickly pulled her back by her hair as he whispered in her ear, "You're not ever leaving me. You got that? Only way you're walking out of here is dead. So don't try no slick shit sweetheart. You're just like my no good mother. Always trying to walk out," Brandon said. She could feel his heart pounding against her back as hers raced faster.

"I'm not leaving, I promise. Forever. Remember?" Cookie spoke, in a frightened tone.

"Shut up!" Brandon slapped Cookie hard with one hand and gripped her by her hand with the other shoulder. She spit in his face and kicked him in the balls. He crouched in pain for a second and then pushed her into the bathtub. Cookie fell, fully submerged, into the hot tub of water. "Did I ask you to speak?! Did I? I already know you're not going anywhere. Stop answering questions I already know the answer to," Brandon said.

Her face was still stinging from the staggering blow of Brandon's hand. After tussling back and forth, trying to free herself from his massive strength for what seemed like an eternity, she was finally able to step out of the water and run past him. But the joy of her freedom was short lived as he picked her up by her waist and slammed her body back into the tub. Her head hit the faucet of the tub as she slumped under the water. There was a slight trace of blood left on the side of the tub. She was still for a moment and started fighting again. Brandon held her head under water, as she struggled for her life. Finally.....she stopped moving.

"Cookie? Get up now. Time to get out of this water, my dear. You've been in here soaking long enough," Brandon said, as if he wasn't the cause of her lying in the water motionless.

"Baby? Cookie? Don't leave me. No! Get up, wake up baby!" he screamed. As the sobering reality crept in that he possibly just killed his own wife, Brandon panicked and tried to think of a plan quickly.

"Shit! What am I going to do now Cookie? Huh?" Brandon said talking to himself, but hoping Cookie would hear him and answer. He propped the top half of her body up out of the water against the back of the tub. "Ok, ok. I'll just call the ambulance, say you fell in the tub, hit your head and just lost consciousness for a moment."

When the paramedics arrived, Brandon made sure his story was as smooth as butter. One of the gentleman asked how the fresh wine stains had gotten on the carper in the bedroom. The two wine glasses were also a good distance away from the bathroom door's entrance. "I was trying to surprise her while she was in the bathroom. You know, ring in the New Year together. It had to have been about a quarter until midnight. I panicked and just dropped the glasses as soon as I heard the noise. I could tell something was wrong and it sounded like she had fallen," Brandon said.

When they arrived at the hospital, he waited until he found out Cookie's status before alarming her parents and Chelsea. After all, his story still had to be tight by the time they showed up. The doctor finally came out and revealed that Cookie was talking now, despite suffering from a mild concussion.

"Hello Mr. Thompson. I'm Dr. Shalik. Your wife is recovering well. She suffered quite a blow though and will need to rest for a couple of weeks. Stay off her feet, only light activity if any. I'm assuming you'll be looking after her?"

"Yes, of course. Thank God she's ok. I was so worried. Thank you Dr. Shalik. Can I go back and see her now?" Brandon asked, laying the concern on thick. Maybe a little too thick. Dr. Shalik didn't quite seem convinced that Cookie's injury was an accident.

"Sure, you're more than welcome, Mr. Thompson. I do have a question though. Is there any possibility that your wife may have been involved in some sort of altercation this evening? Her injuries seemed to be more serious than what you explained. It just doesn't seem to match up," Dr. Shalik said.

"If you're insinuating that I did something to my wife, then you've got the wrong idea," Brandon replied.

"I never accused you. Just know that this doesn't add up to a self-inflicted accident. That's all I'm saying. I'm sure she'll be happy to see you sir," Dr. Shalik said sternly, holding his ground.

Before Brandon walked into Cookie's room, he turned the corner to call Chelsea and her parents. As expected, they were extremely concerned and both said they would be on their way immediately. After he got that over with, he walked back towards the room where Cookie was. Dr. Shalik caught him coming around the corner and gave Brandon a disapproving look.

As Brandon walked into the room, Cookie cringed and felt her body tense up. Her head was still throbbing and she honestly couldn't remember all of the details that got her there, but she knew her and Brandon had gotten into a fight.

"Hey there. Look at my baby. You're going to be ok. You just have to get some rest," he said as he walked over and lovingly rubbed his hand across her forehead.

"Don't. Don't touch me. Stop, before I tell them what you really tried to do to me", Cookie said, fury burning in her eyes.

"Let's just keep this between us. I promise; it won't happen again. I think I need to go seek counseling. Cookie, I know all of this is stemming from my mom leaving me. I don't want to take that out on you. I can't lose you," he said.

Cookie didn't speak a word. She just looked over at Brandon as tears began to roll down her face. She understood that what his mother did to him and Brian was totally wrong. But that was no excuse for what he did to her….twice. She couldn't let another time roll around for this. The next time, she may not be alive to tell it.

Brandon could see Cookie was fading in and out of sleep from the pain medication the hospital was giving her. He watched her as she lay sleeping and almost dozed off himself right before Chelsea walked through the door. "Hey Brandon, got here as fast as I could. Is she ok?! I was so worried. Thanks for calling me. Now what happened again?" Chelsea asked. She had a hunch that some foul play on Brandon's part was involved, so she wanted to hear his story again – this time, face to face.

He recounted the story and although she still didn't buy it, she had to admit he was a damn good liar. She couldn't wait to be alone with Cookie to get the real story. "She just fell asleep. They said she'll need a couple of weeks of taking it easy, which is good for her. She's always so busy and on the go," Brandon said.

"Right," Chelsea nodded with a sarcastic smirk. "Brandon, let's cut the bullshit, alright. I know you had something to do with this."

"Come on now Chelsea. Calm down. I would never do anything to hurt Cookie. You know that," he replied, with a genuinely hurt expression on his face.

"Oh, do I?" she said.

Just then, Cookie's parents walked through the door. They rushed to the bed to tend to Cookie first. Her mother's eyes were bloodshot red and slightly puffy. It was obvious she had been crying. Her father was alert and quiet for the most part, but also asked Brandon how the accident happened. Perhaps he had the same thought Chelsea did and wanted to see if Brandon's story was fabricated or true. But Brandon followed the same story, with no deviation.

While her parents were talking to Brandon softly, as not to awaken Cookie, Chelsea's gears were turning. She would have nearly bet her life that Brandon did something to harm her sister. Chelsea wanted him to feel all of the pain she knew he caused Cookie. Such a liar. She didn't know how or when, but she had to find a way to get to the bottom of this.

SEVENTEEN

Cookie recovered quite well back at home. Her full memory of what happened on New Year's Eve hadn't returned, but bits and pieces of the night kept coming back to her. With each thought, she resented Brandon more and more. No, resentment was too tame of an expression for the way she felt. She hated him. That was much more appropriate. She couldn't believe that he actually tried to kill her. Whether he was in his right mind or not at that moment was irrelevant. She wouldn't have ever imagined he'd something like that to her. One thing was for sure: she had to get away from him this time. She refused to live the rest of her life on pins and needles.

Thankfully, within a few days, she was back on her feet and able to move around like normal. But the doctor warned her that there could be some intense side effects from the medication, so she made sure to pay close attention to any abnormal changes to her body. She didn't do any strenuous physical activity for a while as an additional precaution.

After about a week and a half of recovery, Cookie decided it was time to go back into the office. She was able to work from home, but was ecstatic about going back to work, although this job wasn't exactly her cup of tea. But it was a stepping stone to get her to the job she really wanted. However, Cookie decided she would meet Chelsea to come clean about what really happened on New Year's Eve. It was either that or Chelsea would eventually pull it out of her. She had a knack for seeing right through Cookie, even more so than their parents.

It was her second day back at work and Cookie called Chelsea to meet her for an impromptu lunch. Chelsea was able to meet, as expected, and they decided to dine at a small, privately owned café that served as the midpoint between the two of them.

"Hey girl, give me a hug. I've been missing you. Now what are you doing back at work so soon? Aren't you supposed to be at home for a few more days?" Chelsea asked.

"I'm feeling fine. Back to normal now. I really am. I just needed to get out of the house. Can't believe I was actually ready to get back to work either though," Cookie said.

"Yeah I bet. Look sis, I'm just going to cut straight to the chase. What really happened on New Year's Eve? Did Brandon put his hands on you?" Chelsea inquired.

Cookie took a deep breath before responding. "Yes". She recounted the whole story to Chelsea and before she knew it, she was actually remembering all of the details that happened. Verbalizing the story was obviously helping to refresh her memory. Chelsea thoroughly listened to Cookie before she spoke.

"I knew it! There was just something in his eyes at the hospital that night. I knew he was a damn liar. Always has been." Chelsea said. "Cookie, this is getting too serious. What are you going to do?"

"I don't know. I have to find a way to get away from him for good though. I know I can't live like this anymore. I don't want to be one of those statistics. Sometimes it just feels like the only way I can get away from him is to...." Cookie's voice trailed off and she shook her head, holding back tears.

"What? Kill him?" Chelsea's words cut Cookie deeply. Not so much because of what she said, but the way she said it. Chelsea mentioned killing Brandon like it was no big deal at all. Truth be told, all Chelsea did was take the words right out of Cookie's mouth. She really did believe that killing Brandon would be the only way she could get rid of him....for good.

"Would you judge me if I said yes?" Cookie asked, feeling slightly embarrassed.

"Come on now, who are you talking to? We're blood. No judgment here. I love you. Hell, technically it was my idea right? You can use that to help clear your conscious if that helps. That bastard sure is sleeping well at night. So why shouldn't you?" Chelsea ranted.

"Maybe I can go back to the gun range again. Remember when Daddy used to take us with him sometimes? He always said, "You never know when you're going to need to defend yourself." Well, that time has come. This is all so unreal," Cookie said.

"Bad idea. Not unless you want to sit in court for a year, convincing a jury that you committed a crime of passion in the heat of the moment. Too messy and too predictable. It has to be something well thought out and not easily traced back to you," Chelsea replied.

"True. I definitely don't want that. We have to do this pretty quickly though. I just want to get it all over with," Cookie said.

"I know. Believe me, I probably want him dead more than you do," Chelsea said at a low whisper. No one was sitting close to them, but both sisters were being very cautious as not to giveaway the contents of their intimate conversation. "I got it. Aren't The Red Hot Chili Peppers playing here in a couple of weeks? I'll buy the tickets. Say I won two extra, with you and Brandon as my guests. That's one of his favorite groups, so I doubt he'll want to miss it."

"I like it, but where does the alibi come in? How in the world are we going to pull that one off?" Cookie asked.

"Well, he'll be going with us of course. You drive. He sits in the passenger seat and I sit in the backseat. We have a code, maybe a certain song that plays….then boom! That's when I do it," Chelsea's eyes lit up so brightly that Cookie was a little concerned that her sister was having some sort of deviant fun with it all.

"Do….what?" Cookie asked and gazed intently.

"Let's just say your sister knows a thing or two about prescription drugs. I'll make sure to hide away a special concoction in a syringe. All you have to do is inject it into his neck and he'll be out for the count for at least a few hours. But we'll have to do it on the way back from the concert. He'll be more relaxed then and plus there'll be less people around," Chelsea explained.

"Girl, how in the world did you just come up with all of this on the fly?" Cookie inquired.

"When your sister's life is at stake, you don't have a problem taking the person's life that's threatening hers," Chelsea smiled.

"We need a backup plan though. I'm just nervous something will go wrong and…" Cookie whispered.

"Ladies, is there anything else I can serve you this afternoon? We do have a new wonderful cherry lime cheesecake with graham cracker pecan crust. Really, it's to die for. You'll love it," the waiter interrupted.

"No, we'll be fine. Thanks," Cookie answered.
"Sure, we'll try it. Can we take that to go please?" Chelsea asked at the exact same time.

The waiter pointed to Chelsea and said, "I like her. She's very feisty. One cherry lime cheesecake to go, coming right up. I'll bring the check as well. You can pay whenever you're ready. Will that be separate or together ladies?"

"Together. Thank you. Ben, right?" Chelsea smiled at the waiter.

"Yes, that's right. I'll be back momentarily," Ben answered.

Ben came back quickly with their dessert and the check. Chelsea gave him cash and told him to keep the change. She took a bite of the cheesecake and then handed it over to Cookie. "Wait, just one more. Wow that is so delicious."

Cookie laughed and shook her head. She hugged her sister tightly before they parted ways. "I love you girl," she said as she embraced her.

"I love you too. You think you can leave work early on Friday? You should come by my house so we can finalize all of the details for this plan. I don't trust us talking on the phone about it. He may have your line tapped. You never know. It's better to just meet in person," Chelsea said.

"Cool, I'll go in for a couple of hours and then meet you around 10:00am. How's that?" Cookie asked.

"Sounds perfect. Love you. Hey...you take care of yourself sweetie. Call me if you need anything," Chelsea said.

"I will. Thanks for looking out for me," Cookie smiled as she got in her car. She thought about her and Chelsea's conversation all the way back to the office. She couldn't believe she just loosely developed a plan to kill her husband. Every time she felt uneasy about it, she just felt the scab (thankfully covered by her hair) that was still healing from her hitting her head against the side of the tub.

In the meantime, Cookie made sure she didn't do anything to upset Brandon. She hated the feeling of walking on egg shells, but he also had some major making up to do. When she got home on Thursday, he told her he had an interview that following

Monday with a local accounting firm. It wasn't exactly the position he desired, but it was a job and he was excited about it. Cookie acted happy for him and told him she wanted to take him out to dinner on Friday night to celebrate. She had to tow a fine line between being loving and also a woman scorned that's healing. She couldn't let him figure out her plan.

Friday morning didn't seem to go fast enough. Cookie had already prepped her boss that she had an 11:00 am appointment and she was able to get the remainder of the day off. Cookie called Chelsea to let her know she was on the way.

"Call me when you get here so you can park your car in the garage. These fools are so nosey it's unreal," Chelsea said.

"Ok I will," Cookie smiled and hung up the phone. Once she arrived at Chelsea's house she felt a wave of euphoria and fear come over her. She was coming to grips with the fact that she was actually planning to kill her husband. But her emotions didn't stop her from putting the plan in motion. By this time, she was filled with too much rage and hurt to turn back now.

"Come on in. Hopefully you haven't eaten lunch yet. I ordered some Chinese food. There's fried rice, egg rolls and pepper steak with broccoli in the kitchen. Help yourself. Oh, and I grabbed some extra fortune cookies for you too. I know how much you love those," Chelsea said.

"Aw, thanks. This smells so good. I actually haven't eaten lunch yet either," Cookie responded.

"Alright, well let's eat and get this plan together. I already bought the tickets for the concert, so that's covered. Remember, we have to do it after the show, because he'll be more relaxed and there'll be less people on the road then." Chelsea said. "But the trick is, we'll need a way to get out of there a little early to beat some of the traffic. We'll pretty much be able to feel when the concert is almost over and that's where you come in. Act like you're getting sick and I'll follow you to the restroom and cue Brandon that it's time to go. When we get back to the car, you get in the back seat, I'll drive and…" Chelsea said, on a roll and not coming up for air.

"Wait. Wait. I thought you were supposed to be in the backseat. That was the whole point of you injecting whatever that drug is that you have to knock him out right? And what is this drug anyway. We should at least know what we're dealing with," Cookie cautioned.

"Yeah. Good point. That won't work now. Let's just stick to the plan. But that means now you'll have to inject the drug into his neck. Ok? You think you can do it? Oh and as far as the drug, it will be a concoction of midazolam and hydromorphone. It will make him really relaxed and sedated at first, then he'll be in a lot of pain. But it won't kill him right away. But we have to act quickly to make sure he dies after that," Chelsea said.

"Hmm….sounds interesting. I like it. I can do it. As much as he's put me through, I'll be glad to do it. He'll get just what he deserves," Cookie responded.

"Well we're set then. Now the drug is going to act very fast, so the key is actually holding it in his neck long enough to get all of it in there. About three seconds or so. The needle is very thin so by the time he even feels it, he'll think it was just a mosquito bite. Just make sure you try to find a good vein, which shouldn't be hard for you since he's such an in shape beefcake – let him tell it at least," Chelsea said, rolling her eyes.

"Ok so after all of this happens, then what? What do we do with his body? Wait….I think I got it. You know that big bridge we'll have to cross to get to the concert, with the river underneath?" Cookie asked.

"Yes! Are you saying throw him over the bridge once we inject the drug into his neck? I love it," Chelsea said.

"Yep that's exactly what I'm saying. We'll just swing him over the bridge and let him fall over. Hell we can even say it was a suicide. Just say he was depressed. Sometimes I wonder if he really is," Cookie said, as her voice trailed off.

"What if somebody sees us though?" Chelsea asked.

"Don't tell me Miss-Ride-or-Die is getting scared now? You ok?" Cookie asked.

"Of course I'm ok. Remember I told you to leave him a long time ago. We have to have a solid alibi though. The suicide may work. I don't know. But honestly, there's no way he can survive that drop. It's just not possible. Plus, it will be at night too, which will be to our benefit. I think we have it all set then. Study long, study wrong. Let's go for it," Chelsea replied confidently.

"Let's do it," Cookie said stoically.

"Ok, sounds good. It's almost 3:00. Don't you have to be getting home to your lovely husband soon?" Chelsea asked sarcastically.

"So lovely isn't he?" Cookie chuckled. "Well actually I guess I should get going. He got a job offer earlier this week. He starts on Monday. I'm taking him out to dinner at that new Italian restaurant right outside of downtown."

"Look at you being a sweet little wife. That's good. Your goal now is to just keep him happy until the concert. Don't mention anything about leaving. Don't even say you're leaving to go to the grocery store," Chelsea laughed and then caught herself once she remembered the severity of the situation.

"Where are those fortune cookies? Let's eat them and see what they say," Cookie smiled as she walked over to the counter to grab them. "You go first."

"Alright, don't mind if I do. Let's see here. Hmmm....it says, "Do not walk into perilous potholes." That one's creepy. Let's see what yours says," Chelsea replied.

"I don't know which one to pick. I'll choose this one," Cookie was like a kid in a candy store and Chelsea enjoyed watching her sister express such glee over the fortune cookie. She loved them as far back as she could remember. Cookie's eyes widened as she cracked open the cookie and pulled out the fortune slip inside.

"Well spill it. Come on, what does it say?" Chelsea inquired, with much anticipation.

"Um...it says, "Your big secret will be revealed in due time," Cookie uttered nervously.

EIGHTEEN

Cookie was sitting across from the man she once fell in love with and would do anything for. She played her part well and made Brandon feel like a king. He was pleasantly surprised at their intimate dinner at the new upscale Italian restaurant in downtown Dallas. Cookie had to admit that he was looking damn good sitting across from her with his fitting blue sweater, tan blazer and brown dress pants. His clothes fit him well, showing off his physique in a complimentary way that was sexy, without being over the top.

But she couldn't get off track and forget what her focus was – to make him happy until the time came to get rid of him for good. "Baby, I really appreciate you taking me out. Thanks for supporting me and holding down the finances at home until I found a new job. I actually have a surprise for you too," he said, as they finished the last of their delicious meal.

"You shouldn't have. Look at you. Thank you baby," Cookie replied, with her eyes lit up brightly.

"No. I really did," Brandon said, flashing a seductive half smile across the table at Cookie. He slid, sliding a slim black box across the table. "This is for you baby."

Cookie opened the box and found a beautiful pearl and diamond bracelet inside. "Wow, Brandon this is beautiful. I absolutely love it." Cookie said, as she immediately put it on her bare left wrist.

"Of course, you're welcome. You deserve it. Oh and I did make an appointment with a counselor. I start on Wednesday evening. I'm really trying to make a change Cookie and I promise you're going to see it this time," Brandon said.

"I know you are babe. I really can see it and feel it too. I'm really grateful for it," she replied. After Cookie took the tab on the check, she and Brandon headed outside to get their car from the valet service.

When Cookie and Brandon returned home, he made a couple of advances to let her know that he wanted to make love. She really wanted to make up something – anything, so she wouldn't have to feel him inside of her. She was totally not in the mood for it and he had officially lost that piece of her forever. But she could hear Chelsea's voice in her head saying that she better do all she can to keep Brandon happy in the meantime. So she did just that.

It was the most emotionless sexual experience she ever had with Brandon. She convinced herself that this must be how prostitutes feel. To give of their bodies and have no spiritual ties to their customers. Even they must have had a smidgen more of an enjoyment that she did while Brandon was having sex with her. Ironically enough, she did reach an orgasm – and loved it. Brandon knew her body well and could tell if she was faking it. The thought of erasing his life and all the agony he caused made her shiver uncontrollably inside and lit a fire that turned her on immensely.

When Brandon finally climaxed, she was glad it was over. He went straight to sleep. She stayed awake awhile looking at him, thinking she could bypass the plan her and Chelsea made. She could just strangle him or suffocate him with a pillow. But who was she fooling? He was much stronger than her and would end up seriously hurting her, or killing her, if she tried anything outlandish like that. She smiled as she looked at him sleeping in such a vulnerable state. Pretty soon she was sound asleep as well.

The next few days flew by, especially with Brandon starting his new job. Little did he know the devious plan brewing behind his back. Cookie let him know that Chelsea won tickets to the concert about a week prior to it. He was excited about it and even said he looked forward to spending some time with Chelsea. Either he really was becoming a changed man or he was spewing lies out of his mouth like he always did. Either way, nothing was going to make Cookie change her mind about ending his life.

Before she knew it, the night of the concert had arrived. She and Chelsea met again the day before to confirm everything was set for their planned murder. Cookie filled Brandon in on the travel plans for the night and let him know that Chelsea would be driving to their house and riding with them, since the concert was technically closer coming from their house.

5:30 pm. Chelsea rang the doorbell as Cookie and Brandon were just finishing getting dressed for the concert. She brought a small bottle of Patron and insisted they each take a shot to start the night off right. "Baby, Chelsea really knows how to party. Maybe I chose the wrong sister, you think?" Brandon smiled and nudged Cookie.

"Oh, you've got jokes I see. No that's your brother that's after Chelsea. Don't tell me you too now," Cookie laughed.

"Don't worry about that big sis. He couldn't handle me," Chelsea smirked as she poured three shots for them to take. "Cheers. To love, life, family and just having a damn good time". The three of them raised their shot glasses to the toast and quickly gulped down the Patron.

"Woo….girl, now that is strong!" Cookie proclaimed

"I know, right? Yes it is. So smooth though," Chelsea replied.

"Hit the spot for me. Nice and easy. Pour me another one sister in law," Brandon chimed in.

"Well I guess we know who won't be driving tonight. We should be getting on the road now though. The show starts at 7:00. The great thing is we'll be able to walk straight in. We're VIP for the night," Chelsea said, waving the tickets in her hand.

"Ah, I love it. I can't wait. I haven't seen them in concert in so long. Babe, how about I drive us and you can be my Clyde riding shot gun?" Cookie asked.

"What about Chelsea though? You don't want to ride in front with your sister? I'm cool with that," Brandon said.

"No please. I'd love to sit in the back. Makes me feel like I'm being chauffeured," Chelsea laughed.

As they all piled into the SUV, in their respective seats, they started on the road to get to the concert. 5:50pm. Everyone was buckled in as Cookie pulled out of the driveway. She turned one the radio and heard the DJ talking about the Red Hot Chili Peppers concert. As they started to play "Give It Away", Brandon turned up the radio and started singing along like a big kid; Cookie and Chelsea quickly chimed in.

The song ended as the station went to commercial break. Cookie felt butterflies in her stomach as she drove over the bridge where she and Chelsea planned to throw Brandon over. For the first time, she felt like she could possibly be making a mistake. She felt eerie like something was going to throw a wrench in their plan. They never discussed a backup plan and she could only hope everything would be executed flawlessly.

6:35 pm. Cookie parked in the area marked for VIP guests and got out of the vehicle. "I think we have to walk in this way, through the VIP lounge," Chelsea said. Brandon and Cookie followed her, as Chelsea presented their tickets to the door attendant. Brandon and Chelsea grabbed another drink from the lounge area before they made their way to their seats. The show actually started at 7:30 pm, which wasn't too far past the official begin time.

Red Hot Chili Peppers rocked the house and blazed through their biggest hits along with some more recent songs. They put on such a good show that Cookie almost forgot the concert was just a decoy for their plan. She could tell Brandon and Chelsea were having a good time as well. She checked her phone to see what time it was. 9:05 pm. It was likely nearing the time that she needed to play ill so they could leave early. She toned down her excitement to build up her forced ailments.

9:15 pm. "Under the Bridge" started to cue up and Cookie decided this was her time. She put her hand up to her head and clutched her stomach with the other. "Babe, I'm not feeling too good all of a sudden. I'm really dizzy and nauseated," Cookie leaned over to tell Brandon.

"Oh no, I'm sorry baby. Ok, let's get you home then. Do you think you may need to stop by the restroom first?" Brandon responded, with a genuine look of concern on his face.

"That's a good point babe. Hey Chelsea, you mind coming to the restroom with me? I'm not feeling too good," Cookie asked.

"Right now?! I think this is about to be the encore," she said. "Ok, I'm coming. Brandon, maybe we should go ahead and sneak out through VIP again, in case she doesn't feel well enough to come back in," Chelsea suggested.

"Ok, good idea. I'll be waiting in the back for you and Cookie. You'll be ok baby," he said, patting Cookie on the back as her and Chelsea walked past him.

When Cookie and Chelsea got out of Brandon's line of sight, they still played their roles. Even once they were inside the restroom, Cookie still acted as if she was ill. Chelsea kept rubbing her back and saying, "It's going to be ok." "Here, put a little cold water on your forehead. That should cool you off," Chelsea said. As fate would have it, one of Chelsea's close friends, Tammie Henry walked in and immediately recognized her and Cookie. More importantly, she could tell there was something seriously wrong with Cookie. "Hey girl, what are you doing here!? And....hey Cookie. Haven't seen you in forever. Um, is she ok?" Tammie asked, mouthing the words so only Chelsea could see her.

"Tammie, it is so good to see you. We really have to catch up soon. Cookie's not feeling good. I should get her back out her to her husband before he gets worried. Good seeing you girl. Call me!" Chelsea responded as her and Cookie rushed out of the bathroom together. Tammie stood there with a puzzled look on her face, knowing there was something strange going on beneath the surface of that interaction.

"Brandon, I think we will have to head out after all. She must have food poisoning or something. How about I drive and you still ride shot gun with me? That way Cookie can lie down in the back seat?" Chelsea suggested, sticking with the plan her and Cookie conjured up.

"Ok that should work. You sure you don't want me to drive though?" Brandon asked.

"Oh yeah, I'm good. Thanks though," Chelsea assured him.

As they all got into the vehicle, Cookie climbed into the backseat and laid her head back. She felt around inside her coat pocket to make sure the syringe was still safely secured. Brandon looked back to make sure she was ok. They left just in time as Chelsea noticed several cars coming out of the parking lot behind her. Luckily they had just beaten the crowd and the road ahead of them was pretty clear. There were about 15 minutes before they would approach the bridge, where their plan would be put into motion. The background was perfect; the sky was pitch black with little lighting besides the stars, once they traveled outside of the immediate area of the stadium where the concert was held.

"I'm feeling a tad bit better now. I think that night air hitting my face actually did me some good," Cookie said.

"I'm so happy to hear that. I love you baby," Brandon replied, turning sideways in the front seat to rub her knee. Chelsea looked at Brandon out of the corners of her eyes and turned her nose up at him. He was scum as far as she was concerned and she couldn't wait to get him out of Cookie's life forever.

9:52pm. Chelsea looked up in the rearview mirror and connected glances with Cookie. Cookie gave her a slight nod to let her know she was about to pull the syringe out at any moment to inject the drug into Brandon's neck. He had taken his coat off, with a collarless sweater underneath, so she had a pretty clear shot to a good vein in his neck.

Cookie rose up from the back seat with the syringe in her hand. She wasn't slick enough because Brandon caught a glimpse of it in the rearview mirror. He turned around in the seat quickly saying, "What the hell are you doing!? What's that shit in your hand!? " Brandon said. He slapped Cookie in the face before she was able to inject the syringe in his neck. It went flying from her hand into the front seat, right beneath Chelsea's feet.

"Get your hands off my sister!" Chelsea exclaimed. She punched Brandon in the face while she was driving. "I'll kill your ass myself and not think twice about it." Brandon was silent for a moment and could tell that Chelsea was fuming. Meanwhile, Cookie was kicking at him, infuriated that he just slapped her in the face. She grabbed his neck, dug her nails into it and scraped them across until she felt his skin underneath her nails.

"I hate you!! Come on. Is that all you've got?!" Cookie screamed.

"Whoa. Why are they on this side?" Chelsea said. Brandon and Cookie turned their attention to the road to see what she was talking about. They all noticed a white pickup truck charging rapidly towards them, on their side of the road. Chelsea's eyes widened as she contemplated what snap decision would be best to spare her and Cookie's life, but still erase Brandon's. Before she had a chance to think, the truck's headlights were blinding her and she could barely see anything but the bright white lights.

And then it happened. Chelsea was able swerve into the other lane, which actually made matters worse. The truck clipped the back driver's side of the SUV, causing it to spin three times before slamming into the metal railing of the bridge. Chelsea's head banged against the side of the window. Meanwhile, Cookie laid motionless in the back seat, as the back door on the passenger side was caved in.

Chelsea finally came to and quickly looked around the car. She immediately spotted the syringe under her foot. The top was pushed down as if its contents had already been released. She knew Cookie wasn't able to inject the syringe into Brandon's neck, but the drug must have somehow leaked out. But more importantly, Cookie wasn't moving. Chelsea reached into the backseat and shook her softly at first and then frantically.

"Come on sis. Wake up. Wake up baby. Somebody help me…wake up Cookie! Wake up!" Chelsea pleaded. Just as tears started streaming down her face, she saw Cookie's leg move. Then she sat up slowly and grabbed the side of her head. "Oh my goodness," she said, rubbing her head with one hand and her back with the other.

"Thank God. You ok?!" Chelsea asked.
"Yeah, just hit my head really hard. Oh…look," Cookie motioned towards Brandon's seat. The glass from the passenger window was shattered and the door was ajar, which was seemingly all due to the accident. The car stopped right at the edge of the bridge and the impact bent its metal guardrail. "There's no way Brandon could have made it out of there alive. He must have fallen over the rail and into the water," Cookie muttered.

Chelsea hopped out of the car to open Cookie's door. It was somehow stuck from the inside and Cookie wasn't able to open it on her own. "Come on. Look down there," Chelsea ordered Cookie, as she opened the door for her.

"Why do you want me to look down there? I can't Chelsea. I can't." Cookie sobbed.

"You can't? What do you mean you can't? Pull yourself together! This is what you said you wanted. This is better than we could have ever planned. He obviously fell over the rail. The real work starts now. Call the police. It's over. He's gone now," Chelsea told Cookie.

"I got it. I got it. It just all hit at once. Trying to process it all," Cookie replied.

"No I don't know. You wanted him dead and now you've got it. The driver that hit us is nowhere to be found. So you know that's going to be filed as an uninsured motorist claim. This is the perfect murder! There's no way he's going to survive this. They can't trace this back to us. Is that what you're worried about?" Chelsea asked.

"You're right. I just can't believe....after all this. He's gone. It's over, just like that. Let me call the police," Cookie said. By now, there were several cars slowing down to see what had transpired. Some people even asked if they needed any help. Chelsea deserved an award for Best Distraught Performance. She was pouring tears from her eyes and grabbing her hair, pacing on the side of the highway, just in front of where the crash happened. It was quite disturbing to Cookie just how elated Chelsea was over Brandon's death. But she kept her focus and relayed the story almost verbatim as to how it really happened.

"The syringe!" Chelsea ran back to the SUV and picked up the syringe that had rolled right under her foot when they finally came to a stop after the crash. She threw it over the bridge, into the water. "Thank goodness you remembered that," Cookie said, breathing a sigh of relief. Within the next few minutes, police arrived on the scene. They could clearly see there was an accident and that Chelsea and Cookie had both been banged up.

"Hello ladies, I'm Officer Glenn Mitchell. And this is Officer Jai Jackson. We know you've had a pretty rough night. We have a squad out now to look for your husband Mrs.....?" Officer Mitchell asked.

"It's Thompson. Mrs. Thompson," Cookie replied, in the midst of crying uncontrollably.

"Mrs. Thompson, please, if you can, try to tell us in your own words exactly what happened tonight," Officer Jackson said.

"We were all riding together, coming from the Red Hot Chili Peppers concert. We had just gotten on the bridge when we noticed a white pickup truck coming towards us in the same lane. My sister was driving. She tried blowing the horn and swerving out of their way, but they swerved too and that's when it happened. I don't know the exact order of things but I felt three hard bumps for sure. Chelsea had to wake me up. I think the hit momentarily knocked me out or something. That's when....I can't. I'm sorry..." Cookie sobbed. She truly didn't remember all of the details after that point and didn't want to say the wrong thing.

"I'm so sorry. I know this has got to be difficult for you. I can't even begin to say I know how you feel," Officer Jackson said.

"Mam, do you remember exactly what happened once you were able to bring the vehicle to a complete stop?" Officer Mitchell asked Chelsea.

"Well, I wasn't actually. The rail is what stopped me. I was so wool-gathered when we finally did stop. I looked over in the passenger seat and noticed Brandon wasn't there anymore. The door was open and there was broken glass everywhere on his side. He was gone. We haven't been able to find him since. He's like the brother I never had. I can't lose him," Chelsea immediately burst into tears.

Cookie watched as her sister just stood there and made her lies so believable. Anyone could look at the vehicle and tell the accident wasn't self-inflicted by any means, so she was at least at peace with that.

"Well you ladies did wise by staying away from the SUV. We'll get a wrecker truck out here to pull it back up and away from this railing. You've gotten some pretty serious damages to your vehicle here. Both of you are really blessed," Officer Mitchell said. "And just checking, did either of you happen to see the license plate of the white pickup truck that hit you?"

"No, their lights were so bright, I couldn't see anything. It looked like they had their high beams on," Chelsea answered. "I'm sorry, but I couldn't see it either," Cookie added.

"Ok, understood. We'll give you ladies a ride home. This vehicle definitely isn't safe to drive. Just let us know where we need to go and we'll take care of it from here," Officer Jackson said.

When Officers Jackson and Mitchell pulled into Cookie's driveway, Officer Mitchell immediately recognized the house. "What a coincidence. We were here a few weeks ago for a domestic noise disturbance. Mrs. Thompson, how was your relationship with your husband? Something about the guy really rubbed me wrong when we came by for the noise complaint. I could be way off base here. I'm sorry, that was out of line. Forget I even mentioned it," Officer Mitchell apologized.

"Officer, my relationship with my husband is a loving and loyal one. I love him and he's not dead. He's going to be found. I believe it. Now, if you'll excuse us, my sister and I would like to get inside. It's been quite a long night as you can imagine. Thank you for the ride. It's greatly appreciated. You both have a good night," Cookie answered sternly.

"Mitch, that was out of line man. She just lost her husband in a wreck for Christ's sake! I swear I don't know what's going on in that head of yours sometimes," Officer Jackson exclaimed.

"Yeah, I know. It wasn't probably the best timing, but I just had to ask. I'm telling you, that guy has put his hands on her before. We may never know, but I'm almost positive he has. Let's just say I think she has more than good enough reason to murder him. That's all I'm saying Jai. All I'm saying."

NINETEEN

Cookie and Chelsea were both unable to go to sleep that night. "Wasn't it strange how the officer asked if the accident was really a murder? I can't shake that. It's got me really nervous now. Maybe this was all a mistake," Cookie said.

"Cookie, I'm going to try to say this in the nicest way possible. Who really gives a shit? The important thing to remember is to keep our alibi tight. In hindsight, the wreck was the perfect scenario. We couldn't have planned that better. And hell, if Brandon survived that fall I say his ass deserves to live," Chelsea said.

"Hmmm....well I guess you told me, didn't you? I'm glad one of us isn't worried," Cookie said. Truth be told, Chelsea was very afraid, but she had to stay calm for Cookie. Especially since killing Brandon was really her idea in the first place.

Four days after the accident, there was a knock at Cookie's door at around 9:00 pm. It was Officer Mitchell.

"Good evening Mrs. Thompson. Do you mind if I come in for a moment?"

"Hello Officer Mitchell. Yes, sure that's fine. Please tell me you have some good news for me," Cookie said. Chelsea was in the guest bedroom and came out to the living room to support her sister, and keep an eye on Officer Mitchell. At this point, she trusted no one.

He paused for a moment before answering. "Well, I'm so sorry to say that we still haven't found Brandon's body yet. But of course, we're still trying. I just want you to prepare yourself in case…"
"I…..I got it. Thank you," Cookie replied, holding back her tears. It wasn't long before they started running down her cheeks. Chelsea came over to sit next to her to console her.

"I'm going to keep checking on you. You let me know if you need anything. We're here for you and will help you get through this traumatic experience," he said.

Cookie and Chelsea sat in silence for a few minutes after Officer Mitchell left. They both were in shock. It was one thing to have orchestrated a plan for murder, but a totally different story to have to guess if it really happened. "Wow, um, I think I need a drink. You want one?" Chelsea asked.

"Sure, why not? I'll probably need several. I have to start telling people now. I mean, mom and dad know because we talked to them already. But I have to let Brian know. That's going to be so hard. I'm not ready for his reaction to that. I'll have to go over there tomorrow and tell him. It's almost been a week now. I can't keep letting this drag out, no matter how awkward I feel," Cookie said.

"I don't think my being with you will actually help the situation, but I can be close by in case he tries anything crazy," Chelsea said.

"Oh, would you please?" Cookie pleaded.

"Of course. You know I will," Chelsea responded. "Let's do it."

Cookie called Brian that next morning and told him she had something very urgent to discuss with him. She expected some sort of sarcastic rebuttal, but he surprisingly just said ok and he'd be home after 6:00 pm. Cookie told him that she would stop by at 7:00 pm to talk to him.

Cookie had not been back into the office yet and was working from home until the dust settled from the accident. Her time to head towards Brian's house came much quicker than she would have liked. But there was no choice but to face him and tell him the (semi) truth about what happened to his brother.

"Come on in, Cookie. This is quite a surprise to see you without Brandon. You two are usually attached at the hip. Everything ok?" he asked.

"Well that's actually what I was coming over to talk to you about. You may want to sit down. Brian, Brandon is missing. We've been trying to find him...." Cookie said.

"Find him? Don't tell me you finally ran him off," Brian laughed.

"No. He, my sister and I went to a concert a few days ago. On our way back, we got into a horrible accident on the bridge over the river near downtown. A car was driving on the wrong side of the road and hit us head on. Brandon was ejected from the car when we slammed against the rail." She paused to let Brian gather his composure and to regain hers.

"The police haven't been able to find his body yet. It's been a few days. I was truly hopeful that we would find him. I still am. But I just wanted to let you know what we're facing right now."

"Ah, a concert and you didn't invite me, huh?" Brian responded. His statement threw Cookie for a loop and she was literally speechless. She couldn't help but to chalk up his reaction to him being in complete denial and shock about his brother.

"That's all you have to say? This is your brother we're talking about here," Cookie asked, confused and saddened by Brian's nonchalant response. She shouldn't have cared, but she did. Deep down, a part of her still loved Brandon, despite his cheating and abuse.

"You know Cookie, I think it's time you get out of here before I do something I regret. Thanks for letting me know about Brandon. I'm sure he'll turn up soon," Brian said coldly.

Cookie stared him directly in his eyes intently before she responded. "This is hard for me too. I love Brandon and he's my husband. But he's your brother too and I'll respect your wishes. I'll go now. You take care and I'll let you know about any details I get."

Cookie cranked up her car and waited until she was out of Brandon's clear view before calling Chelsea. "So how did it go?" Chelsea asked.

"You won't believe it. Actually it went better than I thought. The first thing out of his mouth was him questioning why he wasn't invited to the concert. Then he pretty much told me to leave after that and he was sure that Brandon would turn up later," Cookie recounted.

"Don't even mind him. He's just crazy. Seriously, nobody but a fool would respond like that to such news. Good riddance to him too," Chelsea said.

Although Cookie knew Chelsea couldn't stay with her forever, she felt safe and protected having someone else in the house. They both slept together in the master bedroom that night. Cookie felt creepy sleeping in what was once she and her husband's bed knowing he may never be found. Chelsea ended up falling asleep before her and she lay awake for a long time afterwards. Her mind was racing and at the forefront was her conversation with Brian. She wondered if he could see right through her and if he knew that she had killed his brother.

Right before she dozed off to sleep, she felt a hand slipping across her stomach. At first she thought it was just Chelsea moving in her sleep, but she was laying there as stiff as a board. Cookie just brushed it off and tried not to put much thought into it. The next thing she knew, there were fingers grazing her neck. She knew now that it couldn't have been Chelsea touching her. These fingers felt too rough and masculine to be hers. The hand squeezed gently at first and then tightly around her neck until she couldn't breathe. She tried to cry out for help but there was no way she physically could. He took his free hand and covered the pillow over her face, smothering her. She prayed that it wasn't Brandon coming back for her.

"Cookie! Cookie! You almost hit me. Are you ok?" Chelsea asked.

Cookie sat upright in the bed and did a quick scan around the room before answering. "I'm...I'm fine. I'm sorry. Just had a bad dream. It all just seemed so real," she said, rubbing her neck. It actually was tender to the touch as if someone really had tried to strangle her.

"It's going to be ok. It's just a dream. Try to get some sleep. You're probably just delirious from not getting enough rest. That's all," Chelsea reminded her.

Eventually Cookie fell back asleep and so did Chelsea. As days turned into weeks and eventually a few months, Brandon's body was never found. It began to get a little easier go to sleep at night and Chelsea started staying back at her own house on the regular. But none of that stopped Cookie from being paranoid.

Everywhere she went and everyone she knew made her uneasy. She only felt totally comfortable around Chelsea but felt that everyone else would be able to figure her out. As fate would have it, she had been out of touch with Sheila for the last several weeks. Not so much because of them not being close though. They sometimes went in phases like that, but she was actually glad that she and Sheila hadn't talked much during this period. Although Sheila had come by to visit often in the beginning of the whole ordeal, Cookie still felt a sense of nervousness around her.

She knew about the accident but Cookie had that story down pat now. Although she nearly trusted Sheila with her life, she didn't know if she could (or should) trust her with the secret that she played an intricate part in ending Brandon's. But she had told Sheila about the ice cream incident and the night of the bath tub accident. Cookie fabricated the latter story a bit too, stating that she and Brandon did get into a physical tussle yet leaving out the important detail that he pushed her into the tub. Instead she lied and said she fell into it.

Sheila, much like Cookie herself, was extremely perceptive. She was also more vocal about what she thought she knew, even if she was wrong. Most times her intuitions were spot on. That's what Cookie feared the most about their friendship. Sheila was the one person, outside of any family member, that could guess Cookie's secret without ever directly asking her.

To Cookie's surprise, Sheila called her up one Friday afternoon to see if Cookie was free for a happy hour that night. They had eaten lunch and dinner a couple times since Brandon's "disappearance", but not actually going out to a club or happy hour. She brushed aside the thoughts of Sheila having motives to pull information from her and decided to go with the flow. Besides, she could use some time to unwind and really let her hair down.

"So what's been up? I know it's got to be hard dealing with losing Brandon, but a girl still deserves a little fun, right?" Sheila asked Cookie, over their second margarita. "I love you and just don't want to see you get into this dark place, you know. That's not good."

"Yeah I know. It's just been a whole lot to deal with," Cookie said.

"I hear you. Just don't want you to miss out on life. We're not getting any younger. You know 30 will be here before we know it. But for today, cheers to looking good even when we're 50," Sheila laughed.

"Yes, how about even 80?" Cookie chimed in.

"Yes! I love it. Good times. We never miss a beat. I love that about our friendship. But girl, you know I have to ask. With everything that was going on recently with you and Brandon, can you honestly say you miss him?" Sheila asked.

"Sheila?! Yes, Brandon was my husband," Cookie answered, caught off guard by Sheila's statement.

"Well no shit Sherlock. But women, especially abused women, do away with their husbands every day too. You've seen Snapped, haven't you?" Sheila said.

"Girl, you are crazy. Don't get me wrong, at times I hated him. But I would never ever want to take his life. Wouldn't do that. Not ever," Cookie responded. Sheila could see the cold look in her eyes and she knew there was something deeper buried under Cookie's statement. But she didn't push the issue. They had one more drink and got caught up on the brighter aspects of each other's lives in the last few months.

As it neared 11:00 pm, they decided to call it a night. "Sheila, I think all those partying college days have caught up with me. I can't hang nearly as late as I used to," Cookie confessed.

"Who are you telling? You and me both. I feel it now too. It was so good seeing you. And let's make a promise right now to not make it this long before we see each other again. Didn't know how much I missed my sister," Sheila said.

"That sounds like a deal to me. Sounds like we both needed this," Cookie admitted. "Give me a hug. Let me know when you make it home, ok?"

When Cookie pulled into her garage at home, she had to remind herself that she'd be sleeping alone. Although she was well aware that Brandon was dead, she found herself living in moments of the past. Perhaps it was because she stayed uneasy when she was gone for a long period of time, expecting him to be up waiting to interrogate her.

She didn't feel comfortable sleeping in the master bedroom that night and decided to sleep in the guestroom instead. It was practically untouched because Brandon was never one for much company. Cookie was more of the social butterfly. It was at the moment that she realized she would forever feel caged if she remained to live in that house. There was only way to remedy her uneasiness. She had to get out of Chicago and get a fresh start where hardly anyone knew who she was.

TWENTY

As Chelsea looked down at Brian, all the memories she kept locked away for years were suddenly unleashed. There were so many questions running through her head. But the one looming question that she couldn't fathom was why. Why her? Why after so many years? Why did he do this? Had he tried to rape other women too?

Chelsea had to snap herself out of her thoughts. She looked around the room for her things, as she tried to remember exactly how she had gotten there. As she kept walking she stepped on something and looked down to realize it was her purse. Hopefully her phone was still in there so she could call the police. As she dug around inside the purse, she not only found her phone, but a thin sheet of paper against the wall of the purse. It was the receipt from the grocery store. It came back to her now. That was her last memory and she had no idea what happened past that. She kept digging and found her phone. Thankfully, there was some battery life still left on it. Just enough for her to make some phone calls.

She called the police first to report the murder. As she recounted the story to them, she was able to tell this one with no lies, to the best of her recollection. But one bone chilling fact remained. She had a hand in the deaths of both Brandon and Brian. She stepped outside of the strangely designed building the she was in to try to give them her exact whereabouts. She walked out of the bedroom and into a narrow corridor with a glass window that exposed some trees.

She opened the front door and started to step out until she realized there was nothing but rocks, eventually leading to a steep waterfall. She stooped down to look through the trees and saw the grocery store she had shopped at. She knew it had to be it, because of the other landmarks nearby. Chelsea was shocked that this place even existed behind the trees. It was well hidden and was virtually impossible to see from the street. But the police assured her they would find her exact location and be there soon.

In the meantime, she called Cookie back first. She had missed calls from her and her mother. If it had been anyone else, she probably would have called her mother first. But because of who her assailant was, she thought Cookie deserved the heads up.

"Chelsea!!! Thank God you're ok. Where are you? Are you still in Chicago? I'm sorry. Go ahead. You talk….I'm just. Just really glad to hear your voice," Cookie told Chelsea.

"Yeah, I'm ok. Hell, I'm actually right across the street from the damn grocery store I got picked up at," she said.

"You got kidnapped at a grocery store?" Cookie asked.

"Wait a sec. I don't have much battery left. Still need to call mom and dad too. The shit gets worse. Listen. So I woke up in this damn stone dungeon looking thing. I guess he drugged me when I got out of the store parking lot. The guy had a mask on so I never saw his face. He raped me and I stabbed him with a piece of metal I found in the room. I took the mask off and you won't believe who it was," Chelsea said.

"He raped you? Oh my God. I'm so sorry. Goodness, who was it?" Cookie asked in anticipation.
"Brian!"
"Wait a minute. Brandon's brother, Brian?"
"Yes!" Chelsea responded.

"I wanted to tell you first. Hold on, let me call mom and dad too on the other line," Chelsea said.
"Chelsea??? Baby is this you?! Thank God! Come here, Lisa! It's Chelsea!" Bill screamed to Lisa.

"What? Chelsea baby are you ok?" Lisa cried. "What happened?"

"I can't talk long, my phone is about to die, plus the police just got here. Cookie's on the line too. I'm here, right across the highway from the grocery store near our old high school. It may be a little hard to find me, but I'm ok. I'm fine," Chelsea assured them.

"I'm catching a flight out to see you ok?" Cookie told Chelsea.

"And we're coming up there now baby," Bill said.

The phone went dead before Chelsea had the chance to respond. Chelsea's parents arrived on the scene pretty quickly and just in time to hear her tell the story to the police. Bill had a hard time letting her tell her story and he kept interrupting, wanting to know more details of what happened and if the man was still alive. When she revealed that she killed Brian, Bill said, "That's my girl!" The police turned and gave Bill a disapproving look. "Baby, let's wait over here for a minute so she can finish telling her story to the officers. We're just blessed to have our baby safe and in one piece," Lisa consoled Bill to try to diffuse his nervous energy.

The police let Chelsea gather the remainder of her things and investigated the inside of the building, before taking her to the hospital. Bill and Lisa followed behind and stayed while a rape kit was being performed on Chelsea. Once she was released from the hospital, she decided to tell her parents that the man she killed was Brian.

"What?! I can't believe it....we haven't heard from him in years now. How could he?" Lisa's voice trailed off.
"That was Brandon's brother, Brian? I always knew both of those boys were bad news! I tried to tell Cookie that. Serves him right. Nobody messes with my girls and gets away with it. I see I taught you well baby," Bill said proudly.

They drove back to where Chelsea's car should have been to scan the parking lot. Sure enough, her car was still sitting there. "Baby, we're going to get you back home and make you a hot meal ok?" Lisa rubbed her daughter's hand. "Lisa, why don't you ride in the car with Chelsea and follow me home?" Bill said.

When they all arrived at her parents' house, Chelsea took a long, hot shower. No matter how hard she scrubbed and washed, nothing could wash away the filth of the violation she felt inside. This would have been the perfect time for a hit. She knew just where to get one too, but she was determined to stay clean this time. She truly didn't want to go back to that lifestyle.

Chelsea could smell the savory seasonings and herbs from the kitchen. The aroma created familiar memories of warmth. In that instant, she felt like a little girl again. Innocent. Vulnerable. Pure. The very things she wished she could have again, so she could have her own choice to give them up like most young girls. She was stripped of it all involuntarily.

"Chelsea, baby! The food is ready for you," Lisa called. She missed that sound of her mother's voice when it was time for dinner. It felt good being taken care of and this time not because of a burden she had caused with her drug usage.

"Ok, mom. On my way!" Chelsea responded.

When she walked into the dining room, there was a cast iron pot filled with spaghetti and meatballs, a squash and zucchini medley and sliced garlic bread. "I didn't quite have enough time to bake a fresh pie, but I do have a Dutch apple crumb pie warming in the oven that I bought from the store. Dig in sweetie," Lisa said.

Chelsea thanked her parents for the wonderful meal and devoured the food. Even she didn't realize how hungry she really was. Bill smiled as he watched his daughter eat. "I'm so happy you're ok baby. I still can't believe that bastard," he said.

"Bill, let's just be glad that Chelsea's here and enjoy the moment baby," Lisa rubbed his back as she spoke softly.

After the meal, Lisa and Bill asked if Chelsea wouldn't mind spending the night at their place. She welcomed their invitation and watched TV with them in the living room until she fell asleep. Her rest that night was sounder than she felt in a long time. She hugged her pillow tightly and felt safe, a sharp contrast to how she felt while she was trapped inside of Brian's makeshift dungeon.

Meanwhile Cookie had just finished booking her flight to head out tomorrow to Chicago and return on Friday. She was now on her third glass of wine. She talked to her mom for a little while after trying to reach Chelsea and leaving her a voice mail. Lisa assured her that Chelsea was already asleep. They both avoided the elephant in the room; not only was Chelsea almost raped again, but it was by her ex brother-in-law.

So many emotions came flooding back to Cookie's head. All of the thoughts that she was just starting to bury regarding Brandon's death were resurfacing. The shame, guilt, fear, uneasiness and paranoia hit her like a ton of bricks. She tried not to be selfish and just be grateful that her sister was safe. But she realized in that very moment that she hadn't ever really healed or forgiven herself for what she had done. She just swept all of her feelings under the rug. They were invisible to the public and after so long, even to her.

She turned on her radio and heard Mariah Carey's "We Belong Together" spilling out the speakers. That just made her feel worse, so she turned the radio off and decided to just sit in silence. She began to cry uncontrollably and wondered who would miss her if she no longer lived. Remorse came over her as her head began to pound. She couldn't understand why after all these years, she felt as bad about Brandon's death as the same night it happened.

Just then, her phone rang. The sound startled her. She remembered how helpless she felt when the man she later learned was Brian was making demands regarding Chelsea. She looked down at her phone and saw it was Ken. She was supposed to call him back way before now. She started not to answer, but was tired of running. She didn't feel like talking then and likely wouldn't feel like talking later. Besides, maybe hearing Ken's voice would calm her nerves.

"Hello? Hey Ken. How are you?" Cookie answered and tried to clear her throat so he wouldn't realize she had been crying. But she didn't mask her tears well. He could tell something was wrong.

"Just checking on you sweetheart. Don't tell me you're the love 'em and leave 'em kind. My heart just can't take it," Ken and Cookie laughed. "Ah, she laughs. Wish I was there to behold that beautiful smile of yours. Everything ok? You sound a little heavy. Something's wrong. I can feel it. Talk to me."

"Oh nothing. I'm ok, just kind of got caught up with some things. Maybe I've just got the Sunday blues with the new work week coming up and all," she responded nervously.

"Hmmm…..that's all?" Ken persisted

"Oh yes, I promise. That's it. You're so sweet. I probably should get going though. Have a busy day ahead tomorrow. How about I give you a call tomorrow?" She could have kicked herself for saying that, knowing she wouldn't have time to talk to him tomorrow. Her flight left Dallas in the afternoon and she would be solely concerned about Chelsea once she got to Chicago.

"No. I'm not getting off this phone until you tell me the real answer of what's going on with you. I can take it. And I've got all the time in the world. You tell me what's wrong and I'll let you get your rest. But I won't be able to sleep until I know what's upsetting you," Ken responded.

Cookie started crying, barely speaking through her tears. "Why Ken? Why?" She was letting her guard down with him but she couldn't spill out the last decade of her life to a man she was just getting to know. Her intuition told her he could be trusted, but she struggled to keep something for herself.

"Huh? What do you mean?" Ken asked, genuinely puzzled.

"I just don't get it. You've got such interesting timing. I needed to hear your voice. God knows I did. I'm just so tired of walking into one landmine after another you know. My sister was captured this weekend by a man who raped her. She got away and literally fought for her life. And to top it all off guess who did it?"

Ken sat silently on the phone for a moment, not knowing exactly what to say. "Who...who was it?" he asked cautiously. He wasn't sure if it was a rhetorical question that she was on her way to answering on her own and just wanted his listening ear.

"My damn ex-husband's brother. I always knew he was crazy, but this just takes the cake. I still can't believe it. I'm heading out to Chicago to go see her for a few days. Just feels like I can't catch a break sometimes. Me or my sister. I know, go ahead and run. This is a lot to deal with. You're a busy man and you don't have time for this foolishness," she sobbed.

"I actually was going to ask you if I could go with you. I'll free up my calendar at work this week. I can be there as long as you need. And the only foolishness I see is how your ex-husband let such a beautiful, amazing woman like yourself get away. But I'm the lucky one and I'm glad he did. He made room for me," Ken said.

"Do you really mean that?" Chelsea asked, surprised at Ken's statement.

"Of course I mean it. I wouldn't have said it if I felt otherwise. I just want to be here for you," Ken responded.

"What is it about me that keeps you hanging on? A lot of men would have walked away from me by now," Cookie said.

"Well I'm 36 years old. I have everything I want out of life, except a woman to share it with. At this point, I'm done with games. I know what I want and I want you," Ken replied confidently.

"Damn, well ok. I guess I can't argue with that then. It just ….you just seem too good to be true at times. Thanks so much for the offer to come with me. But I think I should probably make this trip alone. It might be a little emotional. I hope you understand," Cookie responded.

"Oh yeah, I understand. That's a pretty traumatic experience your sister has been through. I'm glad you'll be there to help see her through it. She's lucky to have you. My prayers are with you and your family. Let me know when you make it there, ok?" Ken asked.

"I sure will. Thanks for everything. You have no idea how much you've helped me tonight. I look forward to seeing you again soon. Have a good night Kenny," Cookie said.

"You too beautiful. Get your rest," Ken said.

After they said their goodbyes, Cookie started packing her bags for Chicago. As she was gathering her things for the trip, she couldn't stop smiling. She was at the lowest point she had been in years and Ken stepped in right on time. She didn't want to get too excited. But couldn't help but think that it was a sign for something greater between the two of them. Cookie had developed what Sheila coined as "bad bitch blues".

She was an attractive woman, no doubt. She had no problem getting sex, attention, money or even a relationship from a man if she wanted. But the problem was always finding the right man worth developing a relationship with, while sifting through the shallow men who just wanted her body. She couldn't fault them too much though, because she had become accustomed to the no strings attached sexcapades. Deep down, underneath the hard surface, Cookie wanted to be loved just like any other woman.

Thankfully Cookie's job afforded her the flexibility to make impromptu trips like this. She would only miss one meeting that week, which could easily be handled over the phone. When Cookie arrived in Chicago, she texted Ken to let him know she made it safely.

"Hey Kenny, made it here safely. Thank you again. Hope your day is going well ☺," she said.

"Kenny….I like it. Keep calling me that. Glad you arrived safely. I'd love to see you when you get back," Ken responded.

"We'll definitely have to make that happen…..Kenny, lol," Cookie responded. She hadn't even realized until he brought to her attention that she started calling him Kenny instead of Ken. But there wasn't any time to dwell on the puppy love thoughts. She had to go see Chelsea.

Cookie called her parents to let them know she had arrived. Her father answered and told her he would be coming to pick her up.

"There's my first born. So glad you made it in safely. Give me about 10 minutes and I should be there. I'm in the car now. Your flight must have landed a little early," Bill answered.

"Hey Daddy. Ok, it's no rush. I'll just be here. We did land a little earlier than expected," Cookie said.

Bill was there within the next few minutes. He immediately parked, and walked to greet Cookie with a tight bear hug. "Well I hate it's under these circumstances but I'm always glad to see you baby," He said. "Let me get the door for you. I'll put your bags in the backseat."

"Thank you Daddy. I love you," Cookie smiled.

"Your mother is at Chelsea's house. We've been a little paranoid about her being by herself. I just finished tending to the lawn outside and was about to head over there myself, so this is perfect timing. Your sister is really strong. You both are. Just hate that she even has to go through this," he said.

"She is, but I know what you mean. I'm still in disbelief. And to top it all off, the fact that it was Brian makes it even more bizarre," she admitted.

"Yes, but both of those scum bags had what was coming to them," Bill said. Cookie got silent and waited for the conversation to turn to a lighter point. Bill then asked Cookie how her job was going.

"Oh, pretty good, just really hectic. I'll be taking over my boss's spot soon. She's really ill, so it was an unexpected promotion. I'm enjoying it though. No complaints," she said.

"Wow, I'm sorry to hear about your boss. I'll make sure to keep her in my prayers. And I know you will nail the new position. I'm so proud of you baby," Bill said.

"Thank you Daddy. So, what's new with you? I know you and mom are loving retirement. Have you been working on any new projects lately?"

"Actually I have been. I'm working on a new deck for the backyard. I'm about 85% finished with it. Your mom doesn't like all the noise I make out there, but she'll love it once I'm done. I can't wait for you to see it," Bill said with pride.

Cookie and her father kept talking until they pulled in Chelsea's driveway. Chelsea opened the door and threw her arms around

Cookie and told her, "I love you. Thanks so much for coming. It really means a lot."

"Of course, that's what sisters do, right?" Cookie said, squeezing Chelsea tightly one last time before letting her go and greeting her mother as well.

"What's that smell? Are those fresh baked oatmeal cookies?" Bill said.

"Yes, baby, they sure are," Lisa said, walking over to Bill and rubbing his stomach. "Chelsea and I had a bit of a sweet tooth. We actually just pulled them out of the oven to cool. They'll be ready to eat in a few minutes."

"Mmmmm, I can't wait. Those are my weakness," Cookie chimed in.

As everyone started tasting the cookies that Lisa and Chelsea made, Bill decided this was the perfect time to make an announcement to his precious girls. "Chelsea, Cookie, do you still remember how to shoot a gun? I know we went to the gun range a while back when you were in college. But I think it's time both of you started carrying a gun. This maniac Brian coming after Chelsea is just another example that it's not safe out here anymore," Bill said.

"Your father's right. I would feel more at ease knowing you have something to protect yourselves. Of course, nobody wants to have to use it. But, hey if you have to...." Lisa said. The fact that their mom readily agree without hesitation with Bill meant that they were both truly concerned about their daughters' well-being.

"Oh yeah, I still remember how to shoot. That's a good idea. I do need a gun. Cookie, we both do," Chelsea said.

"No objections here. I'll get one as soon as I get back to Dallas. It's so scary out here," Cookie added.

"But baby, we're just so glad you made it out of there alive. That was nothing but God," Lisa chimed in.

They all talked and switched the subject matter to more lighthearted topics before Lisa and Bill decided to go back home. "Alright girls, we're about to head home. Let us know if you need anything, ok?" Lisa said.

"Thanks Mom. I think we'll be ok," Chelsea responded.
"Yeah, I'll just get some long overdue bonding time in," Cookie chimed in.

After Lisa and Bill left, Chelsea and Cookie got down to the nitty gritty of the whole series of events that transpired in the last couple of days. Cookie was on pins and needles to find out the extended story of what happened to Chelsea and how she realized Brian was the person who captured her.

"Okay, so now we can talk freely," Chelsea said.

"Yes, you know I was waiting to hear this one. But I'm just really glad that you're ok. In case I haven't told you before, I really admire your strength Chelsea," Cookie admitted.

"Thank you. That's so funny you say that, because I've always admired yours, ever since we were little. You never let anything hold you back and were so driven. Watching you keeps me going," Chelsea said. "But hey, we've both had enough teary eyes. I don't want to start crying again."

"Yeah I know what you mean. Do you remember anything that happened the day Brian picked you up?" Cookie asked.

"Nope. All I remember is I woke up in this bed, with my feet tied to it. Brian had a ski mask on the whole time. But the strangest thing was the place itself; it was like a stone hut. Very hollow sounds. Hardly any carpet in there and I kept hearing the sound of running water. Once I finally got outside, I realized the place was hidden inside the trees, on a hill, and there was a small creek below it," Chelsea explained.

"Wow, so this is like some secret hideaway he had? Did it look like it was his place or was he just there?" Cookie asked in anticipation of hearing the full story.

"I don't know for sure, but it seemed like it could have been his hideaway. The place didn't really have much furniture, but it did look lived in," she said. "Cookie, I was so scared when he climbed on top of me. He kept making these references about the past and saying that I should know why he had come for me. I started thinking it was someone I knew, but never in a million years did I think it was him."

"Hell, neither did I. But when I talked to him…."

"Talked to him!? Wait a minute. How did you talk to him?" Chelsea asked.

"Yes, he called me from your phone. I'm surprised mom didn't tell you. He called her too. By the time I talked to her she was hysterical. He acted like it was all a big game to him. And he did make some past references to me too, saying something about how I always had a smart mouth," Cookie said. "But, I'm sorry go ahead."

"I had no idea he called you and mom. Anyway, so he climbs his ass on top of me. I found this sharp metal rod next to the bed earlier. I moved it under the pillow. So at this point, I just stopped trying to fight and let him think he had won. He started grabbing me and that's when he started trying to have sex with me. Well, he did. He was forcing himself on me. He raped me. I'm sorry….just have to say that so I can move on from it.

"It's ok….I understand. I'm sorry….I don't. I won't act like I do. I hate him Chelsea. I hate he did that to you," Cookie said, as tears began to stream down her face.

"Now I'm the one that got raped, but you're crying? Come one now, butch up sis," Chelsea laughed, as she tried to hold back tears of her own. "But it gets better. Hold on. So he's pumping and thinking he's really doing something good, you know? I waited right until he was about to cum. That's when I knew he'd be too vulnerable to fight back. I grabbed the metal rod from underneath the pillow and shoved it in his neck. Cookie, I've got to tell you, seeing that blood spew out the side of his neck did something to me. It gave me such an adrenaline rush."

Cookie looked blankly at Chelsea for a while before she said anything. She was actually quite disturbed at how nonchalant she was acting about killing Brian. He deserved it for what he did, but it was as if she had no consideration for his life at all. She felt a wave of déjà vu come over here as she remembered this was the same way Chelsea acted when Brandon died. "Well, tell me how you really feel," she said.

"My curiosity was just eating away at me. I had to see who he was. I found the light switch in there because it was so dim inside. That's when I leaned over and yanked that damn mask off his face. He looked up at me with the coldest gaze. His eyes were still open," Chelsea said.

"I just can't believe it. I know he always had a thing for you but that was so…..no other way to say it but crazy as hell. I'm glad you got rid of him," Cookie said.
"You and me both. But enough about that. He's dead. It's over and now neither one of them can ever harm us again. Somebody over there is glowing though. I did notice that. You know there's

not too much that gets past me. Especially when it comes to you. So what's his name?"

"Who says I have to have a man to look good? I am dating a guy. He's nice. Really nice. But I'm not rushing anything. No expectations. We're just seeing how things go right now. Taking it day by day. Everything is still so new, you know?" Cookie said.

"Oh yeah I know. I know that it sounds like you're already catching feelings. Nothing wrong with that though. I love it," Chelsea responded. She sat back in her chair with her arms folded, in anticipation of hearing more about Cookie's new love interest.

"And why are you looking at me like that?" Cookie laughed.

"Because I'm waiting on you to spill it. Come on. I want to know. How does he look? Does he have any kids? Ever been married? Psycho friends or family? Oh and of course, is he good in bed?" Chelsea asked.

"You are such a mess. Well, he is very attractive. Tall with a big chest and broad shoulders. He has a nice face and really well groomed, but still has somewhat of a rugged air about him. I can't put my finger on it. Nice legs. Cute ass. No kids. Never been married. Not a psycho that I know of. Keeping my fingers crossed, "Cookie exclaimed.

"Sounds nice. But you aren't slick. That's more than a school girl crush glow. You gave it up didn't you?" Chelsea interrogated Cookie.

"Now who said I did such a thing. I'm a good, clean girl," Cookie replied, with a half smirk.

"Right and those good clean girls are always the worst ones," Chelsea laughed.

"He's good…..I mean damn good. Spectacular even. And hung too," Cookie said, as she rubbed the back of her neck and exhaled deeply. "But it's more than that you know. He's very strong, but passionate and not afraid to be himself around me. He's a great guy, but again, I'm not getting my hopes up just yet."

"I hear you. I'm just giving you a hard time. But honestly Cookie, you do have this look about you that's peaceful. I haven't seen that in years. And after all you've been through you deserve it. Don't fight him. But I already know that you are. Let your guard down a little. He may be just what you need," Chelsea cautioned Cookie.

"Yes mam, duly noted," Cookie smiled. "Thank you. That really means a lot and believe me, I value your opinion so much."

"So what are you going to do if he happens to be the one? The right one this time?" Chelsea asked in a serious tone.

"I don't know. I'm honestly afraid. Something tells me he just might be. I just don't know if I'm ready," Cookie said.

TWENTY-TWO

Cookie enjoyed the rest of her time back home in Chicago. It was the refresher she needed and she was glad to be there for Chelsea. In many ways, she felt guilty for some of Chelsea's struggles. No matter how much of a tough girl she appeared to be, Cookie knew that Chelsea was likely battling with the reality that she had murdered not one, but now two people. She hoped the stress wouldn't send her back into a relapse. She was doing so well staying clean and it would break her heart to see her spiral downwards into that cycle again.

She called Ken to let him know that she had arrived back in Dallas. Cookie could tell that he was excited to hear her voice, as she was his. Usually she would act like she wasn't so excited to hear from him, but this time she decided to just go with the flow and let her guard down. It was a scary feeling, but also a welcomed release.

"Well, hello there pretty lady. How was your trip? Is your sister ok?" Ken asked. Cookie adored his attentiveness. All the other guys she dated didn't concern themselves much with how she felt, what made her happy or the things that made her cry. When it came down to it, many of them wanted her for her body and whatever opportunities they thought they could gain from her.

"Such the charmer you are. And you're pretty handsome yourself. It was really good. My sister's ok….well, she will be. I think she's got a bit of a wall up now, but she is really strong. She just needs a little time to process everything and heal," Cookie said.

"I really admire you for being such a great support for her. That's awesome. Many people can't say they have that same support system. I'm sure she was really grateful and happy to see you. I hope to meet her one day. She sounds like an extraordinary woman, much like you."

"Aw, thank you. She's definitely something special. I really love her. I hate it was under the circumstances, but I'm glad I got to see her and spend some quality time with her. With work being so busy, I don't get to go back home too often. I guess life has a way of waking us up and realizing what matters most, huh?" Cookie replied.

"Very true. Cookie, I hope you know how special you are to me," Ken said.

"I'm starting to believe it more and more. It's not easy for a woman like me to let her guard down, but you're making it more comfortable for me to do so. You know, I was wondering...I know it's not quite the weekend yet, but do you have any plans tonight? I was thinking about renting some movies. I know it's last minute, but if you want to join me the invitation is open," Cookie offered.

 "I would love to. I make a pretty good homemade green salsa. How about I bring some over for us to share during the movie?" Ken asked.

"Oh sure, I love salsa. You make your own? I'm impressed. I'll be anxiously waiting to taste it. Oh, and you're welcome to spend the night too. No pressure, just if you want to," Cookie said.
She couldn't believe the invitation that she had just given Ken. She honestly had no qualms about him spending the night. But this was the first time she initiated a man staying overnight at her house when it wasn't right after they had sex. There was something about Ken that made her feel very comfortable and protected.

"Well it sounds like a plan then. What time would you like me there by?" he asked.

"Let's see, it's 3:30 now. How about 7:00 tonight?" Cookie said.

"Sounds great. I'll see you then sweetheart," Ken replied.

At 7:27 pm, Ken was knocking at Cookie's door. It was perfect timing. She had just gotten out of the shower about 10 minutes before and her homemade apple pecan tarts were just done baking. She decided to surprise Ken with her one of her famous desserts, especially since he was bringing his homemade salsa. She opened the door and greeted him with a tight hug.

"Mmmm….you smell so good. It's really good to see you," Cookie said, exhaling deeply as she let go of Ken.

"Likewise and you look amazing. What's that smell…..mmmm…seems like somebody is in here pulling out the kitchen skills," he smiled.

"Well I had to bring something to the table since you were so generous enough to bring your salsa. I can't wait to try it. I have a couple of action movies for us. I figured I wouldn't torture you with a chic flick," Cookie laughed.

"Well I'll be here watching it with you, right? As long as that happens we can watch whatever. But I must admit, I am a big action movie fan," Ken admitted.

"You too? A man with good taste. I like it. Well make yourself comfortable. Take off your shoes. I'll take the food out of the oven now and get the chips so we can dig in to your salsa," Cookie said from the kitchen.

Ken caught himself staring at Cookie's behind in her snug pajama shorts and slight midriff revealing shirt. She was bending down to open the oven, as he fought the urge to pull down his pants and start going to work behind her. "You okay?" she turned around and caught him in mid daze.

"Oh yeah, I'm great. This is a really nice place you have here. I love the art pieces you have. Very eclectic and captivating," Ken said.

"Oh thank you. Just a few things I've collected over the years. I'm glad you like them," she said. Cookie put her tarts out on a platter to cool and opened a bag of tortilla chips to taste Ken's salsa. "Goodness, this is so delicious. I love a man that can cook. This is amazing. I have to get the recipe for this."

"Really? That makes me feel good. I worked hard on it. As far as the recipe, I'll think about it. You know, I only give that out to very special people. But I'm pretty sure you fit the bill," Ken smiled.

 "Oh, well that's good to know then," Cookie laughed. As they started watching the movie, Cookie handed Ken one of the tarts and fed him a spoonful of it. She could tell by the way his eyes lit up that he enjoyed the taste.

"Wow, now you're the real chef. This tart is so good. It just melts in your mouth," he said, kissing her lips softly. Cookie didn't hold back and kissed him back passionately while running her fingers across the back of his head. Ken brought his hand up to the side of her waist and moved down to softly kiss her neck. She brought her leg up across his lap as he slid his down behind her thighs, right underneath the cuff of her behind.

"I missed you," Cookie whispered as she stopped kissing Ken for just a brief moment, just to catch her breath before going back in for more. "I missed you even more," Ken said in between kisses. He slid his tongue down her neck and paused with a gentle kiss on her collar bone, groping her full breasts. He lifted up her midriff tank and pulled her left breast into his mouth, while massaging the right. Cookie was so turned on and her body felt an intoxicating heat wave radiate from the inside out. She could feel Ken's throbbing erection against her knee as they both quickly removed each other's clothes to make love with no restrictions. They started in the living room and then Ken carried Cookie into her bedroom. He sat down on her bed, with his strong arms wrapped around her back, as she moved in rhythmic circles in his lap.

Cookie and Ken moved in sync with one another, enjoying each other's bodies for the next couple of hours before forcefully climaxing. Ken could feel Cookie's legs start to tremble right before she reached her peak. They both laid there listlessly as Cookie's head lay on Ken's chest. His heartbeat felt like home and she wanted to freeze that moment in time.

"So much for the movie huh?" Cookie said.

"It's ok. This one was much more entertaining anyway," Ken smiled, running his fingers through Cookie's hair.

"Yeah…I agree. I could get used to this," Cookie said, as tears began to stream out the corners of her eyes. She was overwhelmed with the new feeling of what could be love with Ken and didn't know how to accept it. It was the first time in her life that she felt she truly knew what love was supposed to feel like.

Ken raised Cookie's head up, as he could now feel his chest getting wet from her tears. "Cookie? What's wrong?" he asked. He had a genuine look of concern in his eyes and sat upright in the bed.

"Ken, can I tell you something that no one really knows about me?" she said, sniffling and wiping tears from her cheeks.

"Of course, come on now. You can tell me anything," Ken said. "Ok, well I've been abused Ken. My ex-husband was abusive to me. It's why I seem so hot and cold with you at times. It's been a long time, but the memories come back when I get close to another man again. It was verbal at first. Then it escalated to physical abuse as well," Cookie sighed.

"Wow, I'm so sorry. I can't believe he would treat you like that. That's insane. I promise you I'm not that guy, if that's what you're worried about. I would never put my hands on you," Ken replied.

"You know what? He told me that same exact thing. He did. He said he would love me, cherish me, and never leave me. But...." Her voice trailed off as Ken showed a frustrated look of disappointment on his face.

"That's not me. I'm telling you. I've never put my hands on a woman and never will," Ken said.

"Well, you didn't let me finish. I was going to say but.....somehow I really feel it would be different with you. Women have that sixth sense you know. We always know the truth, even if we try to ignore it. I had that feeling with him from the very beginning. But I was young, dumb and in love – or so I thought," Cookie said.

"You weren't dumb. It was just your life at the time. I want to make new memories with you. Eventually all of the bad ones can't help but to be pushed out of your mind," Ken smiled. He gently rubbed her back until they both fell asleep.

Cookie naturally woke up the next morning to the scent of Ken. There was a hint of freshly sprayed cologne in the air as she saw him just pull up his pants and put on his shirt for work. "Good morning sunshine," Ken said, smiling at Cookie.

"Mmm...good morning sir. You really put a hurting on me. I slept like a baby. I guess I should be getting up too. What time is it?" Cookie asked.

"It's almost 7:30 am," he responded.

"Ok good, I'll go ahead and get up now, although I would love to spend the day with you instead," Cookie said.

"Who are you telling? You and me both, beautiful. I'd love to see you again tonight if that's ok with you. But I won't wear out my welcome and leave my toothbrush here," Ken laughed.

"You are so silly. Well thanks for not being a stalker," Cookie rebutted sarcastically.

Ken kissed Cookie goodbye before he left. As Cookie started getting ready for work, she checked her emails and noticed she had one from her manager, Tina. She was up pretty early because the email was time stamped at 5:04 am.

"Good morning Candice,

I would have much rather told you this in person, but it's time for the transition to officially begin. My health has not been the best and my doctor is ordering me to cut out any potentially stressful obligations. Let's try to meet sometime soon here in the coming days.

I am totally confident that you will do an amazing job in the role.

See you soon,
Tina"

Cookie felt butterflies in her stomach. She didn't understand why she was nervous. She knew this time was coming soon, but not this fast. There were many thoughts running through her mind. The feeling of euphoria from last night with Ken still hadn't worn off and it helped calm her nerves for the big day ahead she had at work. When Cookie arrived at work, she had a text from Sheila. "In need of some girl talk with my bestie soon. Love you girl. Brunch this weekend?"

Cookie texted Sheila back and said," Yes! Brunch this weekend sounds great. Can we make it Sunday? I'll let you pick the place this time." Cookie purposely set up the brunch with Sheila on Sunday instead of Saturday. Truth be told, she wanted to spend as much time alone this weekend with Ken as she could.

TWENTY-THREE

Cookie walked in the restaurant on Sunday morning right at 11:00 am, the agreed time that her and Sheila confirmed they would meet. Sheila immediately picked up on her pleasant and upbeat demeanor. "Hey there sexy lady. I missed the memo. I didn't know I was supposed to be so jazzy for brunch," she said, hugging Cookie and admiring her outfit. Cookie was wearing an asymmetrical maroon dress that was off the shoulder on the left side with the longer piece of fabric hanging on the right just below her calf. Her hair had been freshly trimmed with dark plum highlights and she accented her outfit with modest yet stylish gold jewelry; not to mention her stunning gold open-toed heels.

"Pray tell Miss Lady. I take it that you and the new man are doing quite well. Should I pull my shades back out? Your glow is blinding." Sheila said.

"Silly. Now why do I have to have everything going right in my love life just to look good? I look good with or without a man," Cookie said assuredly, while she teased the front of her hair with her fingers.

"Well, yes that is true. You're a knockout all on your own. I mean, let's face the truth. You wouldn't be my bestie if you were anything less. But I can tell there's that extra special spark you have there. Definitely looks like you've given him a second chance after that open mic fiasco. So let's hear it. Spill it....I'm all ears girl." Sheila responded.

"I do have to admit, you were right about giving him another chance. He's really been amazing. I even invited him over and let him spend the night. And it wasn't just because I thought we would have sex. The sex is out of this world though. No complaints at all there. He takes his time and just.....ooh, he makes body scream. But even outside of all that, I just feel comfortable with him there. It's strange. I feel really protected when I'm around him. It's kind of a foreign feeling because I never really felt that way with Brandon or anyone else I've been with," Cookie said.

"Well does he have a brother who's single and ready to mingle? I'm out here dating, but all of these guys are such losers. They're either no good in bed, or great in bed with horrible credit, still living with their mom or have no ambition about anything. Maybe I should be a lesbian," Sheila laughed.

"Please, that will happen when pigs fly. Not with the way you love men," Cookie rolled her eyes and laughed with Sheila. "So tell me what else is going on with you."

"Business is really booming. I have a few clients I'm working on events for. So at least that part of my life is going well. It's truly a joy though to be doing what I love. I've been working on some new web development tools to change up my website soon. I'm blessed though. I've got my health, I'm in my right mind, I still look good at 35 and I've got the best sister from another mother on the planet. Oh and speaking of health, how is everything going with your new transition at work?" Sheila said.

"Surprisingly well. Everyone has really pitched in to make it seamless. We'll see when everything settles though. Tina gave me some great coaching; I just wasn't ready for everything to happen so quickly. I can't complain though. She's going through more than I am. She's trying to save up her energy for all of these medical tests she has to start taking. I'm concerned about her. I've been praying for her. She even seems more spiritual now; not saying she was an atheist or anything. I just never really heard her talk about God as much as she does now," Cookie responded.

"You know, they say people always know right before it's their time. Of course I'm not wishing anything on her, but maybe she's getting prepared. It's never too late to be redeemed," Sheila said.

"Yeah....very true. You're right about that," Cookie said, as her voice started to trail off.

"Everything ok? You look a little worried? And where is the waiter? I'm starving. I thought he was coming right back," Sheila said.

"Sheila, there's something else I need to fill you in on too. It's about Chelsea," Cookie said reluctantly. She really was up for recounting the whole story about Chelsea being raped by Brian and her ultimately killing him in self-defense.

"Oh no, what's going on? Is she ok?" Sheila said.

"She is now. She got captured last week. And she got raped. It was Brian that did it. She said she was at the grocery store and...."

"Wait a minute. Cookie, this all happened last week and you didn't tell me!? Come on now. What's up with that? Did you go back home? You know I would have gone with you," Sheila said, genuinely hurt she was just finding out about Chelsea's situation.

"I know. I'm sorry. There was just so much going on at the time. The guy called me and my mom too, threatening us. But Chelsea got away though. She stabbed him with this metal rod she found in the room. You'll never guess who did it though," Cookie said.

"Who? Don't tell me it was her crazy ex-boyfriend Lawrence. That guy was always a little creepy to me," Sheila responded.
"No kidding. I was so glad when they broke up. It was Brian," Cookie answered.

"Brian! Wait, Brandon's twin Brian? What the hell is going on? I know he always liked her in college, but damn that is crazy. Cookie I'm so sorry. I can't imagine how Chelsea must be feeling," Sheila said.

"Yeah I told her she's a very strong woman. Stronger than I would probably be in the same situation. But you know her. She's always had that tough girl wall built up. I just hope she deals with it before she does anything destructive," Cookie said.

"Yeah I know what you mean. She won't. We're not even going to focus on that. Wow…..I just can't believe it though. Brian? Of all people. Why? You think there was some kind of motive there?" Sheila asked.

"I don't know but he had some kind of voice distorter on when he called my mom and I. He kept making these references about the past, letting me know that he knew who I was. He did the same thing to Chelsea too, telling her that she should have seen this day coming. He's crazy. I don't know what his motive was but I'm just glad she got away," Cookie answered.

"Exactly. He deserved it for doing that to her. I really can't believe that bastard," Sheila responded. By this time, the waiter had finally come back to take their orders. They both opted for lunch entrees, since it was nearing the afternoon. Cookie ordered a pesto chicken Panini and a side house salad. Sheila ordered a grilled shrimp Caesar salad with a side of turkey chili. They talked and laughed some more as they enjoyed their food, before going their separate ways.

"We have to meet again soon. Maybe I should get on your calendar now before your new flame takes up all the available spots," Sheila joked.
"I promised myself I would not be that girl. That's so not cool at all. But we do have something planned next Saturday. Maybe we can catch a movie and dinner Friday night?" Cookie said.

"Sounds like a plan to me. I'll check to see what will be out by then. Hey Cookie, I'm really happy for you. Who knows, you may have just found real love," Sheila smiled and hugged her friend.

"You know, it actually feels like I might have. I'm just going to enjoy the moment and see where it takes me. I don't want to get my hopes up, but let's just say I won't object if he happens to be the one," Cookie said.

TWENTY-FOUR

Cookie put on the new black and red dress she bought a few weeks ago and fastened the straps on her red heels. She sprayed a little extra perfume over her body and brushed the sides of her hair one more time. She had let her hair grow out into a longer, layered bob, with a slight asymmetrical cut. It was almost 8:00 pm and Ken would be there any minute to pick her up. It had been seven months since they first started dating and Ken wanted to take her out some place special. She didn't know where they were going, which made her even more excited.

She finally reached a point where she was comfortable with Ken and was able to let her guard down. Her parents and Chelsea all approved of him as well when they came down to visit for the 4th of July. This made Cookie even more excited to have her family's blessing, especially her father's. He was so protective over his girls that virtually no one was good enough to be in a relationship with them.

Cookie reapplied her lipstick once more, looked at herself in the mirror and admired her ensemble. Just then her phone rang. It was Ken and he was in her driveway. "I'm here baby. You can come out whenever you're ready," Ken said.

"Ok I'll be right out in a couple minutes babe. So do I get any clues as to what we're doing tonight?" she asked.

"Well let's just say I'll be enjoying the company of the most beautiful woman I know. How about that for a clue?" he replied.

"Mmmm....I like. You get some brownie points at least for that one. Such a charmer. I'll be right out then," Cookie responded and hung up the phone. She grabbed the gift she had picked up for Ken. She bought him a Beats Pill speaker that she knew he was eyeing. When she walked out the front door, she saw Ken waiting at the passenger side of his car, with the door open and an arrangement of an exquisite bouquet of flowers in his hand.

"Hello beautiful. My goodness. Are you all mine? You look amazing," Ken said. Cookie thanked him for the compliment and blushed like a school girl. "And these are for you. I figured simple roses wouldn't do you justice, so I got these instead," Ken said, handing Cookie the flowers as he closed her passenger door.

Cookie handed him the wrapped box that enclosed his gift. "This is for you to open later tonight, but not right now. I have a feeling you're going to like it," she said assuredly.

"Thank you. I can't wait to see what it is. I have something for you too. You'll get it soon enough," Ken said.

"Hmmm….I like surprises. I'll do my best to be patient then," she smiled.

Ken reached in his back seat and pulled out a black satin scarf. "If you don't mind, I'll put this around your eyes. I don't want you to see where we're going just yet," he said.

"Oh ok. Sure, I'll put in on. I'll only peak a little bit," Cookie said jokingly.

"No peaking allowed lady," Ken laughed. He reached for his radio dash and started playing some soft music. Sade's "No Ordinary Love" poured out of the speakers. "Mmmm….great choice. I haven't heard this in forever. Her voice is amazing," Cookie said.

"I agree. This one is a classic. I love how she takes her time and always releases quality music. You can tell it's not rushed. But I am ready for her to make a new album though," he said. They continued to talk about music, their week at work and how much they were truly looking forward to spending some time alone.

They had both been enduring some pretty hectic schedules and had limited interaction with each other in the last few weeks.

All of a sudden, Cookie felt the car jerk in one direction and then swerve in another. "Just want to throw you off a little bit. Don't want you getting any ideas of where we are before it's time," Ken said. He circled the parking lot before finally parking the car. "Alright, well here we are". He finally removed the blindfold from her eyes.

"Oh wow, the Zentell? Why do I get the feeling you're up to something? If we're going to be here for a while, I'll go ahead and bring your gift too," Cookie said. Cookie was quite impressed. Zentell was a relatively new, five star hotel on the North side of Dallas. The architecture of the building was breathtaking and it included a beautiful infinity pool on the roof.

"Sure, you can bring it with you," Ken said. He got out the car, went around to open her door and took her by the hand. Ken was happy that Cookie was a bit caught off guard and wondering what would happen next.

They took the elevator to the top of the building, walked out into the covered bar area and then towards the infinity pool outside. Cookie immediately noticed that no one else was up there with them. "Do you remember me telling you I wanted to come here? Is anyone else joining us or are we the only ones?" Cookie said.

"Well anything that interests you interests me. I pay attention to you. I'm pretty sure we'll have this whole area to ourselves for a while," Ken said.
Cookie took a closer look around and noticed there was a small table for two outside with a white table cloth, candles and a bottle of wine sitting in a bucket of ice. There were also floating candles on the surface of the infinity pool. The lighting was a little different, with a slight peach hue and there were other intricate decorations laid outside. The weather was perfect for being

outside; something Ken was a little leery of. But the temperature was just the right amount of warmth with a gentle breeze.

Ken pulled out her chair and said, "Have a seat my lady. If you don't mind, I just have to go take care of something for a moment. I'll be right back, ok baby."

"Oh okay, cool. I'll be here. I love you," Cookie said.

"I love you too. I won't be gone long," Ken said.

Shortly after Ken left, music started playing through the speakers. Cookie was so wrapped up in the ambiance that she lost track of time. But something wasn't right. It had to be about 15 minutes that passed and Ken was still gone. She decided to text him to see where he was. "Everything ok?" she said. A couple more minutes passed and no response. Then, all of a sudden she saw Ken turn the corner wearing an apron and holding a large tray in his hand.

As Ken moved closer, Cookie realized that there were two identically plated dishes with one lobster tail, filet mignon with a wine sauce on top and sautéed spinach. "Wow, when did you order that? It looks delicious. I didn't even know they served that here," Cookie said with an impressed look written all over her face.

"Well, actually they don't serve it. I cooked it for us," Ken smiled as he opened the bottle of wine and poured Cookie and himself a glass.
"Wait a minute. This whole time you were gone, were you preparing this?" Cookie asked, her eyes wide with excitement.

"I sure did. I hope I didn't keep you waiting too long," Ken said.

"No I was just getting concerned. But, this was well worth the wait," she said.

"I'm glad to know that then. I hope you like it. I wanted to prepare something special for us," Ken said. They continued to talk as they ate their food over the sensual music in the background.

"You really outdid yourself sir. This is so delicious. I don't think I've ever had filet mignon cooked this well. I've tried to make it at home a few times and it tastes ok, but not like this. And this lobster and spinach are so delicious," Cookie complimented Ken.

"I was really nervous about it. I'm glad it came out to your liking. I'll take these plates for your baby. I won't stay gone as long this time," Ken joked, as he walked back into the kitchen. He returned in a couple of minutes with two small bowls full of vanilla ice cream, with caramel, pecans and freshly cut strawberries on top.

"Baking is not really my forte. I think that's more of your specialty so I decided to keep it simple for dessert," Ken said.

"Well after that delicious meal you just cooked, I think it would be totally unfair to expect you to whip up an apple pie in the back too," Cookie laughed. "I'm just enjoying the moment. It feels so great out here and even better because I'm here with you. Oh, don't forget to open your gift. We can exchange whenever. I mean, I know you said you had something too but I really wasn't expecting a gift."

"Sure, that sounds like a great idea and it's ok to assume that I got you something. I did. I'll go first. How about that?" Ken said. He tore open the wrapping paper of the box that Cookie gave him. Before he completely took off the paper he could see what it was. "What? Wow, thank you so much baby. You remembered me talking about this?" Ken asked, clearly surprised.

"Yes, I did. You're not the only one who pays attention. I take it that you like it. It was the last one they had too. I made it to the store just in time when I got it," she said.

"Oh, you know what. I have your gift, but I left it inside. I'll go get it for you," Ken said.

"Ok, sure baby. I'll be right here," Cookie said.

Ken wasn't even gone a minute before he walked back to where Cookie was sitting. "You know I love you right, Cookie?" Ken said, standing next to her with his hand on her shoulder.

"Yes, I do. Of course. Why do you ask? Is everything alright?" Cookie asked, feeling nervous butterflies flutter in her stomach.

"Oh yes, everything will be perfect if you can do just one thing for me," Ken replied. Cookie had a look of anticipation and slight confusion on her face. Ken got down on one knee and pulled out a black box from the front of his apron. He opened it, revealing a stunning Vera Wang diamond engagement ring with blue accents. "Cookie, depending on what your answer is to my next question, you will make me the happiest man on earth right now."

"Cookie, will you marry me?"

Cookie's eyes widened with excitement. She thought something big was going to happen tonight, but not this. Was she ready to be a wife again? "Of course! Just say yes. Are you crazy?" she thought to herself. She held Ken's face in her hands as tears begin to stream down her face. "Well I think you're about to be the happiest man on earth because my answer is yes. Yes!"

TWENTY-FIVE

Meanwhile, Sheila was just getting home from getting some materials for a birthday party she was planning. It was the exact same night Ken proposed to Cookie, at almost the same time. She had just brought in the last bit of her bags from the car, when she thought she heard a noise rustling in the bushes. She paused for a moment to see if she would hear the noise again, but it stopped. She walked in through the garage, locked her doors and immediately poured herself a glass of wine before she sorted out her purchases.

As soon as she sat on the couch, she heard her phone ring. She didn't feel like getting back up to answer it, so she decided to let whoever it was leave her a voicemail. Just as she laid her head back on the sofa, the phone rang again. This time she thought she should get up and answer, in case it was an emergency. She made it to the phone right as it stopped ringing. It was a number she didn't recognize. Maybe someone dialed the wrong number. She checked the previous call and it was from the same number.

She grabbed the phone and walked back into the living room to turn on the TV. She decided to get caught up on the latest episode of *Scandal* that she recorded on her DVR this week. She was about five minutes into the show when the phone rang yet again. The same number was dialing back. This time she decided she better answer it. "Hello?" she answered.

There was silence on the other end, but someone was definitely on the line because she could hear them breathing. "Um....hello? Anyone there? I think you have the wrong number. Please don't call here again," Sheila said.

"Wait, not so fast. Is that any way to greet me after all these years?" the voice on the other end replied. Sheila felt a chill tap dance down her spine. This couldn't be who she thought it was. There was absolutely no way it could be possible. She stood up from the couch, pacing back and forth, and said, "No, no. This can't be. How?" Sheila replied, bewildered and confused.

"Oh come on now. I thought you would sound a little more excited to see me. That's not the kind of welcome I was hoping for. I still remember how excited you were that night at your house. How many times did you come again? I think it was three, maybe four. Eh, who's counting?"

"Brandon, that was just one time and I've hated myself for it every day since then. Cookie is my sister and that was a huge mistake. Who gives a shit about that anymore? I thought you were dead. What are you even doing calling me?" Sheila responded.

"You don't worry about that. All you need to know is I'm here. Oh and tell Cookie that next time she'll have to try a little harder if she wants to finish me off. I'm coming for her and that little slut sister of hers for killing my brother. It's time for payback. Don't find yourself in the crossfire if you like your life the way you know it today," Brandon said, right before he abruptly hung up the phone.

Sheila felt like she was about to pass out. Why in the hell was Brandon calling her almost 10 years after he was supposedly dead? How could he have really survived that car accident? She had to get to him before he got to Cookie. She would eventually have to come clean about her having sex with Brandon years ago. It only happened once, before they were married, and she had finally psyched herself out to believe she had gotten away with it. Now, not only could Cookie's life be in danger, but so could Sheila's long kept secret.

She tried to go to sleep that night, but couldn't. She kept her bedroom light on and tossed and turned. How could she break this news to Cookie? Where exactly was Brandon? Was he really in Dallas? She remembered something very key in their conversation that Brandon mentioned. She knew about Brian's death because Cookie told her. But she didn't understand what he meant when he said she should have tried harder if she wanted to finish him off. Had Cookie really tried to kill Brandon and he didn't come up missing? She lay awake all night and wasn't able to fall asleep until right before the sun came up.

She had only been sleep about three hours or so when she heard her the sound of her text message alert. She had a special tone set for Cookie, so she knew it was her before she even got up. She reached over and grabbed the phone. There was an unread video message she received from Cookie. She played it back and it was her shouting, "Guess who's getting married?! It just happened last night! Can't wait to tell you all about it! Guess who's going to be a bridesmaid?!" Sheila could see Ken sitting in the hotel room in the background, right before Cookie zoomed in on the beautiful, sparkling engagement ring she was wearing.

Sheila was ecstatic for her friend, but her excitement was bittersweet at best. Now she definitely had to reveal that Brandon was back on the scene, not to mention admit after all these years that she slept with her best friend's ex-husband.

"I'm still so shocked. Wow, this ring is beautiful. I can't stop staring at it. I'm sorry.....man, you have me speechless," Cookie said, laying in the bed on Ken's chest.

"You deserve that and much more. I really love you Cookie. Come on now, you can tell the truth now that it is all said and done. Were you really surprised?" Ken asked.
"Yes I truly was. I've learned not to expect much. When you do, you set yourself up for disappointment. Especially for something like this. You really got me. I'm just elated that you chose me.

Thanks for giving me a second chance. You could have walked away after the way I treated you initially," Cookie confessed.

"No, I doubt it. You would have haunted me in my dreams and I would have had to resort to stalking you and making you mine. Plus, if nothing else I got this amazing Beats Pill speaker out of the deal. I love it baby. Thanks so much again," Ken laughed.

"Silly man. Well I'm so glad it never had to come to that then. And I'm happy to hear you love the speaker. You were so in love with it, I was afraid you were going to buy it for yourself soon," Cookie responded. The two spent the rest of the day reveling in their new commitment to each other. Over the weekend, they even discussed possible wedding dates, although Cookie refused to go into a deep dive conversation about wedding plans. She had just gotten the ring and didn't want to make him think twice about giving it to her. Plus, the advantage was that both of them had already been married before. They agreed that six months would be ample time to plan the wedding. They were going to keep it small and simple. They chose not to focus on the pomp and circumstance for show, but rather their true love for each other.

As they were driving back from the hotel to Cookie's house on Sunday, her phone rang. It was her dad calling. "Let me take this for just a moment. It's my dad," Cookie said.

"Sure baby, of course. Go ahead," Ken said.

"Hey Daddy. How are you?" Cookie asked.

"Ah, the sound of a happily and newly engaged woman. I'm doing well and I don't even have to ask how you're doing. I can already tell you're still on cloud nine. Is Ken around you by chance? I just want to talk to him for a second," Bill said.

"About what Daddy?" Cookie asked reluctantly.

"Don't worry. Nothing to be afraid of. Just a little man to man talk. Just put him on the phone," he insisted.

"Ok, if you say so. Here he is," Cookie said as she passed the phone to Ken.

"Hello Mr. Brighton. How are you sir?" Ken said, not quite sure knowing what to expect from the conversation.

"Oh I'm great and I know you're feeling like a lucky man over there," Bill said. It was a little presumptuous of a comment for him to make, but he was exactly right. Ken did feel like a champion knowing that Cookie would soon be his wife.

"Yes sir, as a matter of fact I am. Truly beaming from ear to ear over here," Ken said.

"Listen, Ken I've never really liked any of the guys Cookie has dated to just be frank with you. And especially her ex-husband, rest his soul. But I digress. I don't play when it comes to my girls. I'm most certain she's already told you this. But there's something different about you. I really think she struck gold this time. Pay close attention; this may be the first and last time you ever hear me say it. The only strike you have against you is that you're a Cowboys fan," Bill laughed.

"That truly means a lot sir. It really does. And if it never comes up again, I'll remember this moment," Ken laughed in return. "About those Cowboys though, I can't turn my back on my team," he exclaimed.

"Well I'll let you love birds get back to it. I just wanted to call and say that. I'll see you very soon I'm sure. Take care and tell Cookie I love her," Bill said.

"Ok Mr. Brighton, I will surely do that," Ken said.
"Bill. Just call me Bill," he said.

"Bill it is then sir. You have a good day now," Ken replied.
"Yeah, you too son," Bill said.

"Ah, what a relief. That seemed to have gone well. What did he say?" Cookie asked in anticipation. "He can be a real bugger at times."

"He actually was calling to tell me that he's never liked any of the other guys you've ever been with, but he approves of me except for that I'm a Cowboys fan," Ken explained.

"Wow, what's today's date? I need to mark this day down in history. He must really like you. My dad has never ever said anything like that," Cookie said, surprised. "That makes me smile." Maybe this time, she had finally found real love.

TWENTY-SIX

After a month in, Cookie still couldn't believe that she was engaged. It didn't quite hit her until Chelsea said she was making a special trip down for a few days to help her go look for her wedding dress. She already decided Chelsea would be her maid of honor and Sheila would be one of her two bridesmaids. Her other bridesmaid, Alexandria Harleaux, was her friend sorority sister that crossed on the same line as her and Sheila. Other than Sheila, Alexandria was the only other one of her line sisters she kept in close contact with. After college, Alexandria moved to New York shortly after graduation to follow her passion for dance. She was always one of those people that followed her heart and it proved to be a formula for success for her. There were a few other female friends who weren't much more than associates. But to have them in the wedding, would have truly been just to fill spots.

She was trying to remain calm and let the sequence of events flow for the wedding. But Chelsea was pressuring her about what kind of dress to get. Sheila already had ideas for floral arrangements and offered her services free of charge. With their added push, she finally started to get in marriage mode. She just didn't want to be one of those Bridezillas that only focused on things going her way.

Lisa was planning on coming at a later date closer in to the wedding. Cookie and Ken decided on an early summer wedding, on June 25th. Cookie thought this would be the perfect time for her, Sheila and Chelsea to get some girls time in and nail some logistics down for the wedding. Chelsea insisted that this would be separate from Cookie's bachelorette party, which she seemed more excited about than Cookie did.

Chelsea arrived on a Friday and stayed with Cookie during the weekend. That night, they spent time alone just getting some sisterly bonding in and going out for drinks at Wing Daddy's, one of their favorite spots whenever Chelsea was in town. They talked, laughed and enjoyed each other's company for nearly two hours before leaving.

"I'm so proud of you girl. I really think you got it right this time. You've come a long way. I'm proud to be your sister," Chelsea said, raising her glass. Cookie raised hers to meet Chelsea's and said, "Aw, thank you. I've always admired your strength. I don't think I've told you that enough. You are truly something special girl. And you've even toned down that temper over the years. Who would have thought?" Cookie laughed.

"We get a little wiser as we get older," Chelsea smiled and laughed back at Cookie.

"Well that temper saved my life. I'm forever indebted to you for that. I love you," Cookie said.

"I love you too. Sisters forever….you don't owe me anything. Oh, but you did say you were driving us back home, right?" Chelsea asked.

"I did say that. Why do you ask?" Cookie questioned.

"Hell that's good because I need to order one more Hurricane before we leave," Chelsea said, slurping the last of her current drink.

"You are hilarious girl. Well good thing I wasn't planning on getting another one," Cookie laughed. "I wonder where Sheila is. I've been trying to call her today but haven't heard back. I'll shoot her a text now so she can be ready for tomorrow."

"Hey Sheila, hope everything's ok. I reached out earlier but haven't heard back. Anyway, Chelsea made it in town and we'll be getting started around 10:00 am tomorrow. Let me know if you're still available. Love you," Cookie typed. Although Cookie enjoyed catching up with Chelsea for the rest of the night, she couldn't help but wonder what was going on with Sheila. It definitely was odd of her not to respond. But she decided not to worry about it and would hopefully hear back from her by the morning.

A little after 8:00 am that next morning, Cookie's phone rang. She thought she was dreaming but then looked over and saw Sheila's face on the screen. She was relieved that she was calling. "Hello? Hey girl, everything ok?" Cookie asked.

"Oh yeah, I'm fine. So sorry to worry you last night. I was just so pooped from the week. Had a birthday party and an engagement party going on at the same time. I've got to get some more staffing or stop double booking. But I pulled it off and they were pleased, so that's all that matters. I came home yesterday and crashed," Sheila said.

"It's ok, I figured you were just caught up or something," Cookie replied.

"But I'll still be there. I'm rested and all yours. 10:00 am at your place, right? If you and Chelsea haven't eaten breakfast, why don't we stop at The Pancake Hut first? My treat," Sheila asked.

"That sounds great. I'll let Chelsea know. We'll see you at 10:00 then," Cookie replied with glee. She couldn't remember the last time she had her sister and her best friend together at once. It was already shaping out to be a beautiful day. When Sheila arrived, they all sat around and talked for a little while before heading out to eat. They reminisced about old times and joked about all of their embarrassing college moments.

"Sheila, will we be hearing wedding bells for you next?" Chelsea asked.

"Oh no bell-ringing here. I'll leave that all to Cookie. I can't pick anybody worthy enough to ring my bells to save my life," she confessed.

"Aint' that the truth. We are in the exact same boat then. Somebody give me an extra paddle. This water's getting thick out here," Chelsea laughed.

"You are still a nut girl. It feels good to laugh. Lord knows I need it," Sheila said. "Come on Cookie, we have some dresses to go look at. We have a mission to keep to."

"I looked up a couple places on the west side of town and one downtown; a vintage dress shop. I just want something simple, but elegant," Cookie explained. "Ken is everything I didn't know I wanted and just what I needed. I don't want the wedding ceremony to take away from that."

"Mission accepted. Let's get to it then sis," Chelsea chimed in.
Cookie had a great time painting the town with Chelsea and Sheila. They actually found a couple of nice dresses, but neither really stood out as "the one" to Cookie. Meanwhile, Sheila was tossing around decorative ideas and logistics for Cookie to ponder for the day of. Cookie already had the day mapped out in her head though, which would make Sheila's job much easier.

Sheila suggested that Cookie at least have a wedding coordinator for the day of the wedding. Cookie knew of a great coordinator named Tambria Barnes that her cousin used a couple years ago for her wedding. Her wedding was flawless, so she decided to give her a call to see what her schedule looked like for the wedding. Thankfully Tambria was available during their time frame.

Before wrapping up the day, which quickly turned into early evening, Sheila suggested that they stop at Loco Taco, a Mexican restaurant they loved that had amazing margaritas. Although Sheila suggested the outing for the group. She needed a drink to take the edge off from being around Cookie and facing the fact that she would eventually have to tell her about Brandon calling her, not to mention her affair with him.

The ladies ordered a few appetizers and had two margaritas each. Everything was going well until Sheila's face flushed in shock during their conversation. "Girl, what's wrong? You look like you've seen a ghost or something. No more drinks for you," Chelsea said.

"Oh I'm sorry. I just….um. Just thought I saw a guy that uh….he looked just like Brian. Well I guess Brandon too for that matter. Just spooked me out a bit. He just walked out but he really resembled them. Really weird…hmmm," Sheila said, sipping on her margarita. "I'm good though. I mean of course it wasn't either of them. Couldn't be, right?"

Cookie could tell Sheila was a little buzzed, but paranoid her actions couldn't all be blamed on the alcohol. Chelsea picked up the same vibe. "Yeah, you sure you're ok Sheila?" Cookie asked. Sheila nodded slowly while staring into space. The guilt smothered her until she could no longer take it.

"Cookie, there's something I have to tell you. Something I've been holding back for a while. But for your safety, I think you should know," Sheila said.

"Ok…..I'm listening. What is it that you have to say?" Cookie said, sitting up straight and folding her arms while Chelsea looked intently at Sheila.

"Well, what would you say if after all these years, Brandon's really not dead? He called me the same night you got engaged,"

Sheila said. "He called from an unknown number. I didn't answer it at first, but he kept calling. When I finally answered the phone, I realized that it really was him. It was his voice. I know it. It's been eating away at me," Sheila said.

"Sheila, you do realize this is extremely far-fetched right? Brandon is dead. He's not coming back. It must have been somebody playing some kind of sick joke," Cookie insisted.

"No Cookie, let her finish. I wanna hear this. Um, sir. I'll take another margarita please," Chelsea told the waiter. "Go ahead now, continue."

Sheila cut her eyes at Chelsea in fear and started to speak again. "He said that he was coming for you and Chelsea. That you should have tried harder to finish him off or something and for me to warn you about it."

"Oh my God, what! Finish him off? This cannot be happening. Not now," Cookie said.

"Wait a minute Cookie. There's something missing in this story here. I don't ever remember you saying Sheila and Brandon were close. Sheila, answer this. What is it about you that made Brandon reach out to you directly? He could have called either one of us (pointing at her and Cookie). Something's not right about this story and we're not leaving here until we get to the bottom of it," she demanded as she finished up the last of her current margarita.

"Chelsea, what are you accusing her of? You know Brandon and his brother were crazy," Cookie asked, directing her attention to Chelsea now.

"Cookie. She's right. There's something else I need to tell you. A long time ago, I slept with Brandon. It just happened once. I've hated myself for it every day since. And no, I wouldn't have told you but he mentioned that too and how he was going to reveal it to you," Sheila spoke and her eyes were filled with fear as she finished spilling out her confession.

"Wait a damn minute. Cookie I told you a long time ago this girl wasn't worth shit!! She's smart though. She knew better than to uncover this behind closed doors. I should walk away right now, just for her damn safety," Chelsea said.

"Sheila, so you had sex with Brandon, while we were married? That's what you're telling me, right?" Cookie asked.

"It wasn't like that Cookie I promise. It was before you even got engaged. I'm so sorry. Please forgive me. Please," Sheila pleaded.

"It wasn't like that? What was it like? You fucked my husband! What kind of friend are you?" Cookie screamed. By now, many of the patrons in the restaurant were starting to turn their gazes towards them.

"I just still can't believe it. This is crazy. Are we done here? It's time to go. Let this tramp find her way back home," Chelsea snarled at Sheila.

"Wait. Wait," Sheila said. "I know your secret too. As wrong as I am, and I know I'm wrong, I know that Brandon wouldn't have said anything about finishing him off haphazardly. There's something more to this. I really just wanted to warn you. He's still alive. Can't you see that?"

"Oh yeah you would know everything about Brandon since you've done everything with him, right?" Chelsea responded.

"Sheila, give me one good reason why I should divulge any of my secrets to you, when you clearly had no intentions of telling me about you and Brandon? Let's cut the bullshit. You only told me to clear your conscious and beat Brandon to the punch just in case we happen to run into each other and he brings it up," Cookie said.

Chelsea paid for her and Cookie's tab, while Sheila paid for her own after pleading to take care of all of their tickets. Cookie dreaded letting Sheila even ride back with them in her car. As soon as they got back to Cookie's house, she told Sheila to leave immediately. Chelsea stared at her with a furious gaze, without saying another word to her.

"Hey baby, how did everything go today?" Ken asked later that evening.

"Oh you know us girls. Just out having a good time, sharing some laughs, painting the town and catching up. That's um....that's pretty much it baby. How was work for you today?" Cookie asked.

"Cookie, today is Saturday. Ok, maybe you might need a little rest. Sounds like you had too much of a good time. My day was fine though. I went to go get a haircut, washed my car and got a workout in at the gym today. I can let you get back to it. Make sure to tell Chelsea and Sheila I said hello, ok?" Ken replied.

"Oh sure baby. I definitely will. I really love you. You know that, right?" Cookie asked nervously.

"Of course baby, I sure do know it. Are you sure everything's ok?" Ken inquired again.

"Yes, I'm sure babe. Just wanted to tell you, that's all," Cookie said. After she hung up the phone she whispered to herself, "Way to play that one off Cookie."

"Huh? What happened?" Chelsea asked.

"Oh nothing, just didn't want Ken to get any ideas about earlier today. But I think he could tell something was wrong," Cookie said.

"We've kept it a secret for this long. We have to keep it up now. You can't ruin your future with him based on something you did to get away from an abusive husband years ago. It's not like you're just some random murderer. I can't believe he's still alive. We never did see him after the accident though and the police never found him. Why now though? Why years later? And I don't even want to think about Sheila. I can't believe you gave her a ride home. I know she's not still in the wedding," Chelsea ranted. Cookie, wrapped up in her thoughts of the day's events, barely heard much of what she said.

"I don't know yet. I just don't know what's going to happen. I'm not going back to living every minute in fear though. I've come too far for that. As far as Sheila, I don't think I can ever forgive her for this. Smiling in my face just to find out she was with my husband all along," Cookie said.

"You know what this means right, Cookie?" Chelsea asked.

"Yep. This time, we'll make sure he's dead," Cookie replied.

TWENTY-SEVEN

Cookie was flourishing in her new role, while juggling wedding plans and the nagging thought that Brandon was on the hunt for her and Chelsea. But she could tell that something adverse was going on with Tina that she didn't want to disclose. Lately, Tina had been more distant, although she was insistent that her health was improving. Cookie was pleasantly surprised when Tina requested that she come see her in the hospital. She was never a woman to complain much and if she did, there usually was a valid reason for it. Cookie knew Tina had something serious to say.

"Tina?" Cookie knocked on the hospital room door, before entering.

"Ah, look at you. You look great. So glad to see you Candice. Thank you for coming here. You don't even look like you're bearing the stress of a woman who's getting married in a couple of weeks," Tina smiled.

"Thank you so much Tina. You look great. How are you feeling?" Cookie asked. It was an awkward question, considering Tina looked tired and visibly sick, like she had obviously been struggling with her health. She tried to come visit Tina before, as she had done regularly. But within the last few weeks, Tina requested that she have no visitors besides close family.

"Oh I'm doing well for a fighting ole lady. How about you? Everything ready for the wedding? I'm so sorry I won't be able to make it. That's part of the reason I asked you to come here," Tina said.

"Everything is going well. It will be a simple wedding. Nothing really extravagant, so it's pretty much all buttoned up. And you don't owe me any apologies. You just concentrate on getting better. Have the doctors given you any new information?" Cookie asked. She noticed there was a small Bible sitting at the side of Tina's bed. She must have gotten serious about seeking God. She could see that there was a book mark placed in the middle of it.

"You know, those doctor's don't really know as much as we pay them for, do they? They've given me a few reports and I've just been meditating and praying. It's amazing the things you can hear in the still silence. The world drowns us out with obligations and foolishness so that we're not able to hear. In times like these, I really think God lays us flat on our backs so we can get the big picture of things, you know?" Tina said.

"Yes, that's so very true. He definitely has a way of getting our attention. Hey, you'd be happy to know that we were able to close that account for KHS," Cookie responded, trying to lighten the mood and fight back tears as she looked down at Tina struggling to be strong.

"Oh really? That's just peachy. Listen, I don't want to hold you. You have better things to do than sit in a hospital all day. I have something I want to give you. These are yours to keep," Tina said, reaching underneath her sheet and handing Cookie a small, white box and a yellow envelope.

Tina immediately opened the box and gasped at its contents. There were two blue diamond earrings with a single hanging pearl. "Oh my God, these are gorgeous. Tina, I absolutely love them. They're beautiful."

"Something blue, something yadda yadda. You know the drill. Hopefully you'll be able to wear them on your wedding day. They've always been a cherished pair of earrings of mine that I only wore on special occasions. I think your wedding day is certainly a fitting occasion, don't you think? Oh, and don't worry about that envelope for now. Save that until after the wedding," Tina mustered up a genuine smile through her pain.

"Ok I will definitely do that. Thank you so much Tina," Cookie said, as she leaned down to hug Tina. "You make sure you get well now. I'll be checking on you and sincerely, thanks for everything."

"You're most welcome my dear. Give Ken my love. I hope he realizes what a lucky man he is," Tina smiled.

"I'll be sure to let him know," Cookie smiled back and waved at Tina before she walked out of the door. She was overwhelmed at Tina's fortitude, despite her failing health. She stopped in the hallway and whispered a silent prayer that her health would make a turnaround for the better. When she opened her eyes, she nearly bumped into one of the staff there. The woman didn't seem the least bit startled and asked if she was ok.

"Oh yes, I'm fine. Just was saying a prayer for my friend that I just left. Please excuse me, I didn't mean to startle you Ms. Hawthorne," Cookie answered. She noticed her badge read Gabrielle Hawthorne.

"Startle me? My dear, I think I'm the one who startled you. It's great to know there are still some praying people out here in the world. I thought we had become an anomaly. Who were you here to see if you don't mind me asking?" Gabrielle asked.

"Oh sure. Her name is Tina. Just a couple doors behind me. And I'm Cookie by the way."

"Tina. Ok, yes she is so sweet. She talks about you often. She's been praying more herself and I'm sure seeing you lifted her spirits. You take care of yourself," Gabrielle responded.

"Thanks. You too. Nice meeting you," Cookie replied.

On her way home, Cookie decided that she would call Sheila to finally hear her out. She had been calling and texting her to try to apologize again, but Cookie wasn't ready to hear it at the time. Seeing Tina today made her realize that life was short and she had to forgive Sheila; not for Sheila's sake, but for her own healing. Up until this point she was still set on not having her in the wedding, although she had been lying to Ken and convincing him otherwise. Naturally, she couldn't tell him about their fight because that would mean revealing to him that her ex-husband that she thought she killed, was actually not dead. Not the kind of thing to bring up two weeks before a wedding.

"Hello? Cookie! Thank goodness. I've been trying to call you. Cookie, I swear I'm so sorry. I haven't been able to sleep at all. I can't lose you. You are my sister. Please forgive me," she pleaded.

Cookie stayed silent on the other end, collecting her thoughts before answering. "Sheila, I didn't call you to hear you apologize for the umpteenth time. Listen, if you're still available you're more than welcome to still be in the wedding. Chelsea and I decided on those peach dresses we saw that day at the outlet. I'm not going to get over this overnight. But I'm not about to dwell on it every day either. I have get ready to meet Ken for a taste testing of the cake but I'll talk to you later," Cookie said.

"Ok, thank you. And I'll be there. I'll go get the dress. I'd be honored to still be in the wedding. Thanks Cookie. I love you," Sheila said.

"Yeah. I love you too," Cookie said. She still had a pang of bitterness towards Sheila, but she did feel much better getting that off her chest and getting part of the awkwardness over with.

Cookie called Ken to let him know she was about 15 minutes out from the cake tasting. He informed her that he would be there in the next few minutes. They tried five different flavors of cakes and both decided on a strawberry cake with cream cheese icing. Cookie found the prefect dress, finalized the guest list, secured the caterer and now had decided on which flavor the wedding cake would be with Ken.

After leaving the cake tasting, Ken and Cookie decided to grab a bite to eat at an Asian restaurant on the way home. With the wedding and both of their jobs in a busy season, they hardly had time to catch up with each other. "Hey babe, all the invitations have already been sent out, right?" Ken asked.

"Yes, baby there are all signed, sealed and delivered. Why is that? Do you have someone you want to add? We received a few declines back so we have room," Cookie confirmed.

"Ok, really? That's good to know then. Jason, the new guy at my job, just moved here from California. He's been a great help picking up some of the weight of the team and he told me he's been looking for a place to meet some beautiful single women. I told him this one is taken of course, but there may be a few to choose from at the wedding," Ken replied.

"Oh yeah, tell him to come on. That should be good. Maybe he and Chelsea could hit it off. She's so picky though. But who knows, he just might be her type," she said.

"I don't know. I'd be scared to play match maker for her. Ok, I'll let him know then," Ken said. After dinner, they both went their separate ways. Cookie had a couple of interested buyers for her house right before she and Ken got engaged. One of them was still hot on her tail and it was perfect timing since she was planning to move in with Ken right after the wedding. She made an appointment to meet with the gentleman and his wife about a week before the wedding.

That Tuesday, Ken spoke to Jason to let him know he was officially invited to the wedding. "Everything's good to go, Jason. The wedding will be next Saturday, so if you're able to attend, we have some extra space for you," Ken said.

"You're the best man. Now what kind of pickings are we talking here? I need to make sure I'm dressed with my A game just in case," Jason responded.

"Yes, definitely bring the A game. Let's just say you'll have a nice selection to choose from," Ken laughed.

"Ok cool, I'm looking forward to it. I have a feeling that will be a good night for me," Jason said.

"It is what you make it right? I'll shoot you the address man," Ken said.

"Thanks Ken. I appreciate it. You know, I've been leery of getting back on the dating scene ever since my divorce," Jason admitted.

"Divorce? Oh man, I'm sorry. I didn't know you were married before. I feel your pain. This is my second go round at it and I'm committed to making this one work. How long ago was your divorce?" Ken asked.

"Oh it's been several years now. She walked out on me. No explanation. Haven't been able to find her since. We were having our rough patch, but who doesn't, you know? I just still can't believe it sometimes. I don't even know what I would do if I saw her today. There's no telling," Jason said.

"Wow, man. I'm really sorry to hear that. Just think of it like this: it's her loss. There's plenty more fish in the sea," Ken said.

"True. You know what? You're right man. I need to stop living in the past and take life into my own hands now. Take back what's mine," Jason echoed.

TWENTY-EIGHT

The day had finally come. Cookie was going to marry the man she truly felt comfortable enough to give her heart to. With Brandon, she always had doubts from the very beginning, but not with Ken. He showed her love, loyalty and trust so that was all she knew to expect from him. However, the tension between her, Chelsea and Sheila was thick. They tried hard to put on a good front for the family, but they all knew there was some unresolved angst there.

"Just in case our little friend decides he wants to show up, I'll have something for his ass," Chelsea said, lifting up her dress, revealing a .22 tucked secretly away underneath a garter belt on her left thigh.

"Chelsea, come on now. We don't need to get Cookie all nervous on her wedding day. Put that away," Sheila pleaded.

"I will not. As a matter of fact, count your blessings that I'm not using it on you. I'm protecting my sister," Chelsea said.

"Come on. Happy day. Good times. Remember? Please let's not focus on that. Today is going to go smoothly, with no drama. Let's just try to have a great day okay?" Cookie asked.

"Of course. Anything for you sis," Chelsea said, cutting her eyes over at Sheila.

"You're right, let's focus. Cookie, you look phenomenal. Ken is going to be blown away when he sees you," Sheila said.

"You do look amazing, if I must say so myself Cookie," Chelsea chimed in. "I love you. It's almost time. We should get ready to be in our places. See you in a bit."
"Cookie, thank you for letting me be a part of your special day again. I don't know what the future holds for us, but know that you are forever my sister and I'll do anything for you. I love you," Sheila followed.

Cookie smiled and hugged her sister and gave Sheila a hug as well. She hadn't fully forgiven her yet, but she was practicing the art of faking it until she made it. She was determined not to let anything shadow the joy of what today represented. "Well, hello there beautiful. You look absolutely stunning. I can't wait until you see everything live and in action. I added a couple surprises for some finishing touches. I hope you like them," Tambria said.

Cookie had another 10 minutes or so before it was time for her to walk down the aisle. She said a prayer and looked at herself in the mirror before going to meet her dad to walk her down the aisle. She paused for a moment to admire the blue diamond and pearl earrings Tina gave her. She smiled and fought back the urge to cry as she touched her ears.

"Now who is this stunning beauty I have the pleasure of walking with today? Oh I should have known. My beautiful daughter. Cookie, you look so pretty baby. That Ken better know he's a really lucky man. I may need to have another talk with him," Bill smiled.

"No Daddy, please don't. I think he knows," Cookie smiled back lovingly at her dad.

The double doors were opened as the music started to play. Unbeknownst to Cookie, Ken called on one of his best friends, John Patrick Adams for a special song for her. John wrote and sang a beautiful song that precisely expressed Ken's feelings for Cookie. Ken nodded at John in appreciation as he could tell by

Cookie's expression that she was pleasantly surprised by the song. She inhaled all of the attention while looking forward to stand next to the man she would soon be able to call her husband. At that very moment, Cookie was really glad that her inner thoughts could not be heard.

I can feel the jealousy burning through me with their stares. But I don't mind it. It actually makes me tingle down below to know that I've beat the odds yet again. I thrive on the impossible and this is just another example of the tables turning in my favor. It hasn't always been easy, but it's damn sure been worth every minute of it. I smile and sway, gliding ever so gracefully along my path. My hips are spread just right. My breasts naturally rise to the occasion and this one suits me so well. My ass is accentuated just enough to let them know I've still got it. Yes, this dress fits me like a glove and I look stunning. No Spanks either.

Ok…..breathe. I've got to get focused again and back to the task at hand. Can I really bring myself to do this? Funny how you can see the wrongs in everyone else's life but be blind for so long when it comes to righting your own wrongs. Am I really deserving of such an honor? What would these people think if they were introduced to the real me? Something feels strange now and the walls are beginning to close in on me. Suddenly I'm seeing things that shouldn't be here and my stomach feels queasy.

My confidence is deflating with each step. My ankles feel as though I'm walking in water with 20 pound weights. My poker face is always on point, but I think they can tell something is not right. Shit! This is the most inopportune time for this. Everything is getting so blurry. My knees are getting weak and I can feel my head pounding as I hit the floor. Please God, somebody save me.

Cookie finally snapped out of her daydream, just before she made it to where Ken was standing. She had just experienced a myriad of thoughts while walking down the aisle and was thankfully starting to feel the butterflies at the pit of her stomach subsiding. She had no doubts about marrying Ken, but was just hoping for everything to go as planned with the ceremony. She wondered if Brandon really was alive and if he was coming back for her and Chelsea. She hoped not and tried to dismiss the thought out of her head. Ken couldn't stop smiling and admiring her. He told her how beautiful she looked while they were standing at the altar. Knowing that she was with a man who truly loved her was like warm honey dripping on her skin; sensational to say the least.

Cookie and Ken both decided on Ken's cousin, Rev. Ethan Williams, to officiate for their wedding. He was a preacher who lived in Austin, Texas. He and Ken were very close so it made perfect sense for their wedding. After Rev. Williams gave a short anecdote about what marriage meant to him and his wife of 20 years, Mrs. Gayle Williams, he read from 1 Corinthians 13: 4-8, then asked the couple to exchange their vows.

"I, Ken, take you Candice, to be my wife, to have and to hold from this day forward, for better or for worse, for richer, for poorer, in sickness and in health, to love and to cherish, from this day forward until death do us part," Ken stated, looking intently in Cookie's eyes.

"I, Candice, take you Ken, to be my husband, to have and to hold from this day forward, for better or for worse, for richer, for poorer, in sickness and in health, to love and to cherish, from this day forward until death do us part," Cookie replied back, eager to officially become Ken's lawfully wedded wife. The words "until death do us part" echoed in her head several times after she said them. She told herself it was just senseless jitters and dismissed the negative thought.

When Rev. Williams finally pronounced them man and wife and commanded Ken to kiss the bride, time seemed to have frozen for that moment. Cookie would have paid to carry that feeling with her in her pocket for easy access whenever she needed it. Mrs. Candice Grant. It had a nice ring to it and she was on cloud nine.

The ceremony flowed extremely well, with no mishaps. Cookie could breathe much easier now. The reception was held at a nearby event center, less than 10 minutes from the church. All of the guests were enjoying the food and beverages, while mingling with each other. John walked up to Cookie and told her how beautiful she looked and said, "You know, Ken was quite the player back in the day. You must have been pretty special to make him settle down," he waited for Cookie's facial expression to show signs of concern. "Gotcha. I'm just joking. You make a beautiful couple. Congratulations again," he said.

"Thank you so much for the song. It was truly amazing. I absolutely loved it. And don't worry. Ken's playboy days are over and done," she laughed.

Bill was so caught up in admiring his beautiful daughter and her new husband that he totally forgot he needed to use the restroom. The garter toss was coming up next, so he thought this would be a good time to make a quick exit. He was happy to have Ken as his new son in law, but he was by no means thrilled to see him, or any man, feeling under his daughter's dress for a garter.

As he was washing his hands at the sink, he looked over and noticed a man that looked very familiar. The guy gazed at Bill a few seconds too long, and quickly turned his head when he realized he had been seen. He looked intently ahead in the mirror at the sink, as if Bill was never there.

"You know, you really remind me of a guy I used to know some years ago. As a matter of fact, you two could pass for twins, except your hair is longer than his," Bill said, drying his hands off at the sink.

"Oh really?" the man answered stoically.

"Yes, funny thing is he even washed his hands vigorously in the same manner you do. I guess stranger things have happened, right? I'm Bill, Candice's father, and you are…?" he asked.

"Jason. I'm Ken's coworker. Nice meeting you sir. I know you've got to be proud. You have a beautiful daughter. Ken is a very lucky man. I guess my twin is out there somewhere. They say everybody has one," Jason laughed.

"Right, that is very true. Well you take of yourself now, Jason. I'm sure I'll see you out there cutting a rug on the dance floor. There are plenty of pretty ladies out here," Bill said, extending a hand shake to Jason. There was an awkward delay that left Bill's hand positioned in midair just before Jason extended his hand.

"Yes, you're right. There are definitely some stunning women here. Especially one in particular," Jason said, as Bill turned around to walk out the door. "Oh Bill, how about those Bears?"

Bill stood there, still as a statue, before he turned around. "Brandon, you can't fool an old fool. I knew it was you," Bill said.

Both men quickly reached inside of their coats. Two shots rang out in the bathroom. Chelsea turned to Cookie with a concerned, but contained expression. The music was loud, but low enough for the shots to be heard by anyone close to the restroom area.

"Did you hear that?" Chelsea asked. "I think I just heard gunshots. Where the hell did that come from?"

"I thought I heard something too. Now, I know I'm not crazy," Cookie said, looking around for Ken. She saw him mingling with some of his family members. Evidently, he heard something too because he stopped in mid conversation to survey the room. He seemed a bit at ease once he saw Cookie was alright and talking to Chelsea.

"Cookie, where is dad? Look at mom. She looks like she's looking around for someone. Dad's not next to her. I'm going to the restroom. Sounds like the shots came from there," Chelsea said.

"I'm coming too. Let's go around the back way so no one sees us walking in. I don't see him either," Cookie said.

Chelsea pushed open the door, foot first, with Cookie close behind her. She nearly stepped on her father, laid out on his back, with a pool of blood forming underneath him. "Oh my God! Cookie no....no. Daddy, get up! Come in Cookie. Don't let anybody in the door. Lock that front one too."

"Chelsea, look! That's Brandon's ass laying on the floor. He shot daddy!" Cookie exclaimed, furious that Sheila was actually right about him coming back for them.

Chelsea stooped over him carefully and nodded. "Doesn't hurt to really make sure," she said, reaching under her dress to get her securely tucked away gun out.

"No, wait! Grab some paper towels," Cookie said.

"What? Cookie, we don't have time for this. Let's just shoot him and be done with it before dad loses too much blood," Chelsea exclaimed.

"This won't take long. Hand me the paper towels and grab dad's gun. No fingerprints that way. I'm going to shoot him," Cookie said.

"Good thinking! Ok, here. Here you go," Chelsea said.

Cookie took the gun out of Chelsea's hand that was wrapped in paper towels and she pulled the trigger. She shot him right in the middle of the forehead and then placed the gun right next to where they found it. "Come on, let's call the police. We gotta get dad to the hospital," Cookie said.

They heard Bill moan as he struggled to get up from the floor. Cookie and Chelsea realized that Brandon had actually shot him in the shoulder and not the chest. Their father, however, had shot Brandon right in the heart. Even in his older age, he was still an excellent shooter.

Cookie went to go find Ken and her mom before the police arrived. Cookie pleaded to her mom not to say anything that the man who her father shot was actually Brandon. She made her way to Sheila quickly and prepped her with the same speech. When Ken saw him, he was livid. "Oh my goodness! I can't believe it. This is Jason! The guy that works with me! Why would he do this? I'm so sorry baby. I never should have invited him," Ken asked, turning to look at Cookie. She stood there silently as her face turned white.

"Get back! Get back! Everyone please clear the way!" The paramedics arrived and they saved Cookie from having to divulge her nasty secret just in the nick of time. They put both Brandon and Bill on a stretcher and wheeled them out. Luckily, everyone else that was also at Cookie's first wedding didn't get to see Brandon's face. The paramedics covered Brandon with a white sheet and gave Bill an oxygen mask, while they were both on their respective stretchers. Lisa was walking next to the stretcher holding Bill's hand, with Chelsea, Cookie and Ken close behind.

Bill waited until Ken was out of earshot, took off his mask and whispered to Lisa through his pain, "Nobody messes with my girls baby. Nobody."

Epilogue

Bill was recovering well at home from the showdown at Cookie's wedding. It turned out to be a moderate flesh wound. Brandon was officially pronounced dead at the scene of the crime. Cookie was finally able to bury her darkest secret for good, but created a new one with Ken. She wasn't ready to tell him that his coworker, Jason, was actually her ex-husband, Brandon that she once tried to kill and eventually did just that. One day she would have to come clean, but not today. She decided to finally read the letter that Tina wrote her after her and Ken returned from their honeymoon in Paris, France.

Cookie didn't think she would be able to handle reading it anytime sooner, considering Tina had passed the day before the wedding. It was almost as if Tina knew her time was up and she wanted to see Cookie one last time. The earrings Tina gave her were now her favorite pair that she kept safely enclosed in their own jewelry box. She opened the envelope of the letter and began reading it, not knowing what to expect.

Dear Candice,

Where did you ever get that "Cookie" name from anyway? ☺ I'm writing you this letter because I know my time here on earth is nearing expiration. In fact, by the time you read this I'm sure I will have transitioned from my outer shell and hopefully into heaven (fingers crossed, right?). I'm at peace with it and honestly, I wish

I could bottle up this feeling and sell it to everyone. I spent the majority of my life being so uptight and neglecting what truly matters. It took God sending me you as a great example of His love and becoming ill to realize that.

On a more intriguing note, I had a strange dream about you and Ken the other night. It was your wedding day and gunshots started ringing out. Everyone was frozen in time while these shots were being fired. I never saw anybody physically shooting, but the strange thing is you seemed happy about it (which I know is so unlike your character to do such a thing). Right before I woke up, someone leaned over to me and whispered, "She can't keep up with these secrets forever." The voice, which didn't necessarily sound masculine or feminine, then let out the heartiest and disturbing laugh. I woke up in a cold sweat and eventually just laughed it off. Maybe it was something I was watching on TV that caused that crazy dream.

Anyhow, I'll bring this letter to a close. Candice, I love you and thank you just for simply being you. Just make sure you stay true to yourself because that's what people will ultimately love you for, just like I did. I hope you really like the earrings and think of me whenever you wear them. Give Ken a kiss for me and cut a rug at your reception in my honor.

Love,

Tina

Alternate Ending

Cookie smiled and exhaled deeply. She had made it through the ceremony with no major mishaps. Most of all, Brandon was nowhere to be found. But, what if it wasn't over? What if Brandon was just lurking somewhere in the shadows, waiting for her to let her guard down? She couldn't worry about the what ifs. Cookie had to remind herself to live in the moment.

"Hello beautiful. Well how do you feel Mrs. Grant?" Chelsea asked, gleaming with a wide smile. "You look so beautiful and you are wearing the heck out of that dress. I see these other ladies in here gawking at you," she laughed.

"Aw, thank you so much. I'm so ready to get out of these shoes and this dress. I feel amazing. For the first time I feel like love has actually returned the favor for me. Ken's the unexpected blessing I didn't know I needed," Cookie said, holding back tears.

"Well, where is your knight in shining armor anyway? Hopefully he's coming this way with some tissue. You can't smear that makeup. There are still pictures to take," Chelsea said.

"I don't know where he is," Cookie answered, slightly concerned as she surveyed the crowd. "Wait, there's Daddy coming out the restroom. Maybe he saw him in there."

"There's Daddy's girls. And how is the most beautiful bride in the world? Where's Ken? Don't tell me he's already slipping up on his duties of taking care of my baby," Bill asked playfully, but with a slightly serious tone.

"You know Ken, I was really starting to think you were a cool guy. I thought maybe we could be friends. But then, I thought, there's no way I'm going to let my baby walk off into the sunset with this weak ass man. Nope. Can't do it," Brandon said, pointing his gun to Ken's head.

"Just put the gun down. Why are you even doing this man? You think you're going to get away with this? I know you may be still in love with Cookie. But I know about you being abusive to her. How could you treat her like that if you really love her so much?" Ken asked, without a trace of fear in his voice. Truthfully, he intensely fearing for his life. He refused to go down without a fight though.

"You know what? To be so gullible, you actually have some balls. Who would have thought? You believed me when I gave you the fake sob story about my divorce and how I was new on the dating scene. And by the way, don't ever call her Cookie again. You got that boy? Her name is Candice to you. I bet she didn't tell you that her and her loudmouth sister tried to kill me. Yeah, that's what I thought. Where's all that tough boy talk hiding now?"

Ken's heart starting racing faster. He couldn't believe that he finally found the true love of his life, only to possibly never live to see her again and face the reality that she could be a murderer. "I don't believe you. And even if she did, I can see why," Ken answered. He had to find a way to break free but also get rid of Brandon for good. If Cookie did try to kill him before, he would make sure to finish him off now.

Brandon still had Ken in a headlock, nearly choking him while his gun was placed to his head. Ken had to think quickly before he lost Cookie and his life. He pretended to slump as though as he was passing out. As soon as Brandon loosened his grip a little bit,

Ken turned and punched him in his stomach with one hand and grabbed the gun from his hand with the other. Brandon barely stumbled and charged back at Ken. Ken kicked him to the floor as the two began to tussle over the gun. Brandon slammed down on Ken's forearm, causing the gun to fall out of his hand. Ken quickly regained his composure and swung a 2 x 4 piece of wood at Ken's head.

Chelsea didn't heard the noises from the closet, as her and Cookie walked closure to it. "Didn't that sound like Ken to you? Let's open the door," Cookie said.

"Yeah, I know. It did sound like him. Wait let's ease it open. What would he be doing in here?" Chelsea asked, as she creaked open the door cautiously as not to be heard or seen.

Ken stood over Brandon as he came to and tried to jump back at him. Brandon was still as strong as ever, but so was Ken. Plus, he was quick on his feet and a man fighting to protect the woman he loves. He pulled the trigger and shot Brandon two times in the chest as he violently fell to the floor.

"Let's see your ass get up now," Ken said, as he stood over Brandon and spit on him before he turned around. Cookie and Chelsea were there at the door. He had the coldest stare and didn't whisper a word. Cookie felt like his eyes were lasers penetrating through her soul, as she felt a wave of crushing fear form at the pit of her stomach.

Before Cookie and Chelsea could really say anything back, Bill, Lisa, Sheila, Alexandria and many of the wedding party attendants slowly trickled in to towards the side of the building where the storage closet was. "Oh my goodness. Bill, come here," Lisa said.

"Ken, what's going on here?" Bill said.

"I was just protecting my wife sir. Trying to protect my wife," Ken replied, with beads of sweat and tears rolling down his face. That was all he could say. He couldn't tell the truth that he just killed his wife's ex-husband who she possibly tried to kill years ago. Or could he? For the first time he wondered if his decision to spend the rest of his life with Cookie was a mistake.

Just a few minute ago, Ken was willing to fight for Cookie and literally lose his life for her. He didn't care what she may have done because that was the past. Now, with Brandon lying there in a pool of blood, Ken realized that he never would be in this mess if Cookie was absent from his life. "I'm calling the police so they can come pick this scoundrel up. Whoever he is that tried to harm my daughter," Bill said. Although Bill believed his story, he was now cautious of Ken and the kind of man he was. "You're a courageous man. I respect that," Bill added, looking Ken directly in his eyes.

Cookie walked towards Ken and stretched out her arms to embrace her. He welcomed her embrace because he loved her. He also embraced her because he didn't want it to look strange that he was processing the whole situation and didn't know if he should trust right now. "Baby, I'm so sorry. Who was that? What happened to you?" Cookie asked, picking up a towel to wipe Ken's forehead.

"Funny you ask. I think you know him pretty well. Turns out he was posing as my coworker," Ken said.

"Wait, are you telling me that Jason was really Brandon?" Cookie asked.

Ken just stared blankly back at her, as she burst into tears. "Cookie, we have a lot to talk about. How could you lie to me? You have some major explaining to do. I can't believe this," Ken whispered, making sure no one was within earshot of his voice.

Thankfully it was dark in the closet and people couldn't really make out Brandon's face. Plus, he disguised himself to look different than he did years ago. Truth be told, Cookie was glad no one could really see his face. She would eventually have to come clean to her parents, but she would cross that bridge later. For now, at least she didn't have to worry about the shame of someone else at the wedding possibly recognizing Brandon's face as he laid there bleeding in the closet.

When the police came, Ken covered for Cookie well. He did majority of the talking and told the story just as it happened. All with one very important detail excluded. His coworker that attacked him and was invited to the wedding was actually Cookie's ex-husband Brandon. As the crowd began to thin out, Sheila walked towards Cookie. She was waiting for the perfect time to talk to her friend. Although it was the most inopportune time, she felt compelled to tell her. This one thing could truly damage her friendship with Cookie forever, but she had to inform her of what was really going on.

"Cookie, I'm so sorry. I can't believe he actually showed up here. Ken's a very brave man. Hold on to him. He's good for you," Sheila said, looking around to make sure no one was close by.

"Thanks Sheila. I just really don't know what to do now. It seems like it would be so easy now that it's all over, but I don't know if Ken can love me through this," Cookie said, pulling away from Sheila.

"No wait. Keep hugging me please. There's something I have to tell you. There's something else you don't know. Cookie, it's not over yet," Sheila leaned back and stared in Cookie's eyes, hoping she would be receptive to what she had to say.

About The Author

Carlos Harleaux is a native of Houston, TX. He is a poet, with three books published, including *Blurred Vision*, *Hindsight 20/20* and *Honesty Box*. Fortune Cookie is his very first novel. Carlos also has a Masters in Emerging Media and Communication (EMAC) from The University of Texas at Dallas and is a member of Alpha Phi Alpha Fraternity, Inc. He currently resides in Dallas, TX with his wife, Alexandria.

For more information and to purchase other books from the 7th Sign Publishing catalog, visit www.peauxeticexpressions.com.

www.ingramcontent.com/pod-product-compliance
Lightning Source LLC
Chambersburg PA
CBHW072357110726

47909CB00003B/731